A Family Affa   forgiveness,
and redemption, a   e people we
love to love, and e

Harry Blacksw   , the ultimate playboy
with a killer smile a   ever wit. He's fought it, denied it,
ignored it, but the damn truth won't go away: He's fallen in
love. And just when he's accepted that fact, Greta Servensen,
the only woman he's ever trusted, breaks his heart.

Christine Blacksworth and Nate Desantro beat the odds
when they fell in love and married. But staying married is
threatened when the foundation behind every good
relationship—trust—is challenged.

Gloria Blacksworth descends upon Magdalena in all of her
designer-clad arrogance, determined to make Christine change
her course and return to Chicago and her old life. It may take a
well-planted lie or two, but Gloria doesn't plan to fail. When
she finally confronts Miriam Desantro, the "other woman",
Gloria discovers more than she ever wanted to know… or
admit.

Angelo "Pop" Benito is The Godfather of Magdalena.
Nothing happens in that town without his knowledge or
approval. And Pop doesn't do anything without a long sit-
down with his dead wife, Lucy, and a half dozen pizzelles by
his side. He'll need a lot of lung power and a tray of his
favorite treat to help Nate and Christine out of a real mess.
And he may need the help of his checkers buddy and
Magdalena's shining star, Lily Desantro.

Truth In Lies Series
A Family Affair, Book One
A Family Affair Spring, Book Two
A Family Affair Summer, Book Three (2014)
A Family Affair Fall, Book Four (future release)

A Family Affair: Spring
Truth in Lies Series, Book Two

by
Mary Campisi

A Family Affair: Spring is a work of fiction. Names, characters, and situations are all products of the author's imagination and any resemblance to persons, locales, or events, are purely coincidental.

Print ISBN: 978-09857773-4-0

The Story Behind the Story

I never intended to write a sequel to *A Family Affair*, let alone a series. For me, the story was done and I moved on to my next book. Readers had a different idea. I began to receive emails, Facebook comments, and blog posts, asking to know more about these characters. Did Nate and Christine marry? What about Harry and Greta? And heavens, did Gloria Blacksworth ever get her comeuppance? The correspondence from readers requesting more was heartfelt and humbling, and yet, turning a book into a series that was never intended to be one is a huge and daunting task. I wasn't going to do it unless I could feel the passion for the continuation of that story. It was a struggle, yet it remained in the back of my mind as I wrote one book after another.

I do some of my best thinking when I'm walking my dog and during a particularly cool morning walk, I started playing around with scenarios and characters. I let my imagination go and didn't try to shut anything down. I did the same thing the next day, and soon Lily, Nate, Christine, Harry, Gloria, Greta—the whole crew— had taken residence in my head. They wouldn't go away and that's when I knew I *had* to write about them and gave the series what I think is an appropriate name: *Truth in Lies*.

I have absolutely loved every part of this process and the characters have entertained me as well as broken my heart a time or two. Long before I wrote "The End", I'd already decided what the storyline would be for *A Family Affair: Summer*. If you guessed Cash Casherdon and Tess Carrick, you are exactly correct. I hope you've enjoyed this journey and before long, we'll take another into *A Family Affair: Summer*.

Thank you to all the dear readers who wrote to tell me they

wanted a continuation of *A Family Affair*. I have indeed heard you!

Dedication

To all of the readers who wanted to know more about the Blacksworths and the Desantros...because of you, this book exists. Thank you.

Chapter 1

"I ain't leaving this place again, Lucy. I promise you that." Angelo "Pop" Benito sighed and sipped his root beer. Nothing better than a cold "beer" after a morning walk, especially now, with spring emerging like a baby bird, mouth open—eager, excited, joyful. There was none of that in the place he'd just escaped. The only sprouts he ever found there were the ones in those fancy grocery stores, all packed up and marked "organic". His son almost croaked when Pop demanded he stop the car to look for dandelions and mustard greens.

What are you doing? Why would you eat weeds? And then, *They're probably coated with insecticide and dog urine.* Pop guessed his son didn't remember all those years ago and the baskets of "weeds" they'd picked and brought home to his mother for cooking with oil and garlic. His son forgot a lot of things that tied him to his roots. Or maybe he just didn't want to remember.

Well, the boy could choose his own lifestyle and what tickled his taste buds, but he sure as hell wasn't trapping Pop in that California dungeon he called home ever again. If Pop hadn't wanted to see his granddaughter so bad, he'd never have agreed to flying to California for Christmas, and then he would have been in his own home when he had the trans ischemic something or other—dammit, it was *not* a stroke. And he would not have taken a header on the bottom step and broken his hip because Pop's house was a ranch and nobody in Magdalena had fancy, slippery steps glossed with five inches of varnish. *That* was his son's wife's doing, her and her designer must-haves. And *that* is what landed Pop in surgery and rehab, and for the first and only time in his seventy-three years, thinking about taking his last breath.

Pop remembered those days and even now found it hard to believe he'd come so close to giving up. Lucy wouldn't like hearing that but he had to tell her. "I had a long conversation with the Man upstairs, and I vowed if I made it back to Magdalena from that godforsaken place your son calls home, I'd turn a new leaf, eat more greens, put a nightlight in the hallway, everything to keep me regular and upright." He clutched the arms of the rocker Nate Desantro had made him two years ago and closed his eyes. "I'm going to keep my promise, Lucy, don't you worry about that, okay?"

Pop didn't wait for an answer. No matter what some of those New Age types preached, he didn't believe loved ones talked from the grave and that's where his Lucinda rested these past twenty months, weathering mounds of snow, fresh blades of grass, parched roses, and scattering leaves. Only to begin all over again, season after season.

The cancer took her, ate her female parts and stole every last red curl. But even on that final day, with her plump body worn to the size of a No. 2 pencil, her lips bare of the poppy lipstick she loved, her olive skin bruised and paper thin, he could still see his Lucinda.

He opened his eyes and reached for his mid-morning snack, a pizzelle, which might not be on the heart-healthy eating list but had its own restorative powers. It was a pizzelle that got him his first date with Lucinda Vermici. It was a pizzelle that had a part in making their son, Anthony, and it was also a pizzelle that became the solace for news of the cancer. Lucy's last taste of solid food was an anise pizzelle that Pop had cut in bite-sized pieces and carefully placed on his wife's parched tongue.

There was nothing better than a pizzelle, except maybe a good bowl of pasta in marinara sauce with a side of bracciole. His thought processes kicked in as memories of Lucy bombarded his brain. He'd only been home four days, but word had it Nate Desantro had taken another wife and not just any wife, but Christine Blacksworth. Hah! How long did the boy think Pop would let it go before he requested a visit with her? Just because Pop was one of the only residents in Magdalena who had not held a soft spot for Charles Blacksworth did not mean he would shun the man's daughter. If she gave the boy a smidge of the happiness Lucy had given Pop, that would say something, and maybe then Pop would keep his thoughts about her father and his cowardice to himself. But probably not, which was why Nate hadn't called. Didn't matter. As soon as he polished off his snack, he'd head out back, check his hostas and tulips to make sure the deer hadn't chomped them last night, and then he'd make the phone call Nate knew was coming.

***

Christine read Uncle Harry's email, the third one this morning with the first delivered at 5:45 A.M. Uncle Harry, sending messages at 5:45 A.M.? These last several months he'd become the person she'd known was inside the drinking, carousing, swearing, just-turned-fifty man she called Uncle Harry. He'd become responsible. That was a word not often associated with Harry Blacksworth. *Dependable* was another unfamiliar term. Of course, *she'd* always been able to depend on him; it was the rest of the world he'd shut out, intent to let them think he was not reliable and therefore incapable of making a decision that was not connected to fitness, food, or attire. But he was an integral part of Blacksworth & Company these days with a sign on his door that read Chief Executive Officer. He called her with questions now and again, sometimes about the small set of clients she maintained, other times in regard to broader issues. Truthfully, he'd slid right into the high-powered position as though he hadn't spent the last twenty-plus years perfecting his golf game and enjoying a workout and long lunch during business hours.

Maybe the change had to do with her leaving the company and moving to Magdalena. Or it could be tied to the secret he'd carried for so many years: He might be her father. Hadn't he said that if he'd known she'd look to him as a father figure he would have done things a bit differently? As in the running around, swearing, drinking, and overall debauchery he so enjoyed for too many years. Or did the miraculous change in her uncle have to do with Greta Servensen, her mother's cook-turned-manager at Harry's Folly, one of Chicago's new trendy restaurants? Uncle Harry avoided questions pertaining to Greta, but Christine didn't miss the faint pink that crept up his neck when he talked about her, or the way his voice dipped, like he was thinking about her and not as a manager.

The truth would spill out eventually. It always did.

Nate said she shouldn't try to play matchmaker for the rest of the world, that some people really *did* want to be alone. What did he know? When they first met, he'd tried to push her away with his harsh commentary on her life and her family and given her a thousand reasons why she should leave Magdalena. But the pull to find the truth about her father's secret life had proved stronger than Nate's insistence, and once she'd glimpsed the real Nathan Desantro—kind, gentle, trustworthy—she'd acknowledged there was nowhere she'd rather be than beside him. Safe. Secure. Committed.

She traced the intricate design of the wedding band on her left finger. They'd exchanged vows in the living room of Nate's log cabin ten days before Christmas, surrounded by red and white poinsettias and the people who meant most to them. Uncle Harry was there, gold pocket watch dangling from his jacket, his tanned face serious. Lily stood next to him, dressed in green velvet and patent leather, her smile brilliant, her

Blacksworth eyes bright. Miriam had swiped at her face and sniffed a few times while Winston Hardin, Magdalena's justice of the peace, recited the vows.

And then it was over and Nate had taken her in his arms and kissed her with such reverence, Christine cried. Big tears, the kind that smeared makeup and created streams of mascara on a woman's cheeks. Nate hadn't cared. He'd wiped her tears and whispered in her ear, *I love you, Christine Desantro. Today and always.* The tears multiplied and spread to Lily and Miriam, and she hadn't been certain, but Uncle Harry had appeared wet-eyed as well, though he attributed his to an allergic reaction to the pine from the Christmas tree in the corner.

The ceremony bore no resemblance to the high society affairs Christine had attended in Chicago: silks and satins, vases with orchids and roses smothering entire rooms. Chateaubriand, Swarovski crystal table arrangements. Limousines. A flutist. A pianist. A harpist. Champagne and chocolate fountains. Diamonds, rubies, emeralds, glistening and glimmering on hands and necks and wrists. Outdone and overdone. That was the type of wedding her mother had planned for Christine and Connor Pendleton. Fortunately, *that* wedding hadn't happened. Fortunately, the Desantros crept into her heart and claimed it, making her one of them.

"Are you working or daydreaming?"

Nate's voice still made her tingle, even after all these months together. She guessed it would be this way ten or twenty years from now. "A little of both."

"Ah." He slid a plate in front of her and set his own down before sitting next to her. "I thought only writers and creative types stared off into space and called it 'work'."

She laughed. "Maybe I'm turning into a creative type."

His dark gaze settled on the top button of her shirt. "You're creative." His gaze slid lower, settled on her breasts. "No doubt about that."

When he looked at her that way, she almost forgot to breathe. It was unsettling and exhilarating and no other person had ever been able to do that. She cleared her throat and struggled to change the topic.

Nate forked a piece of egg and sausage and said, "I have an appointment with the bank this morning. Stan said we could look at the numbers again."

"Ah." Stanley Ketrowski, assistant bank manager, captain of his bowling team, lector at St. Gertrude's. Nice guy. Uninformed banker. "Still don't want me to take a look?"

"Nope."

She nodded and picked up a slice of orange. "Even though I could analyze the numbers and make a recommendation before Stan adjusted his reading glasses?"

Nate's lips twitched. "He's just old school. He'll figure it out."

"Eventually, he'll come up with something." She shrugged and pulled a smile across her lips. "But you'll be too old or too arthritic to carve a simple spindle."

"Have a little faith. Stan's a good person."

"So am I, and I'm your wife. Your partner. We're supposed to talk and decide things together." Just because she'd never seen her own parents sharing anything didn't mean it wasn't what a marriage should be. Couples talked and shared and gave to one another. Why did it have to be "mine" and "yours"? Nate still hadn't bought into the idea of "team", if it had to do with money or obtaining it. She'd tried to tell him that her money was his money, and she wanted to provide the cash to set up his furniture business, or at least cosign a loan. He'd refused, saying he already owed her for the loan her father had given ND Manufacturing.

"Stan and I have a history. He helped my dad out of a tough spot a long time ago. I owe him."

"Hmm. Well, I certainly can't compete with that." His words hurt and the fact that he might actually believe them hurt more.

Nate clasped her hand. "Look, I know you want to help and I appreciate it. Really. Give me a little time to see what Stan comes up with, okay? If I can't get the loan or the terms don't make sense, we'll talk about it." He squeezed her hand. "Deal?"

She shrugged. "You're making me look bad. How am I going to continue in business if my own husband is determined to stay with someone who still believes in passbook savings? I've had people approach me about investing in you: Rex McGregor three days ago and last week it was Nanette Giraldi. They're watching, Nate. They want to see what you're going to do, and more importantly, if you're willing to back Charlie's daughter, a city girl with big ideas for their town."

The left side of his jaw twitched, twitched again, a sign she'd come to recognize as controlled annoyance. "It's not that simple. If you come in and take over, I might as well put on a skirt, because the town you think you know so well will view your help as weakness on my part. And ineptitude." The jaw twitched again. "And I'm neither."

Christine leaned forward, closing the gap between his reticence and stubborn conclusions. "I know that. I also know that I can help you realize your dream, if you let me. The people in this town have been kind and welcoming. They've accepted my suggestions on financial matters, turned over their money for me to invest. They aren't as judgmental and unaccepting as you think."

He laughed and shook his head. "A ruse. All of it. Sure, they're accommodating and polite, but don't think they don't have a bead on you, waiting to see if you'll mess up. They might not wear fancy suits and drive big cars, but they know people better than most therapists. You're still on the outside and if I let you just take over my business, they won't respect me." He paused, his voice fell. "Or you."

"I think you're wrong about them. I haven't seen anything to indicate wariness."

"That's because you don't recognize it." He pulled his hand away and crossed his arms over his chest. "How many have asked about me, or Mom, or Lily?"

"All of them. But what does that have to do with trust?"

"And how many made mention of your father, even though they know you're Charlie's daughter?"

"Well…" Surely someone had made reference to him in some capacity. Hadn't they? She'd been so busy trying to win them over with her background and expertise that she hadn't noticed their reticence in regard to her father. This was crazy. Just because she couldn't recall an inquiry did not mean these people were wary of her and her intentions.

"Exactly. And what kind of business dealings are you having?" A faint smile slid across his lips. "I'm guessing they're bringing in their kids for Investment 101 strategies or it's a young couple trying to consolidate debt, or maybe even Vinnie Zaffino still looking for a loan to get his Bobcat going. I know you can't tell me, client privilege and all that, but you don't need to. Betty Rafferty, my very own reporter, fills me in weekly on the comings and goings from your office."

"Betty's spying on me?" She liked Nate's receptionist. Betty with the sweet smile and cat-eye glasses who greeted her with high-pitched excitement whenever Christine called? Why on earth would the woman do such a thing?

"It's not called spying in small towns. It's known as information gathering."

"I don't appreciate that." *Not one bit.* "Okay, I'll give you that maybe the majority of my clients are currently fighting bad credit scores and high debt, but I'm trying to help them dig out. And maybe they are not investment savvy." She paused. "Yet."

"Uh-huh. Like I said, kids with bad spending habits."

"Who will become conscientious, dollar-cost-averaging adults."

His lips twitched. "So you say."

Just because she had not been born into their small community did not mean she couldn't be trusted by them. She had clout. She had credentials. She had been named one of the best businesswomen in Chicago. It was not about her. Christine narrowed her gaze on her husband and offered a tight smile. "I've come to the conclusion the reason I'm not seeing more investment money is that there isn't any."

Nate scratched his jaw. "Come again?"

"It's obvious and it's not something I can say to anyone but you, and maybe your mother, if the subject comes up. Magdalena's residents don't have extra money to invest. They're living paycheck to paycheck, probably mortgaged out, and scraping to pay the utility bill."

He scratched his jaw again. "You think so?"

She didn't like the way he said that, as though he believed she were miles off track with her evaluation. "I do think so. They can't invest if they have to worry about school clothes and orthodontia bills and repairing the family car." Her voice softened as a new plan formed, took root, and spread through her. "I need to hold meetings in the town hall to educate the community as a whole. Debt reduction, that's the key." Her smile morphed into a burst of excitement and opportunity. "I'll show them how to reduce debt, realign spending, and then we'll talk about investment vehicles and retirement opportunities."

Nate's expression turned serious. "You think these people have no money because they drive ten-year-old cars, buy reduced produce, and haven't made an appointment with you to talk about investment strategies? You are so far off base, you have no idea. This town has money, don't think they don't. That's not your problem."

"I don't doubt your calculations on the community's wealth, but I've seen no evidence of it, in any form, and if they were truly in tune with their portfolios, they would talk to me about increasing returns and making their money work for them."

Nate shrugged. "Unless they didn't trust you."

"For heaven's sake, do you have any idea what kind of deals I was involved with in Chicago?" *Was he serious?* "Megamillion ones, big companies." She clenched her teeth and bit out, "Huge profits."

"I'm sure." He nodded his dark head and looked at her as one does a child who still doesn't understand that a bee carries a sting. "But you aren't in Chicago anymore. You're in a small town where people want to know your word is good before they hand over their life savings."

This was ridiculous. No one had ever questioned her integrity, and she resented the implication that she lacked it. "People trusted my father. Why can't they trust me?"

Nate hesitated before answering. "They trusted him to a point. He was a spokesman for those who were taken advantage of by shady businessmen, and he did help people dig out from debt and get loans. But he did not invest their money."

"But I can help them, I know I can."

His voice gentled. "Sweetheart, maybe they don't want your help."

"Are you saying they don't want to increase their wealth?"

"I'm saying they don't want to hand over their money to someone they don't really know."

She supposed she could see the backward justification of this. Still, there had to be a way to gain their confidence. Christine studied her husband; he had the respect of the town, and their loyalty, too. He'd gone without so his employees could keep their jobs, and from the whisperings about town, most people knew the stories of his empty paychecks, long hours, and sacrifice. "If you let me help you get financing for the furniture business, it would send a message."

He frowned and picked up his fork, twirled it between his fingers. "And what message would that be? Nate Desantro relies on his wife's money to get ahead?" He shook his head. "I won't do it. Besides, it wouldn't matter. You need to partner yourself with someone who has a lot of clout in this town and get him to back you."

"They really don't trust me?" The notion was almost incomprehensible, but the solution was not. If Nate could point her to the town's spokesperson, she'd convince him to support her. "Did you have someone in mind?"

He cleared his throat and looked away for a few seconds before meeting her gaze head on. What she saw in his eyes confused her. Concern and dread. A faint pink crept from his tanned neck and settled on his cheeks. "I do, but…"

"What? Tell me his name and I'll call him right now." She leaned forward. "Nate? Who is it? Do I know him? Or her?"

Her husband sighed and ran a hand over his face. "You don't know him, but he's heard all about you."

"Oh." And then, "Well? Who is it?"

"We call him The Godfather, but his real name's Angelo Benito, Pop for short." He twirled the fork again, studied the tines. Apparently a utensil was more interesting than looking at her. Or maybe he didn't want to claim what was coming out of his mouth, and it was easier to look at a piece of stainless steel. "He just got back from California. His son lives there with his family, some big advertising guy. Pop took sick and then broke his hip, landed in rehab for too many months. Mom said the son tried to get him a condo near San Diego, but Pop said he wasn't living anywhere that wouldn't let him grow basil and sit on his back porch in his underwear." He laid down the fork and slid his gaze to hers. "He got back four days ago."

"He sounds like a character in a book. I'd love to meet him."

Nate danced around the question and finally said, "He's kind of got an interesting perspective on life and people, and he's not afraid to say what he's thinking."

"A man who speaks his mind?" She threw Nate a pointed stare. "I know someone like that." Pop Benito sounded like a gentle, grandfatherly type. The only grandfather she remembered was her father's father, Randolph, founder of Blackworth & Company Investments, and she doubted anyone had ever seen him in his underwear.

"Yeah, well, when he speaks, everyone listens, and sometimes that's a problem because it can stir things up around here."

"Then I definitely want to meet him." He might be just the person to give her his blessing *and* his approval. With him behind her, she could begin to earn these people's trust and eventually their business, along with her husband's. It was a solid plan, one she wanted to implement right away. She tried to keep the excitement from her voice when she asked, "Can you set up a meeting? Today?"

Nate picked up that darn fork again and twirled it three times. "Actually, he called this morning. He wants to meet you, but there's something you need to know." The twirling stopped. "He never liked your father. No matter how much good your dad did for the town, Pop called him a coward. I'm not sure he'll be willing to help Charlie Blacksworth's daughter."

Chapter 2

Nothing compared to a bowl of penne pasta smothered with spinach, garbanzo beans, and chunks of beefsteak tomatoes. The crushed red pepper was the key, and if you didn't add a healthy smothering of Pecorino Romano cheese, well you weren't going to get Harry Blacksworth's "keeper" vote.

Greta knew this dish was one of Harry's favorites and made sure she brought him a side of it, no matter what he ordered. There was something to be said for anticipating his desires, and she'd done a good job of that since he opened the doors to Harry's Folly last November and put her in charge. The woman was a natural: in the kitchen, prepping alongside the staff, taste-testing for improvement; in the dining room, chatting with the guests, welcoming them to the restaurant with a sincerity that could not be practiced or pretended. Greta was the real deal and he wasn't the only person who recognized that. Men flocked to the restaurant, asking for her under the guise of a food issue and once she appeared, scrub-faced and natural, these men who expressed concern for an ill-prepared dish changed their tune and threw her compliments and phone numbers.

It was damned annoying and Harry had told her more than once that she needed to shut it down. Of course, Greta merely smiled and shook her head, insisting she had no interest in any of the men, her blue gaze meeting his a second too long when she spoke. What did that look mean? And dammit, why was she giving it to *him*? Hell, he knew what it meant, had been getting those kinds of looks for years. It was a green light to pass "Go" and collect whatever the hell he wanted.

Harry swore under his breath and sipped his iced tea. It had not been easy working alongside Greta these past months, pretending he wasn't attracted to her wholesomeness, that he didn't think about sex and lots of it when she brushed her arm against his. Granted, he'd done a bit of reforming since Chrissie packed up and headed to Magdalena, dumping the company on him. He hadn't minded the extra work, though he missed Chrissie so much his chest ached when he thought about it. Still, what could he do? She'd fallen in love with a mountain man-turned-gentle giant who worshipped her and now they were married. Kids would be next, then the dog, or maybe the dog and then the kids. It didn't matter which came first because Chrissie wasn't coming back. Damn, there was that pain, right in his chest. He guessed poets and writers called it a broken heart. What a bunch of bullshit. Too many minutes on the rowing machine is what did him in and a hot stone massage would set him straight, or maybe he'd skip the hot stone and get straight to the massage, with Bridgett, his sex partner. Interesting term: sex partner. It implied a detachment that did not include emotion or feelings, and if Greta found out, she'd clock him over the head with one of her stainless-steel skillets.

He pushed the menu aside and waited for her to appear with his salad—iceberg and red onion—*no radicchio, thank you very much*. Why was he thinking of Greta and sex again? It wasn't going to happen. Ever. She was a nice lady. Period. He was a deprived individual who didn't know how to have a relationship with someone like her. End of story. Bridgett was convenient, young, undemanding. She had no expectations for a meet-and-greet with the family. If he got involved with Greta, he'd have to contend with that bird-eyed witch of a mother and those two kids who would rather puke than speak to him. And he'd have to clean up his act: no more swearing, though he had toned it down quite a bit, and scale back on the drinking. That would require work. And taking an interest in the kids and the old lady. Even conversation. *How are you today? How was school?* He almost gagged on his lettuce.

Who was he kidding? He could clean up his mouth and maybe sanitize the lustful thoughts that roamed his brain when he spotted Greta, but for how long? And for what? Greta would want a commitment, a curfew, a toothbrush at his place. *Hell no.*

"Hello, Harry." Greta's slight German accent spilled over him, hot and tempting, making him forget why he could never get involved with her. She stood before him in a red shirt and black skirt, a bit snug around the breasts and hips, just enough to emphasize her curves. He was positive the tight fit was not by design, more positive still that a nun should coordinate her wardrobe.

"Greta." He tried to keep his voice businesslike because he noticed it had a tendency to slip into hunting mode if he weren't careful. That occurrence perplexed him. He was not "hunting" Greta and why various parts of his body insisted he was proved a damn annoyance. One of these days, his body parts would have to grow up. All of them. Even the ones he wanted to remain youthful. Her smile spread, her eyes grew brighter than an angel's on her way to heaven. Pure. Honest. Good. He cleared his throat, allowing enough time for a string of curses to pulse through his brain and transform him into the man with a reputation for debauchery and carelessness.

"I'd hoped you'd stop by today," he said. "It's been a while."

Four days, that's how long it had been. "I've been busy."

Her smile faltered but she worked it back into place. "You have a lot of responsibility these days. It's hard to go it alone without someone by your side."

What did she mean by that comment? Was she talking about herself and this business, or was she referring to her personal situation? If it were the first, it required his attention. If it were the second, he'd jump into a freezing lake before he'd touch that one. "Is everything okay here? Jimmy working out in the kitchen? Produce and meat deliveries on time? New menus look good?"

"Of course." She nodded and the blonde bun flopped on top of her head. He'd always had a fondness for that bun, had wondered many times what it would look like unraveled and wrapped around his hand. "I miss you, Harry."

Shit. "Don't start with that."

"I know what you said." She bit her bottom lip, probably to keep from crying, and nodded again. "It's just that I see what's inside you, even when you try so hard to keep it hidden." Those damn blue eyes turned bluer, brighter. "The real Harry Blacksworth has a heart as big as this room." She pointed toward the kitchen, then the dining area of Harry's Folly. "Who else would give a young man with bad job references a second chance and make sure he had a ride to work every day?"

Harry shifted in his chair and shrugged. "Rocco makes the best linguine and clams with white sauce in the city. It was a self-serving move."

Her voice softened. "And Leo? I heard you're paying for him to take night classes at the community college. And you said if he did well, you'd hire him on as an intern." Her voice dipped lower. "Is that self-serving?"

It was getting damn hot in here. Hadn't he told Greta not to worry about saving on the utilities? Couldn't she follow a simple direction and listen to him, even once? He threw her a cold stare and said, "Cheap labor."

"Ah. And Diana? The singer you brought in when we have no need for one? And you bought her a piano and pay her a daily rate whether she sings or not? Is *that* cheap labor?"

He'd had enough. "Why is it I can't come in here and have a simple bowl of pasta without you battering me about my hidden qualities? You think I'm a friggin' god, but I'm not. I'm a selfish, manipulative bastard and the sooner you realize that, the better."

The damn woman actually had the audacity to laugh. In his face. Not just a giggle, but a full out, teeth-showing laugh. "Of course you are. You are so big and mean and cruel that little children run and hide when they hear your name." She laughed again. "One day you'll stop being afraid, Harry Blacksworth. And when that happens, I'll be here."

He glared at her, for what good it did. "I'm not afraid of anything but starving."

She smiled. "I'll tell Jimmy to get going on the penne."

"Light on the garbanzos, heavy on the spinach."

Giant sigh. "I know."

Damn right she did. Harry shifted in his chair, grinned. "And let's take a look at the new menus."

"Yes, boss."

Boss. He liked that. Liked it even better when she slipped back into Greta Servensen, manager of Harry's Folly, instead of Greta Servensen, temptress extraordinaire. "All right. Hurry up, woman. I have a busy afternoon." She saluted him, which made him laugh. Greta was good for his soul, what was left of it.

"Harry!"

His smile slipped. He'd recognize that voice anywhere, even attached to a body *with* clothes. "Your secretary said I could find you here." His brain shut down, strangled by that voice that inferred carnal familiarity. He kept his eyes on Greta who had turned stone-faced still as the woman attached to the voice slid into the seat across from him with her jasmine perfume and suffocated the last few bits of logic that might help him out of this mess.

"Bridgett! What a surprise!" *A disaster was more like it.* He forced himself to look at her. Tall, leggy, killer tongue. "What are you doing here?"

She flashed him a smile and reached across the table to clasp his hands. French manicure. Diamonds. Bronzed skin glistening under the subdued lights. "I had to see you." She ignored Greta as though she were part of the décor and pulled her lips into a pout. A practiced expression, he could tell by the perfection of it. This wasn't his first rodeo with someone like her, a barterer of goods for services rendered. Women like Bridgett provided the sex and Harry provided payment in the form of fancy dinners, clothing, and jewelry. Occasionally, trips. A win-win situation for those with black hearts and empty souls—like him. Bridgett brushed her blonde hair behind her right ear and said, "I can't seem to find one of my diamond studs? Have you seen it?"

"No." Had Greta figured out who Bridgett was and what he'd been doing with her?

"Hmm." She tapped a finger against her chin and sighed. "You haven't seen it anywhere? Did you check the sheets?"

The gasp pierced his left ear. Harsh, painful, shocked. Harry turned to find Greta rushing toward the kitchen, head high, step filled with purpose and no doubt a desperation to get as far from him and his deceitful self as possible. There was no question Greta had figured out his relationship to Bridgett. *Dammit.* He grabbed his iced tea, drained it. Why did do-gooders always act like they'd had their heart gouged out when the person they refused to believe ill of disappointed them? Hadn't he told her straight up he was no saint, didn't even deserve a second thought because his soul was black and twisted and he was beyond redemption? Because that's the way he wanted it? Hadn't he been up front about it? And what had she gone and done? Believed in him. That was the worst thing she could have possibly done. He'd stepped up for Chrissie, but if people thought he was going to make a regular habit of it, they were going to be very disappointed.

"Harry? Baby. Can you check the sheets?" Bridgett laughed, low and sultry, a sound filled with promises of sensual escapades. "Maybe it slipped to the bottom of the sheets when we were," she paused, ran her tongue over her glossed lips and said, "pleasing each other."

On a usual day the lips and tongue and voice could get him going, especially if he pictured the aforementioned coming from a feisty German woman. But today was different; today was nothing but an exposure of his sick mind, with Greta as witness of his debauchery. He thought of her standing before him in shock and pain. Strings of curses bombarded his brain, big and bold and crude, plastering themselves all over his psyche, festering until they poured out. Unfortunately, Bridgett was the recipient of the curse-laden barrage.

"Harry? What did I do?" She eased her hand from his and pushed back her chair. "Why are you so angry?"

"I need a drink. A double."

"In a minute. Talk to me. What's wrong?"

Okay, she wanted him to talk, he'd talk. "You've got a master's in psychology, right?"

She smiled, her eyes lighting up. "I do."

"Next up is the Ph.D. so you can discuss Freud and all that other crap in a college classroom, right?"

The smile brightened, the lip gloss shimmered. "You *do* listen."

"So, why are you with me?"

She laughed. "I like you."

Right. "You like me or my money?" Now there was the question.

She spread her hands flat on the table, leaned forward until her boobs squeezed into the opening in her shirt and she murmured, "Is there a difference?"

"There should be." What the hell kind of psycho-bullshit answer was that? Greta would never spit out that kind of twisted garbage.

"I don't see the difference. You're a fun guy, handsome, entertaining." She paused, licked those damn lips again, and said, "Sexy as hell."

"And you're half my age."

"Doesn't feel that way when we're in bed."

Had he really fallen for such bullshit? Of course he had. Men thought with the wrong head most of the time and then wondered how they ended up getting screwed by someone like Bridgett. Not that she'd tried to screw him over yet, but she would. Eventually. They always did. At some point, she'd want him to put her up in a condo, visit her every night, or maybe she'd expect a drawer at his house—even a bottom drawer would do as long as she had her scent there. And little by little, the expectations would mount and if Harry didn't deliver accordingly, sexual favors would be withheld, and then the pouting would start. What man didn't recognize pouting for what it was, especially if delivered after a firm *No, you cannot put your stuff in the bottom drawer. No razor either. Nothing but the bag you come in with every night and leave with every morning.*

"And you take care of yourself." She fluffed her hair over her shoulders, studied him. "You could pass for thirty."

"You are so full of bullshit."

She smiled. "Okay, thirty-five."

"Are you sleeping with anybody else?" He'd never have to ask that with Greta.

"No." She lifted her chin in what might be defiance or

challenge. "Are you?"

Only in my head. "No."

She let out a breath and clutched his hand. "Something's bugging you, Harry. I can always tell."

"I've got a lot on my mind." Beginning and ending with women who tried to turn him into a saint.

"I can take your mind off of your problems. Why don't we go to your place?"

He shook his head. "No time."

"Your office then? You can sit in your chair and do your work while I climb under the desk…"

"Uh, no. But thanks."

"Well." The tone said *pissed*, even if she served it with a smile. "You've never been one to turn down *that* offer before."

Over the past few months, Bridgett's offers had been increasingly difficult to accept. It didn't matter the time, the position, the location; he'd not been as interested or as engaged, which often led to *other issues* of a very personal nature. Dammit, he was not taking that pill, not yet, at least not until he determined which head was causing the real problem. Somewhere in the mix of all of this was a blonde-haired woman with a bun and a German accent.

"You're really turning me down?" When he didn't respond, she sniffed and said, "Can I at least have lunch with you?"

"Sure." *Damn*, now he couldn't confront Greta and tell her to stop thinking whatever it was she was thinking.

"I do like spending time with you, Harry." She paused, lowered her voice. "Even out of bed."

The rest of the lunch followed the same rhetoric. Harry spoke, Bridgett answered with a sexual innuendo. Maybe he was just tired or needed a good workout to relieve the stress pulsing at the back of his neck and temples, but he wasn't interested in her or what she had to say. About anything. He eyed her plate, tried to determine how long it would take her to eat the rest of her angel hair pasta. There'd only been about twelve strands and she'd been playing with them for a good ten minutes. No wonder she was so thin, except for the boobs and that had more to do with a good plastic surgeon than a good diet. She could use a few more curves…soft and supple…like Greta…whom he hadn't seen since she pulled the disappearing act into the kitchen.

"Okay." Bridgett pushed back her plate, which still had three strands of pasta on it, and stood. "You're preoccupied and I've got class." She leaned forward and placed a soft kiss on his temple. "Call me." She straightened and flung her designer bag over her shoulder. "And let me know if you find the earring."

Then she was gone, leaving Harry with a half-eaten bowl of penne with spinach and garbanzos and a stomach full of regret. He should just leave and to hell with Greta's sensitivity. What did she really expect from him, and worse, why did it bother him so much? He wiped his mouth, tossed his napkin on the table, and headed for the kitchen. "Where's Greta?"

"On the patio." There were three people in the kitchen, Jimmy, Leo, and Rocco. Jimmy was the one who spoke. Short, wiry, a ball of energy with a wife, four kids, and the face of a rock star, he was fiercely loyal to Greta. She'd given him a chance when all he had as a reference was a short stint at an Italian restaurant chain and two wedding receptions. But he'd had a shitload of confidence that stretched from Chicago to Los Angeles, his hometown. He'd come into the kitchen and nailed three of Harry's favorite dishes: penne with spinach and garbanzos, veal saltimbocca, and mushroom ravioli. How could you argue with that? The kid was a genius in the kitchen. Success didn't always follow a straight line, littered with advanced studies and fancy résumés. Sometimes success grew from a burn in the gut and determination. Hell, in Harry's dim estimation, the ones walking the tightrope without a net below—no family money, no bailout plan—were the ones who refused to accept defeat.

He worked his way past the aroma of garlic and marinara, and through the door leading onto a fenced-in patio with stucco walls, terra cotta pots, and six wrought-iron tables with matching chairs and a removable umbrella. In a few weeks the place would be crammed with urban professionals sipping daily specials. But not today. The square of stone and stucco was empty, except for Greta, who sat at the farthest table, head bent, hands folded. She didn't move as he approached. "Are you sleeping or praying?" She inched her head up and he wished she hadn't. Damn but she'd been crying and he didn't need to be a rocket scientist to know he was the cause. Harry moved a step closer, remained standing. "What's wrong?" It was a conciliatory question, not one he particularly wanted answered.

The blue eyes watered. "Why didn't you tell me you had a girlfriend?"

"What?" *Girlfriend?*

"Why didn't you just tell me, Harry?" She straightened in her chair, her voice growing stronger. "Instead, you let me act like a fool."

"Are you talking about Bridgett? She's not my girlfriend." Her eyes narrowed, the eyebrows shot up. "She's not."

"Then you should tell her."

That made him laugh. "She knows. I've never pretended to be anyone other than who I am, and she gets that." *Unlike you, who believe I'm some other person: better, honest, trustworthy.*

Greta's next words pinched his crotch. "If she's not your girlfriend, what is she?"

A sex partner. A call at three in the morning to ease my needs. A substitute for a woman I have no business wanting... "A good time." He stuffed his hands in his pockets and planted his feet like a soldier readying for battle.

"A good time who lost a diamond earring in your bed."

"Stop it."

"I thought if I gave you time, you'd trust me enough to give me a chance. I see the way you look at me, the way you watch me cross a room or eat a bite of food. You want me, Harry Blacksworth, and you've wanted me for a very long time. You're just too much of a coward to do something about it."

Her accusations blasted him back a step. "Yeah, I want you, but so what? Nothing can happen."

"Why not?" She stood, hands on hips.

"Because you'll want more than a romp in bed. Dammit, you'll want a friggin' profession of love and until death do us part."

She opened her mouth and spit fire. "Did I ever once say that?"

Who was she kidding? They all wanted a ring, even the ones who said they didn't. Actually, *especially* the ones who said they didn't. "You didn't have to."

"Apparently I did." She moved toward him until she was close enough for him to smell her honeysuckle scent. "I don't want to marry you. I don't want to marry anyone. But I have needs too, Harry. Physical ones."

He took another step back, trying to block out her words. "Don't talk like that."

"Why not? I'm a woman, I have needs, just like you do." Her voice turned hard. "Just like your Bridgett and all of the 'Bridgetts' before."

He stared at her. Where was the mild-mannered cook who drove a dented Toyota and couldn't look him straight in the eye? He wanted her back. Now. Not this she-wolf who wanted to have sex with him for the pure sake of ….well, sex. That was like hearing your mother say she liked sex. "You want sex? That's it?"

She sighed and her voice dipped, deflated and sad, as though she'd used up all of her oxygen with her sex rant. "I wanted you to be honest with me and let yourself want me. Be a man. Make love—"

"I don't 'make love'. I have sex."

Her lips flattened. "Of course you do. Excuse me, I wanted to have sex with you." For a half second, he shut down his brain and enjoyed what she'd just said. Sex with Greta. It would be passionate and pure and …. "But not anymore."

"What does that mean?" He was still stuck in the passionate and pure mode.

"You're never going to give us a chance. And I'm tired of living moment to moment, hoping, waiting, praying even, that you'll look at me and say 'What the heck? I'm going to stop being afraid of this thing between us.' But you won't and it took that woman and her missing diamond, which I'm sure you bought for her, to open my eyes."

His chest tightened, squeezed hard until it hurt. He wasn't afraid of starting something with Greta, he was trying to protect her because he knew he'd only hurt her. Didn't she see that? Dammit, he was not afraid. But there was a tiny piece of him that knew she was dead-on; he was scared shitless of caring about her. And if he showed her, then what? He knew what—he'd find himself picking out china patterns and buying an SUV and ten years later he'd wonder how the hell he'd ever gotten into this mess.

"Don't answer, because there's no need." She cleared her throat and continued, "I'd rather not see you unless it's about business."

"What the hell does that mean?" *What the hell did that mean?*

"No more Sunday dinners. No drop-ins to bring Arnold a DVD or Elizabeth toy ponies. I'll meet with you about menu changes or building issues." Those blue eyes zeroed in on his, and her next words gutted him. "But I won't sit with you and ask you about your day, make you pies, or wait for you to show up for lunch. I'm moving on with my life and you're not going to be part of it."

Chapter 3

Angelo Benito lived on the east side of town in a white shoebox-sized house with a white front porch and matching railing. The structure itself was quiet and unassuming, but the flowers and shrubs that surrounded it were not. They spoke of skill and patience, care and passion. Nate had told her Pop Benito had two green thumbs and a way with growing things that stumped the horticulturists. According to Nate, the old man didn't subscribe to store-bought fertilizers or expert recommendations on grafting, pruning, or deadheading. He did his own thing and while he shared a few tidbits, most practices he only shared with Lucy. His dead wife.

At two minutes before three o'clock, the time Pop had instructed Nate that Christine should arrive, she parked her car alongside the curb and got out. Why had he asked to meet with her? Did it have to do with her father? Her marriage to Nate? Or had he heard that despite her background, the townspeople were not willing to trust her with their money? None of the possibilities were good and each would foster its own brand of discomfort. Still, there was no avoiding The Godfather of Magdalena.

Christine climbed cement steps that had been gouged and cracked from one too many harsh winters and heavy applications of rock salt. She knocked on the weathered oak door with the scratched brass kick plate and matching knocker engraved with a bold *B*. A few minutes passed and she was about to knock again when the door creaked open. A small man with a shock of white hair and silver glasses that took up a third of his face stared back at her. His eyes were dark and intense, his eyebrows bushy, his mustache pencil-thin. She guessed him to be in his mid-seventies, but when he smiled, ten years washed away. Or maybe the confusion arose when she glanced at his attire: a football jersey, sweatpants, and high-top tennis shoes. Blue, black, and red. He wore a training wristwatch on his right wrist and a gold wedding band on his left finger.

The Godfather of Magdalena thrust a bony hand at her, looking more like an aging sports advertisement than a spokesman of the community. "Angelo Benito. Good to meet you, Christine. Come on in. We'll go sit out back." He held the door open and ushered her into a room covered in roses: cream wallpaper scattered with crimson roses, couch and chairs in a subdued floral design with a cream backdrop. And more cream and roses, this time with end tables on either side of the couch. There were vases on the mantel stuffed with bunches of silk flowers; blood-red, whisper-white, soft peach. Hanging above the mantel was a portrait of a woman about Christine's age, her long fiery curls a stark contrast against the whiteness of her dress, her smile bold and vibrant. But it was the woman's eyes that pulled Christine in: a brilliant blue that followed the viewer about the room. At the woman's feet lay a blanket of blood-red roses.

"That's my Lucy." Angelo Benito spoke in a hushed tone of reverence and longing. "She'd just given birth to our son, Anthony. She's beautiful, isn't she?"

The woman's almond-shaped eyes held Christine's. "Yes, she is."

He motioned for her to follow him. "She was my angel. Loved roses, insisted we plant all different colors: red, orange, yellow, white, pink. Lucy said the food we grew filled our bellies, but the roses filled our souls." The back door opened onto a small wooden deck with a green and white striped awning that provided protection from the sun. When Christine had settled into one of the rocking chairs, Angelo sat down next to her. "You've got your father's eyes."

"Yes, I do." She hadn't planned on asking about the issues between him and her father until she'd enlisted his help with the townspeople. Apparently, Angelo Benito believed in dealing with unpleasantness straight up. Fine with her. "Nate said you knew him."

The look he gave her was direct, powerful. "Then that husband of yours must have also told you I didn't like him."

"He did." She fidgeted with her watch, wished she did not have to have this conversation. "Can you tell me why?"

"I'll be happy to. As a matter of fact, that's why I called you here, Christine. I want you to know why your father and I never saw eye to eye, and why I'm going to see to it you don't hurt Nate or Miriam, or God forbid, Lily."

"I would never hurt them."

"Hmph. That's what everybody says, but it happens all the time. Give a person a chance to do the right thing or the easy thing, and they'll pick the easy one most of the time. That's what your father did." He scratched his head and frowned. "He hid behind his good deeds, and maybe he did help the town with money, advice, and kindness. But that didn't make up for the other family he had tucked away in Chicago, or the one he had here and kept from you. And what about Lily? Four days a month for a father?"

"I don't know why he did what he did. When I first found out, I hated him for destroying the memories of the father I thought he was." Her voice dipped, softened. "And then I forgave him, because if I hadn't, it would have destroyed me."

"He was a coward. Pure and simple." Angelo gripped his rocker and sucked in air. "Miriam is a good woman. It wasn't right what your father did, no matter the circumstances. He took the best of what he had in Chicago and mixed it with what he had here and it was wrong. Miriam didn't see it that way, but why would she after being married to a bastard like Nick Desantro? I didn't like hearing you and Nate got married. That's a powder keg waiting to explode if you ask me, which nobody did."

"We love each other and we are not our parents."

He studied her long and hard, in a way that made her wish she were hidden in his garden and away from his scrutiny. "Love has nothing to do with it. It's commitment and toughness when your world shatters around you. It's losing babies and jobs and hope. It's sickness and pain, and disillusionment and broken dreams." He leaned forward until he was inches from her face. "Do you and Nate have *that* Because if you're gonna survive, you'll need it. He already sent one wife packing. You might be number two."

"If you think that, Mr. Benito, then you have clearly underestimated me. I'm going to make this marriage work, and I don't care what you think." She stood and grabbed her handbag. "I mean you no disrespect, but you don't know me. Nate said you're The Godfather of this town and I needed your approval to get people to trust me with their money. Well, you know what? You've already made up your mind about me, so let's not pretend whatever I do won't be overshadowed by your issues with my father. Good-bye and thank you for your time." She'd made it to the third step with the intent of rounding the house when Angelo Benito's laugh reached her: full-bodied, loud, pleased. Christine swung around and faced him. "I wasn't trying to be humorous."

He stood and held out a hand, motioning her back. "Nobody but my Lucy ever gave me lip like that." He laughed again. "She would have liked you. Maybe you will be good for Nate. Strong-willed, like him. Like me and Lucy. Come on, sit down, and we'll agree to disagree about your father."

Christine made her way back up the steps and sat in the

rocking chair she'd vacated moments before. Angelo pointed to the garden in front of him. It was a 12x15 raised bed surrounded by small wire fencing with random tin pans dangling from the top of the fence and strips of white cloth. Inside the fence were several rows of what appeared to be tomatoes, zucchini, and peppers. She would not have been able to identify any of these vegetables if she and Lily hadn't spent last summer planting their own garden. Lily had taught her the names of each plant, helped water and weed, and eventually harvest the bounty.

"Chicken wire and tin pans are a gardener's secret weapon. Yup." Angelo scratched his head and squinted at the garden. "No four-legged creature's gonna steal Pop's tomatoes. You ever grow anything, Christine?"

Yes, I grow personal portfolios; can I show you what I can do? "Um, last year Lily and I planted a garden."

"Lily." He said her name with great affection. "She'll teach you a thing or two if you open up and pay attention."

"I know." Lily had taught her about forgiveness, hope, and unconditional love, but the first time she'd met her half-sister, Christine had seen nothing but a Down Syndrome child.

He switched the subject back to gardening. "I used to tend a football-field-size patch of land. And then those dang ladies of The Bleeding Heart Society cornered me and wouldn't let me go until I agreed to help them out."

"That's the perennial garden club Miriam told me about." Miriam had given her an earful, starting and finishing with how the members were in everybody's business, offering suggestions on problems related and unrelated to gardening, whether the advice was solicited or not.

The dark eyes grew wide behind the giant glasses. "Miriam told you about them?" His thin lips pulled into a smile. "Was it a warning to stay away? She's never been keen on that group, says they're busybodies, which they are, but in a concerned way." He rocked back and forth, considered his next words. "Or maybe they have too much time to yammer on and on about other people's worries. Or they read too many 'feel-good' books and think people all deserve a happy ending."

Curiosity got her. "You don't seem like a man to get cornered into anything you don't want to do. Why did you join the group?"

His voice downshifted. "Because of Lucy. She was one of the first members and when she passed, they just couldn't let her go." He cleared his throat and settled his gaze on a planter at the foot of the steps. "I couldn't let her go either, so I joined and it helped ease things a bit. Lucy was a character, always getting mixed up in one thing or another, but with a heart as big as a watermelon. The society says it fosters a 'passion for perennial gardening' but what it really does is helps people in need. You know, mends things like broken hearts, shaky marriages, empty bank accounts...It's made up of a conglomeration of people, all pitch-patch, some descendants of the founders, others brand new to the community. It's by invite only, so you can't join just because you want their recipe for corn chowder and a vote on the flower of the month calendar."

"Can you get me in?" If these people had a say on what happened in their community, they could convince people she was trustworthy even if her education from Wharton and her vice president's title at Blacksworth & Company could not.

"Maybe. But if you go in there and give them your 'Hand over your money and I'll show you what I can do', they'll vote you out before the hibiscus tea is served."

"Oh." And then, "Do you have a better approach?"

He smiled and tapped his tennis-shoe-covered feet against the deck floor. "Pop Benito always has a move."

"So, will you help me?"

The smile spread. "I can offer a suggestion or two, make them think they need you. But you're gonna have to do the real convincing. What's in your bag of tricks besides a calculator and a business card? Can you raise money for their causes? Sell flowers at the annual garden event? Bake cookies?"

"I …I guess I could. I don't know about the cookies, but Miriam could help." She shook her head and said, "But how is this going to make any difference? Baking cookies has nothing to do with dollar cost averaging."

Angelo Benito tsk-tsked her as though she'd failed the test of a lifetime. "This is about building relationships. You do that, the trust comes, and if the trust comes, they'll do business with you." He sighed and said, "Enough of that. Let's talk about Lily. She's one of my favorite people, right up there with my own granddaughter. I've been gone a long time, but from the stories she used to tell about you, I'll bet Lily almost flew when she met you. And then you went and became her sister-in-law? Doesn't get any better than that in her book. I'm sure she'll tell me all about it when she comes tomorrow. We've got a checker tournament, best of seven." He winked at her. "Winner takes home pizzelles."

"She's very good at checkers." Her thoughts wandered back to what he'd said about The Bleeding Heart Society. Angelo had offered to help her but he'd neglected to provide specifics. How was this all going to work? She was a detail person, not a fly-in-the-dark, see-what-happens-next-Tuesday kind of girl. Surely he had a thought or two about what he planned to say. "About my introduction to the society, how is that going to happen, and when?"

"We'll have to strategize and that requires my brain to think." He eyed her and grinned. "I need something to make my brain synapse. Will you go into the kitchen and look on top of the fridge? There's a shoebox filled with pizzelles. Bring out four; two for me and two for you."

"Oh, no thank you, Mr. Benito—"

"It's Pop, or Angelo. No mister. And if we're gonna work together, you're gonna learn to eat pizzelles."

***

Harry yanked his tie into place and grabbed his suit jacket. He had an appointment across town in forty-five minutes and it would take fifty-five minutes to get there. Damn. This being in charge and accountable bullshit was messing with his head and his body. How was a person supposed to get in a decent workout, eat a meal, and take a good crap if he had to fly out the door and into rush traffic? Only to sit there like an imbecile, creeping along until some jerk tried to cut three lanes to the exit? Maybe he should reconsider his start time *and* his end time. Ten o'clock to two o'clock had always worked in the past, and no outside appointments either. He was the big cheese now; people should come to him. And Belinda could continue to run to the corner shop and bring him his coffee and oatmeal. Why not? He paid her well; she should sing "John Jacob Jingleheimer Schmidt" if he asked her to.

He'd been in a foul mood for the past twelve days and it had nothing to do with work or appointments or breakfast. It had to do with *her:* Greta Servensen. Two Sundays had passed with no visit to the tidy bungalow, no lemon meringue pie, no mother cutting him the look with her voodoo eyes, and no kids staring at him as though they couldn't quite make out why he was there. Hell, he couldn't fault them on that one. He'd never been able to figure out why he ended up at the Servensens' dinner table every Sunday like friggin' clockwork, but he had. And damn, if he hadn't looked forward to it, especially when the mother was flitting off with her old cronies to some knitting party where they made a bunch of socks and scarves for the needy. Then, he could relax and Greta's smile would spread and light up his heart. Even the kids, Arnold and Elizabeth, acted happier when the "police" wasn't in residence. But it didn't matter now because he'd gotten the boot.

Three hours and a speeding ticket later, Harry slammed the door to his office and tossed his client files on the desk. He eyed the decanter in the corner and glanced at his watch. Before Chrissie left and put him in charge, he would have been on his third scotch and to hell with drinking before noon. But now he had other things to consider, like being a responsible adult whom people depended on for paychecks, insurance, 401K's. If he were honest about it, which he often wasn't, he'd admit he liked people needing him. It felt good, especially when he could deliver, which he'd been doing since the day Chrissie handed him her father's pocket watch and headed to Magdalena for good. He missed Chrissie, wished she'd take a trip here with that husband of hers, Lily too, so they could see what The Windy City was all about. Lily would love seeing the city from the rooftops. And Michigan Avenue? What wasn't to like about that. Even Nate, hermit that he was, would enjoy a good bowl of penne or a plate of beef carpaccio.

Of course they wouldn't come, not with Gloria breathing the same city air. The one upside to Chrissie's move was not being obligated to attend those blasted, ridiculous dinners Gloria insisted on, even after Charlie's death, as though she were serving two dozen people. It wasn't as if she actually prepared anything or ate more than a bite here and there. The woman just liked the idea of pretending she was a showcase for family and commitment. And control, couldn't forget that. Gloria Blacksworth was all about bending people and situations to fit her needs.

But she hadn't been able to control Chrissie. The girl had escaped and found a life far from the destructive grasp of a manipulative mother. Still, he missed Chrissie. A lot. Harry picked up the phone and punched out her number, relieved she was only a phone call away.

"Hello?"

"How's my favorite girl?" Harry settled in his chair and kicked his feet onto the edge of the desk.

"Uncle Harry! I was just thinking about you."

He smiled, his mood lifting as he thought of her in the small office she'd rented, or off with Lily as the child click-clicked her way to new memories with the early birthday present he'd sent her last month: a camera. "And what were you thinking? How sad you are to have abandoned this old fool?"

"Actually, I was wondering if you planned to visit this summer because Lily's been asking. She wanted to call the other night to tell you about a movie with a talking dog named Harry, but I told her it was too late."

"She can call whenever she wants. I like talking to her. We understand what it's like being the youngest kid."

"Oh, please. And don't you dare tell her to call whenever she wants, because you have no idea what you're saying. I once told Lily I'd make her breakfast whenever she wanted, meaning after seven. She woke me up at three in the morning, begging for pancakes."

Harry pictured that scene and smiled. "Unless you've improved, you had a hard time in the kitchen when you were fully awake. I can't imagine what you'd produce waking up from a dead sleep."

"Well, it was only toast. The pancakes had to wait a few more hours." She laughed. "And I'm getting better. Miriam and Nate are very patient teachers."

Her voice slipped into his heart and pulled it apart. He really missed her, and talking on the phone actually made it worse. Still, it wasn't about him or what he wanted. It was about Christine and her life. "You sound happy, kid."

"I am." She sighed. "A little aggravated with some narrow-minded thinking in this town, but I've figured a way around it."

"No doubt."

"So, will you come visit? I miss you."

"Me too." He hesitated, figured what the hell and said, "Any chance you might consider a trip here?" He'd been really good about not asking, but this thing with Greta had him off his game and vulnerable, though he'd be damned if he'd ever admit it. Christine waited so long to answer he almost asked again, but before he could, she spoke.

"I'm not ready."

That meant, *I'm not ready to face my mother.* "She try to contact you?" When Chrissie first left, she told him that her mother called five and six times a day, then five and six times a week, then letters, and who knew what Gloria's current modus operandi was? He'd bet she had the private investigator tailing Chrissie. That would be Gloria's style, all wrapped up and served to her in a monthly report.

"No, she hasn't tried. And you?"

"Nope." *Thank God for that.* "Okay, now that I completely ruined this conversation, I might as well toss it in the garbage and light a match. Are you ever going to be ready?"

***

Gloria Blacksworth sipped her coffee and flipped the page of the magazine. She'd stopped reading the newspaper years ago, too much doom and gloom, and all before lunch. Who needed that when there was enough tragedy in a person's life to fill a Dumpster? She bit into her toast, rye with cherry jam, spread thin. The new girl had almost figured out Gloria's food specifications. She was not quite as adept as Greta Servensen, but then she wasn't eyeing Harry Blacksworth either. Since

Greta's forced departure, there'd been four cooks. Why was a cook so hard to find? The requirements were not that complicated or unattainable, were they? One must possess a general knowledge of kitchen appliances, have an aptitude for baking, and know how to prepare a good roast. One could certainly refer to a book for guidance, couldn't one? And a cook must understand politeness, modesty, and what constituted an overall geniality. Was that so very difficult? Apparently locating such a person was a monumental task and one that should not be treated lightly. The first cook after Greta had thought it acceptable to try on jewelry found in the master bedroom, as long as she didn't leave the premises with it. The second had the disgusting habit of sampling everything she made, to the point of presenting a meal that had been decreased by half. The third asked if the young woman in the picture on the mantel was Gloria's daughter. Of course it was, but that was not the point. Gloria did not need a reminder of the hole in her heart, especially when delivered by a servant.

This new one was a quick learner. She was twenty-three or -four, young enough to serve as a brutal reminder that Gloria's skin wasn't as firm and supple as it had once been, her hair unable to achieve the color and luster of a younger version without hours of treatment, and her eyes were no longer those of a hopeful twenty-something. Age and living had trounced Gloria, sat on her with such heaviness she'd not been able to spring back as quickly or as well as she'd once done.

No matter, the girl displayed respectfulness, punctuality, and adequate culinary skills—ha! How sad that the term *adequate* would be applied to Gloria's vocabulary. Her name was Elissa Cerdi, but it was easier to think of her as merely "the cook" unless it was necessary to address her directly.

"Mrs. Blacksworth?" The cook stood a few feet away, arms at her side, a cautious smile on her face. "I need to run to the store to pick up a few things for tonight's dinner. Would you mind if I left now?"

"Aren't you supposed to prepare for the week to minimize trips?" Greta had never left her post and run willy-nilly all over town in search of food items. She'd made lists, been organized, and efficient. And Harry Blacksworth had ruined it all. Damn that man.

"I'm sorry. I didn't realize we were low on strawberries. If you don't want me to leave, I can substitute the frozen ones." The girl's voice softened. "My grandmother used to do that, said it worked in a pinch if money was short."

"Well. Money isn't short and frozen isn't fresh, is it?"

The girl blushed. "No, Mrs. Blacksworth."

Gloria sighed. "Go if you must, but don't get lost and check the menu for the rest of the week. I don't want you coming to me tomorrow because you've run out of lemons."

"Yes, Mrs. Blacksworth." She nodded, backed up toward the kitchen. "Thank you. I'll be back in a jiff."

I'll be back in a jiff. Christine had used that phrase when she was a teen and wanted to convince her parents to let her take off to this place or that, citing her leaving would barely be noticed because she'd return so quickly, they wouldn't even miss her. *I'll be back in a jiff.* Gloria's breath caught in her throat, sucked out by the cook's words and the horrible realization that Christine would not be back in a jiff. She would not be back at all.

"Mrs. Blacksworth?" The girl inched toward her. "Are you unwell?"

Yes, yes dammit, I'm bleeding inside, my heart torn apart and left in shreds. Gloria cleared her throat and sat up straight. "I'm fine." As fine as a mother could be when she had a daughter who shunned her. How could a child pretend a parent didn't exist? Gloria sniffed. How indeed? Did Christine merely transfer the title of "mother" to that Desantro woman? Did that woman enjoy special dinners with Christine, even a Mother's Day card as Gloria once had? The thought of Christine attempting to replace her birth mother with her father's mistress was unconscionable and disgusting. But the truth lay in the empty seat next to her. It had been months since she'd seen or heard from her daughter, and it would be many more before she did—if at all.

No one could replace a mother; didn't Christine understand that? Had pride and that damnable Harry Blacksworth convinced her she was better off pretending Gloria didn't exist? There was one way to find out, and confrontation was more friend than foe right now. Yes, indeed it was. A kernel of a plan burst through her, spilled out.

"I'm planning a trip out of town for a few days. I'd like you to stay here and tend to my orchids." It was not a question, but a statement. *I'll be out of town. You'll be watching my orchids.* No one ever challenged her, at least not since Harry Blacksworth, and she hadn't seen that sad excuse for a human being since Christine left.

The girl bit her lower lip, hesitated. "Do you know when you'd be leaving?"

"I haven't decided yet. Does it matter?" How could she know when she'd only conjured up the idea a minute ago?

More lip biting, accompanied by a brilliant flush and a bit of hand wringing. "It's my parents' twenty-fifth wedding anniversary next weekend. I told them I'd babysit my little sister so they could celebrate. They're staying downtown."

"How nice." Twenty-five years. Comprised of what? Love? Hate? Compromise? A mistress or two?

The lip biting stopped. "They're so excited. They never go anywhere and this is a big deal." Her eyes grew bright, her voice soft like she was recalling a fairytale. "Dad ordered a dozen roses for the hotel room and plans to attach a pair of diamond-chip earrings to them." The fairytale continued. "Mom got him a watch and had the date inscribed and a message that says, 'Here's to twenty-five more'."

"How romantic." Charles had purchased her a two-carat diamond pendant for their twenty-fifth anniversary. She'd chosen it, of course, but he'd been more than willing to visit the jeweler's and pick it up. *Happy Anniversary, Gloria.* Charles had held out the silver-wrapped box and given her a smile that was reserved, withdrawn, and empty. She should have snapped the box shut and thrown it at him, spewing a line of curses that would shock him. Oh, she'd certainly wanted to, yes, she had. But then what? Then he might have done the unthinkable—he might have left her. And so she'd lifted the necklace from the velvet-lined box and handed it to her husband. He'd gently placed it around her neck, fastened the clasp, and not once did he touch her. Not a hand on the shoulder, a brush of fingers across her neck, certainly not a kiss. There had been nothing but the weight of the diamond necklace and years of discontent holding them together. *Happy Anniversary, indeed.*

"I'm sorry, Mrs. Blacksworth, but I have to babysit my little sister next weekend, so if that's the date and you can give me specific times, I'll see if I can fit it in."

Gloria blinked. "Fit it in?"

A nod. A bit of lip biting. "Yes. I'll try very hard to accommodate you."

"Why, thank you." The girl was accommodating her? Well. "I'll wait until after your parents celebrate their anniversary so you won't be distracted. Orchids require great care. I have several of them." One for every month Christine had been gone.

"Yes, Mrs. Blacksworth. How long will you be away?"

Gloria slid her gaze to Charles's empty seat. "Four days. I think that will be sufficient."

Chapter 4

Christine removed four plates from the cupboard and set them on the table next to the silverware. Miriam had invited her and Nate for chicken and dumplings, one of Nate's favorites. At least that's what he'd told her, but maybe he simply wanted a respite from the treadmill of nightly cooking. She was getting better in the kitchen, but he had a twenty-year head start on her. It would take time and lots of practice. Unfortunately for her husband, he was the resident guinea pig. When she cooked, which wasn't more than once every two weeks, he ate everything on his plate, chewing and swallowing with such deliberation that talk was confined to one-word comments and nods. She'd offered to cook tonight, a chicken and broccoli dish Miriam said he loved, but when she suggested it, he paled and declined, muttering in a rush about an invitation from his mother. Well, she couldn't be good at everything, but that didn't mean she was going to give up. Nate was getting that chicken and broccoli dish next week and it was going to taste like his mother's, even if Miriam had to provide onsite supervision.

"There's something you should know about Pop," Miriam said.

"Oh?" Christine wanted to learn everything about the man who would be the catalyst to get her town support. Plus, a person who dressed like a billboard for major athletic companies required further conversation.

"Last Christmas, he visited his son in California. Pop hates traveling five minutes, let alone hopping a plane and heading two thousand-plus miles. But he did it for Lucy, his granddaughter." Miriam poured a glass of ice tea and took a sip. "He had a stroke while he was there, right after Christmas.

His son, Anthony, brought in specialists and Pop fussed at all of them, refusing to listen until Doc Needstrom, who lives here, called and told Pop to settle down and follow instructions or he'd end up meeting his wife before next Christmas." She shook her head and smiled. "That got him in line, but then he fell and broke his hip. He almost gave up. Anthony made big plans for Pop to sell his house, move into a condo or an assisted living home in San Diego. That idea did not sit well with Pop. He got all feisty and pushed himself through rehab so he could get back here."

"He does seem very driven." That was an understatement.

Miriam's brow furrowed. "Anthony isn't going to give up. He'll keep pressing to get Pop out of here, and you can probably tell, Pop isn't one to be pressed." Her voice softened. "Getting old is difficult, on the person and the family. There's such a fine line between maintaining independence and knowing when you aren't independent anymore."

"I think it would be hard for both sides, but Pop sounds pretty spry, with a wicked sense of humor and some keen insight."

"Oh, he's got insight, sometimes too much. He and Lily have been good for each other. She keeps him young and he sends her home quoting Mark Twain."

Christine traced the apple pattern on the plastic tablecloth. "Speaking of insight, he wasn't big on my father, was he?"

Miriam sighed and looked away. "No, and he's told me for years, in English and Italian."

"He seems tough, but I think he's the kind of person who will do anything for you once you win him over."

"Hmm."

Christine had heard that small sound enough times in the past several months to know it meant Miriam was plotting and planning. "Okay, what are you thinking about?"

"Pop has always been a softy for a person in need. He and Lucy were always diving into one cause or another." She paused, threw Christine a pointed look. "And if it wasn't a cause, they could convince you it should be."

"So now I'm a cause?" No one had ever considered her a "cause" except maybe her mother as she tried to secure a marriage to Connor Pendleton. Gloria had also taken up a personal crusade to convince Christine that much happiness and self-worth could be found in clothing, jewelry, and personal pampering, even though her mother had failed on all fronts.

Miriam shook her head. "A cause? Of course not. But you're a woman in need and Pop does love to save his damsels. Just don't let him drive you crazy with those pizzelles. He's got Lily hooked on them and you know how she can be when she sets her mind to wanting something."

"You mean she gets stubborn, like her brother?"

"Exactly. She was after me to take her to Pop's since 7:00 A.M., but I told her Pop had a routine that included reading the morning paper, eating his oatmeal with raisins, and twenty minutes in the bathroom." Her lips twitched. "Not necessarily in that order."

Christine laughed. What would Pop do if he knew they were discussing his morning rituals, including his bathroom habits? From the little she'd learned about him, he'd probably put the rituals in order for her. "So Lily's there now?"

"Oh, she is, and I told her she'd better not come home with a belly stuffed full of pizzelles and no appetite for dinner." Miriam glanced at her watch. "Nate said he'd pick her up after work. They should be here soon."

"Good, because I'm hungry." And she missed her husband. When he walked in the door, her world shifted, her heart swelled. What would it be like in five years, ten? After a child or two? Their love would only grow deeper, their bond stronger. A few minutes later, Nate's truck rumbled up the drive. Doors clanged shut, footsteps raced up the path and onto the back porch.

"Christine!" Lily flung open the door and rushed inside waving a paper bag and wearing a huge grin. "Look what I won!"

"Let me guess. Is it something I can eat?"

"Uh-huh." Lily gave her a quick hug and shook the bag. "You can eat it."

"Is it yellow, flat, and crispy?"

Lily giggled. "Yup." She began to slowly open the bag, paused. "Keep guessing."

Christine tapped a finger to her chin and frowned. "Is it…could it possibly be…." Another giggle from Lily, followed by more bag shaking. "A pizzelle?"

"Yes!" Lily dove into the bag and pulled out three pizzelles. "How did you know?" She glanced at Nate who stood in the doorway, watching them. "Did you call and tell her my surprise? If you did, that is not fair. You're not supposed to tell secrets."

Nate moved toward his sister, knelt down, and looked her in the eye. "I did not tell Christine, silly. Did you ever think maybe that buddy of yours told her all about how you two bet on these things when you play checkers?"

Lily peeked in the bag, nodded, her lips pulling into a wide grin. "I bet it was him. He thought he was going to win, but I got him. Took all his kings."

Nate flipped one of her braids over her shoulder. "I'll bet you did." He stood and leaned toward Christine. "Close your eyes, Lily."

She giggled. "You're going to kiss her."

"I am." He cupped Christine's chin and placed a soft kiss

on her mouth. "We have an audience," he murmured. "We'll finish this later."

Later was good. Later, with Nate, was perfect.

"Lily," Miriam interrupted the moment with sternness in her voice. "How many of those things did you eat and how many are in that bag?"

Lily turned and held out the bag for her mother to inspect. "There's only three. See?" She dumped the contents of the paper bag onto the kitchen table. "There were four, but Nate ate one on the way home."

Miriam slid a glance in her son's direction and sighed. "And how many did you eat at Pop's?"

"Only one."

"But I sent you with two dozen. Where are the rest?"

Lily looked at her mother and said matter-of-factly, "He's keeping them for me. Said they would be safe and I didn't have to worry about Nate sneaking any."

"He said that?" This from Nate.

Lily nodded. "Yup. Said Christine might want them. too, so we should keep them at his house."

"The proverbial fox in the hen house," Nate muttered.

Miriam's lips pinched. "If that man thinks he's going to live on those darn things, I swear, I'll march right over there and tell him exactly what's on my mind. He needs to get his fruits and vegetables." She shook her head and snatched Lily's winnings from the table. "That man's going to turn into a pizzelle."

"No, he's not," Lily said. "He can't."

"Don't worry about it, Miriam." Christine trailed a hand along her husband's arm and stood. "Pop and I are meeting tomorrow to go over strategies. I'll find out what's going on."

***

Four days later, Christine and Pop entered the Magdalena

Towne Hall, a spacious old house built of white brick, covered in ivy, surrounded by azaleas, rosebushes, and boxwoods. Pop told her the house had belonged to Mimi Pendergrass's family. Mimi was the mayor of Magdalena and a founding member of The Bleeding Hearts Society.

"Mimi's a real dynamo," he said as they climbed the creaky stairs to the second-floor meeting room. "Lost a husband to a heart attack, a son to an auto accident, and a nephew in the service." He paused on the step, leaned close, and whispered in a voice that was not a whisper, "There's a daughter, too. Hasn't heard from her in seven years. Something about a man."

Wasn't it always about a man? Maybe Mimi was like Gloria; maybe she'd tried to manipulate her daughter's life and her choice in men. And maybe it hadn't turned out well for her.

"And there's Will Carrick. He's a widower, owns a piece of land outside of town. Got a niece that's been giving him trouble, but he might not say anything about it with you there." They reached the top of the steps and Pop hitched up his sweatpants and lifted his arms over his head in a stretch. "Staying limber's the key to getting old. And sleep, lots of it, not just the dozing in the afternoon. Eat right, too."

"Does that include pizzelles with every meal?"

Pop eyed her from behind his large, silver frames. "If need be." He grinned. "Lucy used to give me the most horrible time about it. 'You're gonna end up with the diabetes,' she'd say and 'How are you gonna work in the garden when you can't fit between the rows?' She worried me to death. But in the end, God took the good one and left me behind. Sometimes it makes no sense, no sense at all."

The second floor was high-ceilinged, with dangling globed lights, dark wooden floors, and burgundy walls covered with photographs. The photographs did not contain people, other than a random hand or finger, or perhaps a foot on a shovel. They did, however, share their own particular form of beauty: a dissemination of the flower, from petal to stem to root. Dark, rich soil stuffed in a clay pot. A bulb, thick and meaty, ready for planting. Seeds: thin, flat, hard, tiny, thumbnail size.

"Pretty good, aren't they? That's Mimi's work; she spends hours lining up a seed and a pod. This leaf, that stem. Calls it therapy." He lowered his voice, muttered, "I call it just short of crazy, but it gives her a few minutes of peace and sometimes that's all you can ask for."

"They're very interesting." Such intricate detail. So precise. She was anxious to meet Mimi Pendergrass, not just because she was the mayor and an important person in the community, but because the woman obviously had a passion for her work and excelled at it. Christine followed Pop toward a hand-painted sign that read "The Bleeding Hearts Society". For a man in his seventies who had recently suffered a broken hip, Pop could move. "Let me do the talking. I know how to work this crew. And don't pay no never-mind to Ramona Casherdon. Grief has turned her plain mean. You just smile and follow my lead." He threw her a wide grin and removed his baseball cap. "Let's go."

It was obvious in the span of two minutes that Pop had neglected to tell anyone she'd be in attendance. He didn't seem to notice the pointed stares or if he did, it had no effect on him as he took her arm and led her straight to a woman dressed in jeans, clogs, and a T-shirt that read "Plant Power".

"Mimi, this here's Christine Desantro," he paused, added, "Charlie Blacksworth's daughter."

Mimi Pendergrass was small-built, with cropped salt-and-pepper hair, and a firm handshake. Red glass earrings in the shape of a triangle dangled from tiny lobes. "Welcome," she said in a voice that held a hint of a drawl. "I heard about you and Nate. Good luck to you." She said the last part in such a way that Christine didn't know if she meant good luck because you'll need it, or simply, good luck.

"Thank you."

"I believe I've seen you about town a time or two. Maybe at Sal's Market." She rubbed her jaw, apparently considering where she might have seen Christine. "Or St. Gertrude's. Hmm. You and Lily sure do have the same eyes." And then, "I'm real sorry about your father." She shook her head. "Damn shame. He was a good man."

"Yes, he was." For a small town, there were still a lot of people she hadn't met. Miriam knew the whole town but hadn't seemed particularly eager to thrust Christine into Magdalena society, and Nate certainly hadn't jumped to provide a bounty of introductions, not when he still got looks from women he'd dated—or whatever he'd done with them. He'd told her he'd lived here all of his life, and most of the people annoyed the hell out of him because they couldn't mind their own business. They poked, prodded, asked too many damn questions that were none of their business. Yes, he did have a point, but a sentiment like that just wasn't human. Christine glanced at Pop Benito who stood next to her, smiling. Miriam and Nate could keep to themselves because she had her own Magdalena Welcome Wagon right beside her.

"Christine's in business," Pop said. "She's renting an office next door to Barbara's Boutique and Bakery."

Of course, Mimi must already know that, being the mayor and all. She eyed Christine over her lime reading glasses. "I heard you helped Richard Voormen get a loan and gave him a budget."

How had she heard that? "Well, I can't really say."

The woman waved a hand in the air. "Don't need to. I'm

friends with the boy's aunt and she told me all about it. Says there might be hope for him yet."

"See there?" Pop nodded. "Christine's a financial whiz."

"Good to know. Now, go grab yourself something to eat. I brought those sugar cookies you like and there's hibiscus tea over there, too. And Ramona brought sweet rolls." Mimi excused herself and moved toward the oblong table.

"That didn't go very well." Christine said in a low voice. She'd had more success in a boardroom filled with top executives than she did with the mayor of Magdalena.

Pop shrugged. "It ain't over yet. Give it time to percolate. Now, let's get some sugar cookies."

The meeting began and ended with plans to plant flowers in the wooden boxes alongside the business locations downtown and in the hanging baskets near the coffee shop. Suggestions for specific flowers were given and noted, votes were taken, and petunias, impatiens, alyssum, and tuberose tuberous begonias were the winners. There were nine people in attendance, including Pop and Christine. Will Carrick was the only other male. He owned a stretch of land outside of town and the society used a patch of his property to grow and harvest perennials. When Mimi Pendergrass introduced Christine, the members mouthed their welcomes, some even smiled, but the wariness in their eyes said they didn't know Christine Desantro any more than they knew Christine Blacksworth.

The majority of The Bleeding Hearts Society monthly meeting had nothing to do with planting, propagating, or harvesting. In fact, it had nothing to do with anything related to plants. It did, however, have to do with Will Carrick's niece, age fifteen, sneaking out after curfew, threatening to run away, disrespecting the rules of the house. In other words, being a teenager.

"What can you do about it?" Will rubbed his temples with callused hands. "My sister is beside herself with worry that Megan is just going to take off one day, and if she does she'll have gotten into deep trouble." Code for pregnant.

"Where's her father?" Christine asked.

They all looked at her as though she'd asked about running a highway through their town.

"Gone," Ramona Casherdon said between pinched lips.

"Amen to that," Will muttered.

"It is so hard to be a parent today," Wanda Cummings said. "Almost worse to be a grandparent and witness it all." Pop had told Christine that Wanda had eight children and sixteen grandchildren, all living within a ten-mile radius of Magdalena. "Do you think we can invite someone to speak at the library about troubled teens? They brought in that social worker last year and I thought she was real helpful."

"I suppose we could have a plant sale and put the proceeds toward the cost of the speaker." This from Mimi. "Even a bake sale would help. Ramona," she turned to the woman with the solemn expression and said, "maybe we could coax you into baking a few dozen sweet rolls?"

"And I'll make pizzelles," Pop piped in. "But if we want to raise serious money, we need the help of a professional." He grinned and extended a hand in Christine's direction. "This little lady knows all about raising money and she's going to teach us how to do it."

***

The most valuable lesson Gloria learned from her father-in-law, Randolph Blacksworth, was to employ the element of surprise whenever possible. It worked in battles fought on the field, in the boardroom, and in life. For this reason, Gloria did not announce her impending arrival in Magdalena. Rather, on a sunny Tuesday in early June, she drove her black Mercedes sedan through the streets of the small town and straight to ND Manufacturing. She didn't expect to find Christine there. She did, however, expect to locate her target: Nathan Desantro, Christine's husband. If Gloria had any say in the matter or could manipulate the situation to her satisfaction, the man would not possess that title much longer.

Gloria parked her car in the truck-filled lot and entered the low, squat building. She'd never been inside a factory, and while there was no distinct odor to the place, she wrinkled her nose. What would Charles have said if she'd made the trip while he was alive? Would he have begged her to leave, promising to end his relationship with Magdalena and everyone associated with it? Or would he have stood beside that woman and their child and told Gloria he wanted a divorce? She couldn't say, even now after his death, and that was why she'd never entered Magdalena while Charles was alive.

But now he was dead and Christine had married the mistress's son and practically disowned her mother. It had to stop, no matter what methods need be employed, and Gloria was quite good at inventing ways to get what she wanted. It was ultimately for Christine's own good. Mothers always knew what was best for their children, and it was a mother's duty to steer the child back onto the right track, especially if said child had gone astray—which Christine had.

The Desantro man was the key. She'd read enough about him in Lester Conroy's report to know he was fiercely loyal, proud, hard-working, loved his sister and apparently Christine. Damn to the last one. Maybe Lester was wrong? Just because he saw a couple holding hands did not mean love. Or kissing or cooking a meal together. But the man usually had a keen sense about these things, so it might be true. Even if love were involved, Nathan Desantro was a hothead with trust issues, and

Gloria would make those work to her advantage.

"Ma'am, can I help you?"

A thin woman with tight curls and cat-eye glasses peered at Gloria from across the receptionist window as though she'd just spotted a lioness and couldn't put a name to it.

"Yes." Gloria advanced toward the window and offered a smile in the woman's direction. "I'm looking for Nathan Desantro. Is he available?"

"I don't know. I can check." She lifted the receiver on the phone and paused, her small face a wrinkle of confusion. "Who should I say is calling?"

"Gloria Blacksworth. His mother-in-law."

***

Nate had been working on a machine that went down on second shift when Betty called to tell him his mother-in-law was waiting for him in the lobby. For a half second, he thought Jack Finnegan was playing a joke on him as he did now and again, but the nervousness in Betty's voice told him this was no prank.

What the hell did Gloria Blacksworth want with him? Did Christine know her mother was in town? He bet she didn't, and if he had anything to do with it, the woman would be heading out of Magdalena in fifteen minutes or less. He thought about washing the grime from his hands and face, changing into a shirt that wasn't rimmed with sweat, but figured the hell with it. The woman would consider him low-life scum even if he greeted her in a tuxedo. Nate grabbed a rag, wiped his hands and face, and headed toward the lobby.

He spotted her before she saw him, which gave him a half-second advantage. Small, petite, blonde, a real blue blood with the education and manners to go along with it. Clothes, too, designer, no doubt, and he knew the glint of diamond on her ears was not cubic zirconium. She turned and her gaze met his, equally assessing, equally disdainful. The woman didn't need designer duds to ooze wealth; it spilled from her pores. She moved toward him with casual grace and elegance, in a sleekness that proclaimed, *I'm rich, more than rich. And you're not.* "Hello, Nathan."

"Gloria." Oh, but those damnable eyes were cold. "What a surprise."

Her laughter filled the tiny lobby, swirled and grabbed him around the neck. "I'm sure it is."

He crossed his arms over his chest, forcing her to take a step back. "Does Christine know?"

"No." She sighed and lifted a delicate shoulder in a gentle shrug. "As much as I'd love to see my daughter, it's obvious she's not interested at this point in time."

Betty gasped, dropped a basket of paper clips on the floor. "Oh, oh, oh." Nate glanced over to see her scrambling after them.

"Let's go in my office." He shot one more look at Betty who pretended to zip her mouth closed and led his mother-in-law into his office. He'd never been much good with in-laws. Patrice's father was dead and her mother had been a money-grubber who'd expected to move in with Nate and Patrice or at the very least, receive a monthly check from them. It hadn't happened. If the woman could spend half her paycheck on lottery tickets and smoke a pack of cigarettes a day, then she could figure out her own issues. It was a damn sure bet Gloria wasn't after money. What did she want? His help repairing the mother-daughter relationship she destroyed with her manipulative bullshit? She could go to hell and back if she thought he'd help her do anything other than point her out of Magdalena. Nate snatched a stack of papers from a chair and said, "Have a seat."

Gloria Blacksworth eyed the vacant chair a second too long

before she sat down. "Thank you."

Nate leaned against the desk, determined to gain any leverage over the woman he could. A standing position dominated a sitting one; he'd take it. "Why are you here?"

The smile she offered was forced and fake. "Maybe I wanted to get a first-hand opinion of the man who stole my daughter from me."

"I didn't steal her. You lost her."

The lips pinched, the eyes narrowed. "That's not true." She sighed, tucked a stray lock of blondish hair behind her ear. "Christine and I shared a special relationship that only mothers and daughters can share." She paused, bit out her next words. "Until she came here and this town destroyed it."

Was she for real? "You make it sound like we're the plague."

Her chin inched up. "This town and the people in it ruin lives. They latch onto unsuspecting victims and destroy them."

"I think you're the one who does that."

She ignored him. "Christine should have married Connor Pendleton, not someone like you."

"From what I've heard, the guy was more in love with his clients than he was with Christine."

"Because he knew restraint? Because he understood lineage was important in a relationship? You're nothing but a shot of testosterone in a flannel shirt and your mother's no better."

So there it was. She wanted to zing him about his mother. Well, he wasn't biting. Nate pushed away from the desk and towered over her. "You need to leave. Now."

The damn woman didn't budge. "I'm not afraid of you, but you should be afraid of me." Her lips curved into the faintest smile. "I might look small and fragile, but I have a lot of power."

"I don't think there's anything fragile about you, Gloria.

You're as dangerous as a rattlesnake."

"I'm glad you realize that." The smile spread. "Do you have any idea where Christine comes from, the opportunities she's passing up to remain in this backward town with a husband who sweats for a living and," she wrinkled her nose in disgust and pointed to his clothing, "dresses like that?"

"I don't give a damn what you think about me. Christine and I love each other and that's something you damn sure know nothing about." There. He'd said it. Gloria Blacksworth paled, sputtered, then calmed so quickly, he wondered if he'd imagined her earlier upset. Goading her had been low and cruel, but dammit, she'd pushed him.

"I'll make you regret those words." She stood, smoothed the wrinkles from her slacks, and gathered her handbag. "Good-bye, Nathan." Her tone was cool, assessing, dismissive. She turned to leave, stopped and shot him a parting glance. "Tell your mother I think of her every day."

She swept out of the room before he could ask her what the hell that comment meant. Gloria Blacksworth really was a miserable person with her superior attitude and arrogant demeanor. So what if he hadn't been born with a stock portfolio and his father had worked a blue-collar job? So what if Nate used his hands and his brain and wore jeans to work? Did that make him inferior to a suit like Connor Pendleton? Well, did it? Of course not. But Gloria's insidious comments crept past his logic and common sense to take a front and center spot in his brain. *Christine should have married Connor Pendleton, not someone like you.* And, *Do you have any idea where Christine comes from, the opportunities she's passing up to remain in the backward town with a husband who sweats for a living...* By the time he made his way to the lobby, he'd begun to wonder if Christine hadn't been crazy to marry someone like him. And he didn't like that feeling, not one bit.

"What in the hell was that about?" Jack Finnegan pointed to the front window and shook his head. "Betty said that was Charlie's widow."

"Yup." Nate rifled through a stack of mail in the basket beside Betty's desk.

"And?" Jack made his way toward Nate and waited.

"She wasn't very pleasant," Betty chirped. "I mean, seeing as how she's from the city and all, you'd think she'd have had better manners." She lifted her bony shoulders. "Didn't even ask who I was."

"Betty," Jack said in a gruff voice, "those kind of people ain't askin' about the likes of you and me. They get a bead on something and they don't see anything else. Not you, me, a dog. Nothin' but their target." He scratched his stubbled jaw and pushed back his ball cap. "Something tells me you were the target, Nate."

"Pretty much." And she'd nailed him, dead on.

"Gonna tell us what she wanted?" When Nate didn't spit it out, Jack added, "Want us to guess?"

"Nope." Would Gloria try to see Christine? She might have said she'd only come to see him, but a woman like that couldn't be trusted with anything, especially the truth. "I've got to go. I'll see you tomorrow."

"Nate? Aren't you even going to give us a tiny clue?" Betty's question reached him but he was out the door and in his truck before she could try to corner him for details. He had to get to Christine in case Gloria tried to see her daughter. But even as the idea flitted through his brain, he admitted the bigger reason he needed to see his wife: He needed reassurance they were in this marriage together, for better, for worse, and she wasn't going to leave him once she realized he didn't deserve her.

Chapter 5

Christine sat beside Nate on the piano bench while he played Beethoven's "Moonlight Sonata." She rested her head on his shoulder, her hand on his jean-clad thigh. This was peace, pure, absolute. Nights like these calmed her more than any massage or yoga class ever had. When she was with Nate, life made sense. He wasn't big on words or showy gestures, other than the ones that counted like *I love you*, and *You're a part of me*. There were times when she caught him studying her with such intensity, it unnerved her ,and while Nate had opened his world and his heart to her, there was still a part of him that was a loner. Maybe he'd always be that way, or maybe it would take years and a history together before he'd truly open up. But the thoughts were there, the yearning brushing the surface of his emotions even if he couldn't always voice them. One day he would. She believed this as much as she believed in him and his steadfast commitment to do the right thing. Christine closed her eyes and drifted with the music, her body growing languid, her breath matching the soft cadence of the melody.

"Your mother visited me today," Nate said, his voice blending with the notes. At first she didn't think she heard him correctly, but then the music stopped and he repeated the words in the same tone of casualness. "Your mother visited me today."

She straightened and stared at him. "My mother?"

His dark eyes turned opaque, his expression closed. "Oh, yes. Gloria was in Magdalena. She came to the shop."

She sipped in air, tried to focus as visions of her mother and Nate in the same room took shape. It was not a welcome sight. "I haven't spoken to her in months, and she just flitted in to see you?" Why would she do that? Christine knew why, had wondered if her mother would have the audacity to actually make an appearance in the town her father considered "home". The more important question was, Where was she now?

Nate's jaw tensed, the lines around his mouth hardened. Whatever Gloria had "flitted" in about had not been a happy occasion. "I guess I wouldn't use the word *flit*; that's too low-brow for your mother. She's first-class all the way." He paused, his gaze even more unreadable. "And she made sure I knew that."

Christine stroked his stubbled jaw. He had no idea how quickly or viciously her mother could let someone know his insignificance. "Oh, Nate, I'm sorry you had to deal with that. My mother is very difficult in the best of circumstances." What an understatement. "She's got a lot of issues, and with me leaving, I'm sure she's looking for someone to blame." She could not tell him about her mother and Uncle Harry. If she did, she'd have to confess the rest, and that was too painful and surreal to acknowledge. Even now, all these months later, Christine kept that secret in the corner of her subconscious, pulling it out in the blackness of night when she was certain no one would catch a glimpse of her face and guess the truth. "She's trying to punish me for choosing you and this life over the one I left in Chicago."

He eased her hand onto her thigh and looked away. "She was pretty damn convincing."

"What did she say?" It wouldn't take much to guess what her mother had said in her sophisticated voice, her gestures and non-gestures equally demeaning.

He studied the music in front of him as if the notes held the answers to her questions. The only answers would be from a psychiatrist's evaluation and her mother would never submit to one of those. "That you're too good for me, that you don't belong here." He paused, squinted at the pages in front of him. "That you married the wrong guy. You know, typical mother-in-law stuff."

More like typical Gloria Blacksworth. Any thoughts of mending her relationship with her mother disintegrated the second Nate started talking. He was her husband, she loved him, and she would not let her mother's manipulative attempts ruin her life or those she loved. Christine clasped Nate's hand, leaned in and kissed his temple. "Don't let her get inside your head. She's a very unhappy person and she'll try to ruin us."

He let out a laugh filled with disgust. "That's an understatement."

"She's not going to get away with treating you this way." Damn her. Did she really think this type of behavior would make Christine want to mend their relationship? "Did she say where she was staying?"

"I got the impression she made the trip to meet me and you weren't part of the equation." He shrugged. "Of course, we both know you're the whole equation, while I'm merely irrelevant data."

"You have to forget everything she said."

Nate turned and looked at her, his dark gaze burrowing straight to her soul. "She was right about one thing." His voice dipped lower. "You do deserve better than me." He swept a hand around the room. "Better than this."

Panic swirled through her, settled in her chest. "Don't say that."

"Why? A log cabin that's probably smaller than your mother's foyer? A town that likes you but hasn't decided if you're worthy of their trust?"

"Nate—"

"A husband who will never be able to buy you what you're used to, what you deserve?"

Now he sounded like the old Nate, the one who didn't want to need anyone.

"That's absolutely not true. We're meant for each other." She placed a soft kiss on his mouth. When he didn't respond, she pulled back and thrust her disappointment at him. "You're going to let the words of a bitter woman come between us?"

The left side of his jaw twitched. "The bitter woman is your mother, and while I knew she was a tough lady, I didn't expect her to have the ability to make me feel like a hillbilly piece of scum."

"It's what she does and why everyone always scurried around so they wouldn't upset her. Heaven forbid if Dad was a second late for his welcome-home dinner. I went on shopping trips with her and bought clothes I knew I'd never wear again because I didn't want to disappoint her. Even poor Uncle Harry tried to keep his mouth shut so she wouldn't throw a tantrum. Appease, appease, appease. I was even going to marry a man I didn't love, just so I wouldn't upset her." The anger she'd held inside for so many months burst forth, coated her next words. "But guess what? It wouldn't have been enough. She would have continued to insinuate her disappointments on everyone around her, especially me, until I had the number of children she wanted, named them the names she selected, even signed them up for her preferred schools. And I would have ended up just like her: drinking and self-medicating while I stumbled through a designer-clad life, disconnected from my husband and children, disconnected from myself."

Christine swiped at her eyes. "I am not my mother and I will not be defined by her." Her voice turned cold, challenging. "And if you think so little of me, so little of us, that you would believe her sick words, then maybe I am too good for you."

Anger flashed across his face, but he remained silent, assessing her words, drawing his own conclusions. Nate was a hard man to love, and an even harder one to convince he was wrong. She waited for him to say something, anything, even a nod so they could start to talk about it. But he didn't, or maybe he couldn't. The anger on his face smoothed and shifted into something altogether different: fear. Was he afraid she'd leave him?

"I'm not going anywhere. For better, for worse, right?" She offered him a smile, touched his arm. "I'll be here for you, even when you're a thick-headed idiot who doesn't recognize commitment when it hits you in the face."

His lips twitched, his dark eyes grew bright. "Now that's a phrase that will win me over every time." He pulled her to him, framed her face with his large hands and kissed her. "I guess I can be an idiot once in a while," he murmured, nipping her bottom lip.

Christine sighed and pressed her body against his. This conversation wasn't over, even if her husband thought it was. Time and patience would show him there was no need to worry; she wasn't leaving him. "I said a thick-headed idiot."

He laughed and slid a hand up her thigh. "Do you think this thick-headed idiot can entice you to bed?"

"Hmm. Let me think." She traced the zipper of his jeans. "Oh, I absolutely think he can."

**

Harry stood outside of Greta's tiny house and studied his list. Who knew spilling your guts could be confined to a 3x5 lined note card? Not him, that was for sure. But here he was, a fool in a gray suit and a lavender tie, squinting at the card because he'd left his readers in the car and dusk was settling in. Oh hell, he'd practiced the damn speech so many times he didn't need the card to prompt him. He'd come here because the last eighteen days had been a mix of torture and agony, with Greta in the middle of it all. From that fatal luncheon when she'd witnessed Bridgett purring and pouring herself all over him, Greta hadn't spoken one personal word to him. What do you think about adding portobello mushrooms stuffed with zucchini and topped with Parmesan cheese to the menu was not a conversation starter. He'd attempted a few jokes, even recycled ones that had once made her burst out laughing, but he got nothing. Dead stare, pinched lips, nose in the air. She could do a good impression of Gloria without even trying.

And forget the Sunday dinners. She'd shut those down so hard and fast, he'd have better luck getting a seat at Gloria's table. The whole thing didn't sit well. He'd told her he wasn't the commitment kind, and she'd gone and spouted off about what a good man he was, yada, yada… But she'd changed her tune when Bridgett strolled in with her skin-tight dress and five-inch heels. He might have been able to pass her off as his assistant, though probably not, but once she started on about the missing earring—in his bed—he was cooked. It's not that he wanted to lie to Greta, but he hadn't wanted to throw his depravity at her. He'd done more than that; he'd dunked her in the stench of his deeds and held her there until she'd emerged filled with repulsion and disbelief. And that had given him more to think about than he cared to admit.

Maybe it was time to change his act, grow up, become a caring human being. Hell, maybe even attempt an adult relationship that started and continued past the bedroom. He wouldn't be pushed, though, not by Greta's disappointment or her expectations. He scanned the note card once again. *Your absence has caused me to reconsider my actions, which were a grievous offense against you.* What the hell did that mean? He must have been kicked when he wrote it. *Can we start again, fresh? See where it takes us?* See where it takes us? That sounded like code for heading down the aisle. How had that snuck in there? Harry yanked at his tie and vowed to scratch it from the list. *I miss you.* Nope. *Why don't we spend some time together, start slow?* Argh. *How about we take the kids to the zoo on Sunday and then out for pizza?* Okay, now he was going to puke. He could not picture himself on the best of days taking a kid to the zoo to watch a bunch of stinky animals fornicate and crap.

He crammed the note card in his pants pocket and turned to leave, pissed that he'd let an errant emotion like loneliness slip through and land him on Greta's doorstep. Just because he'd broken off his sleepovers with Bridgett didn't mean he'd done it for Greta or that he wanted her to invite him in for coffee and conversation.

"Harry?"

Damn. He swung around and there she was, the thorn in his conscience; blonde, curvy, dressed in jeans and a T-shirt, and looking more delectable than a golden pound cake topped with blueberries and cream. "Hello, Greta." Harry shoved his hands in his pockets and moved toward her as though he were out for a stroll and had just happened upon her street. "Looks like another nice day."

She stepped outside and closed the door behind her. Her feet were bare, her toenails a bright pink. Dainty. Sexy as hell. "Harry? What are you doing here?"

"Me?" Trying not to look like a jerk. "Oh, I don't know." He shrugged. "I've always liked driving this time of year, seeing the landscape turn green, the flowers popping, you know. Kind of picks you up." What kind of bullshit just fell out of his mouth? She looked at him like she thought he was a whack job. Damn, but she had the bluest eyes he'd ever seen. He could get lost in them, float around like he was in the Caribbean…

"Harry? Harry!"

"What?" He cleared his throat and pretended he'd been deep in concentration, not daydreaming about her like some schoolboy imbecile.

"Is something wrong at the restaurant?" Her eyebrows knitted together and she bit her lower lip. "I hired a new waitress. Did you meet her? Was she not acceptable?" Before he could think of an answer, she barreled on. "I know she's young but I'll work with her. She needs this job, Harry. Please don't be harsh on her. Everyone deserves a chance."

"What are you talking about? I didn't come here about a waitress." He rubbed his temples and sighed. "If you say she'll learn, then she'll learn. Just make sure she knows the difference between Pecorino Romano and Parmesan cheese."

Greta offered a faint smile. "I will. Thank you." And then, "Why are you here?"

Her voice was soft, close to a caress if he had to categorize it. Damn tempting. That was the problem with Greta Servensen: Everything about the woman was too damn tempting. Oh, what the hell? A tiny bit of honesty wasn't going to kill him. "I came because I missed you."

He coughed, waited for her to smile or maybe slug him in the gut. She did neither. Merely stared, her expression as closed as a poker player's. Harry shifted from one foot to the other, dug around in his pants pocket, and pulled out the crumpled note card. "I figured you'd give me that look, you know the one that says you think I'm full of bullshit. I made a few notes so I could keep it all straight in my head: the reason I came, what I wanted to say, why I wanted to say it." He stopped, scanned the other sentences he'd written and determined they were equally ridiculous. "Oh, hell, I don't know why I'm here. I want things to be the way they were." He gestured toward the house. "The dinners, the late-night snacks." He paused, his voice gentling. "Talking to you. I miss that. Can't we get that back?" She squared her shoulders and studied him, her bottom lip quivering the tiniest bit. What was wrong? Had he frightened her? Said too much? Maybe he should have—

"I think you should bring your appetite and your talks to the young woman who lost her earring in your bed."

So much for Greta being afraid of him. He'd mistaken the quivering for fear when it was anger disguised behind those full lips. She was still pissed about Bridgett. Maybe he could cajole her into a good mood. "Bridgett isn't much in the kitchen or in conversation."

She snorted. "Obviously."

Obviously? What was he supposed to do with that comment? It was pure sarcasm, filled with female venom. "I haven't seen her in weeks." Was he, Harry Blacksworth, actually confessing this? She raised a brow that implied he was lying. "I'm done with her." There. Read between the lines. *I'm interested in you. Can't you see that?*

She sniffed. "And what on earth does that piece of information have to do with me?"

Okay, that was enough. This was why he avoided long-term relationships and female entanglements that led to comments like Greta's. She knew exactly what it had to do with her and yet she expected him to sit down, pat her hand, recite a sonnet or two, and tell her exactly what it had to do with her. In great detail. Repeatedly. Harry met her stare and said, "You're right. It has nothing to do with you. Thanks for reminding me. I'll see you around." He turned and started for his car, anxious to get the hell out of here. Who said a man couldn't be comforted by a drink and a stranger? He planned to do both tonight, anything to not think of Greta Serevensen.

"Harry." She was beside him, close enough for him to

smell her honeysuckle scent.

"What?" He would not notice the wispy strands of blond hair trailing along her neck, or the flush of her cheeks, and certainly not the timid smile hovering about her lips. Full lips. Pink lips. Lips that could take him to heaven.

"May I see your card?"

"What?" He stared at her, confused.

She pointed to the crumpled note card in his hand. "The card. May I see the notes you wrote for me?"

"I didn't write notes for you." Damn straight on that. "I wrote them for myself." He paused, stumbled around, and ended with, "So I could keep my head together, but it was all bullshit anyway." He laughed, folded the card in half, then half again. "You know me, Harry the bullshitter. You deserved better."

She ignored his attempt at humor, kept her gaze glued on his. "May I read what you wrote?"

No. If she read it, she might notice how desperate he'd become and how it all started and ended with her. "It's nonsense."

She held out her hand, small, efficient. "Please?"

It was the *please* that did it, coupled with the sincerity in her voice and the honesty on her face. This was about trust and Harry hadn't seen much of that in his life aside from what he shared with Christine. Still, for some bizarre and totally unfathomable reason, he wanted to trust her. He placed the crumpled-up, folded card in her hand and looked away. "It's just bullshit," he muttered.

She unfolded the note card and attempted to smooth it out. "Sometimes, if you look hard enough, you can pick out bits of truth from the, uh," she paused and finished with an uncharacteristic, "bullshit."

"Or sometimes it's just straight bullshit." He vowed to keep his thoughts in his head from now on, not in any written or verbal format, which could then be retrieved and misinterpreted or properly interpreted by someone else. Namely, someone who was not meant to see or hear what was going on in Harry's messed-up head. He slid a glance her way. What the hell was taking her so long? Was she memorizing every word? Damn. They were only notes, nine of them, and most weren't even complete sentences. "Can't understand my writing, can you? Mrs. Gimball flunked me for penmanship and Mr. Torpin told me I did not possess the proper skill set to create a sentence, let alone a story." His attempt at a laugh fizzled. He couldn't take it any longer. "I lied to you," he said.

That stopped her. She glanced up, brows pinched, eyes wide. "About what?"

Harry pointed at the note card in her hand. "That. It wasn't for me. I was trying to help a friend." Yeah, he liked the sound of that better, made him appear noble, strong, not a gutless wimp with poor penmanship and a bad case of the hots for a woman he shouldn't want. Greta's lips curved at the corner. Was that a smile? Why? She didn't believe him? Thought he was making the friend story up? Give him a minute and he'd railroad her with his sweet talk. Before he could get a line out, she butted into his thoughts.

"This friend, does he have a name?"

Harry shrugged. She was a shrewd one. "Of course he has a name, but I can't divulge it." He paused, added, "You've met him."

"Ahh. From the restaurant?"

She sounded intrigued. Good. He'd play along. "Right. He only came in a few times but he was having real problems with this one woman." He shook his head, falling into the tale. "He had it bad, but he was not the settling down type."

Greta nodded. "Was she?"

"Hell, yeah. She was the kind you took home to your mother."

"And that was a problem?" Her voice turned soft, encouraging.

"For a guy who flunked relationships 101 and had women lining up for him since he was fifteen? Oh, that was a big problem."

"But he wanted to be with this woman?" Her eyes grew bright. "Maybe have a relationship with her?"

"He never came out and said he did, but you don't give up the twenty-five-year-olds and start and end your day thinking about this woman if you don't want a relationship." He paused, met her gaze. "Do you?"

Her mouth opened and he honed in on her tongue. Pink, wet, tantalizing. "No, I don't think so."

"What?" Damn, he couldn't think with her so close, talking in that soft voice, that tongue darting in and out around her words. And that honeysuckle scent grabbing at him…Harry loosened his tie. "Don't you think it's hot out here?"

"I think it's perfect."

The way she said it made it sound like she was talking about a lot more than the weather. Did he want what she might or might not be offering? Of course he did, but with a woman like Greta, it came with conditions. Lots of them.

"'I'm turning over a new leaf. Obviously, there was a misunderstanding. Let's get coffee.'" Her lips twitched, but she kept on reading that damn note card. "'Trust me, this time for real. I miss the times we used to spend together, don't you? I miss your pie.'" She looked up and said, "I miss your pie?"

Heat rushed from Harry's neck, splattered his face, made his eyes water. "What do I know about that kind of stuff? I told you I was helping a friend." He let out a laugh. "He was so desperate, it was pathetic. What kind of guy gives up a steady bed partner who makes no demands on him other than an occasional piece of jewelry and dinner?"

Greta's lips pinched. "Someone who wants more in life than sex and penne with spinach and garbanzo beans."

"What?" That was his favorite dish and she knew it. "Are you talking about me?"

She folded the note card and stuffed it in the back pocket of her jeans. "Oh, I think we are talking about you. I think we've been talking about you, don't you, Harry?"

He stared at her, debating how to answer. Before he could convince himself that admitting anything resembling an emotional attachment spelled disaster, he sucked in a deep breath and said, "Yeah, I guess so."

When Greta smiled, her eyes lit up, her face turned pink, and she actually sparkled. She leaned up on tiptoe and kissed him softly on the mouth. "Don't be afraid. We'll go slow." She spoke as if he hadn't bedded hundreds of woman, as if she was the first one. Maybe in some ways, the important ways like honesty, trust, and fidelity, she was.

"I like slow. I can do slow."

"I'm sure you can," she said in a soft, sultry voice. "I'm sure you do it very well."

Was Greta making sexual innuendos? His Greta? She'd never done that before. He smiled. Maybe this relationship thing wasn't such a bad idea after all.

Chapter 6

Harry sat in Greta's kitchen with a glass of iced tea and a ham and Swiss on rye. He'd tried to tell Greta he wasn't hungry, but the woman had the sandwich ready for him two minutes after he walked through the door, so what choice did he have but to eat the damn thing? She'd been so pleased when he'd taken a bite and given her the thumbs-up. He guessed this was new territory in building a "relationship". Thinking about the other person and wanting to please her, out of bed.

Since the afternoon he'd made a fool of himself at Greta's front door with that ridiculous note card, she'd been extra gentle with him, like he was a wounded duck who couldn't find its way back to water. He was no damn duck and he wasn't wounded, but there was something about her warm hand on his and that smile that calmed him more than a double scotch.

He'd been to her house four times since "the talk"; two of those included dinner with the whole clan. Elizabeth was a miniature version of Greta, blonde, blue-eyed, but damn those sticky hands. She giggled every time she called him Mr. Harry, so much so that Greta blushed and explained when a four-year old called someone Mr. Harry, it meant just that, Mr. Hairy. Whatever. As long as the kid didn't throw up on him or expect him to read bedtime stories, he was good. The boy, Arnold, was eight and a bruiser but shy and clumsy. Poor kid needed some work in the self-esteem area. Maybe he could start by ditching his name and using initials instead. Harry would have to find out the kid's middle name and maybe he could make a few suggestions.

And then there was Helene. The witch of Chicago. Harry didn't care if she thought he was a degenerate; he was a degenerate. Or had been, until recently. It would take a good amount of scrubbing and a few hundred hours of practice to make him a decent human being, but he'd give it a go. The old lady could look down her wide nose at him, mutter in German, and never address him directly, and he was fine with that. But screw around with Greta, demean her with snide comments about her clothes or the meals she prepared or didn't prepare? Those were fighting words. The old bag even picked on poor Arnold and little Elizabeth, calling them brats and ungrateful. Harry vowed the next time she started up, he was going to forget his pledge to clean up his mouth and let her have it, starting and ending with the F-word.

"Mr. Harry?" Elizabeth stood in the doorway, dressed in pink shorts and a purple polka-dot top. "Mama said you're taking us to the zoo today."

"That's right." How the hell he'd volunteered for that job was not worth considering. Wouldn't a shrink have a blast with that one?

"I like the elephants." She took a few steps toward him, her sneakers lighting up as she moved. "Do you like elephants?"

"Sure." Damn, he should have gone on that safari to Africa when he was twenty-five. Then, he'd tell her a thing or two about elephants. Instead, his knowledge was limited to what he'd seen on television and the circus he'd attended as a kid. He'd never made it to a zoo, never had a desire to see animals locked up and kept from roaming free and doing what they would. Maybe it reminded him too much of marriage, cage and all, especially the part about not being able to roam free and do what came naturally.

"Arnold likes the monkeys. They poop all over the rocks."

"You don't say." Harry scratched his chin and nodded. "Guess they don't have toilets, huh?"

She giggled and bounced toward him, stopping when she

was a step away from his feet. Her blue eyes sparkled, just like her mother's. "No, silly. Monkeys don't use toilets."

Harry grinned. "At least they don't have to wait in line."

She giggled again, her face lighting up. "Mr. Hairy," she said in a singsong voice. "He's kinda scary." Next came the hopping from one foot to the other and hand clapping. "Mr. Hairy, he's kinda scary." She held out her hand and said, "Dance with me."

"That's okay, I'll just watch."

"No, I want you to dance. Arnold won't ever do it. He's no fun." She hop-hopped back and forth, twirled around and clapped. "Mr. Hairy, he's kinda scary."

It was catchy in a ridiculous way, but so what? He'd known entering into a "relationship" with Greta, whatever that meant, was going to be foreign, and hell, maybe ridiculous. At least the kid had rhythm, and she could hold a note. Harry shook his head and stood. What the hell? Elizabeth clutched his hands and hop-hopped. "Now you, Mr. Harry. Hop on one foot, then the other. And sing, 'Mr. Hairy, he's kinda scary.'" The first hop was the worst because he knew he looked like a fool, but after that, it was kinda fun.

That's how Greta found them, hopping around the cracked linoleum kitchen, singing a silly song about Mr. Hairy being scary. The second Harry spotted her standing in the doorway dressed in white shorts and a blue top that matched her eyes, he clamped his mouth shut, planted both feet on the floor, and cleared his throat.

"Mama!" Elizabeth clutched Harry's hand and tried to make him move. "Mr. Harry was dancing with me."

Greta's lips twitched. "I see that."

The child smiled up at him, her small hand lifting his in the air so she could twirl underneath his arm. "Singing, too. He's a good singer. Do you want to hear him sing?"

"I'm sure she doesn't." Harry twirled her once more and released her. "Unless she likes the sound of a sick frog." Elizabeth giggled and grabbed his hand. "We're going to see the elephants, Mama. Mr. Harry likes elephants, too. Not monkeys, like Arnold." She scrunched up her nose. "They poop on the rocks. Mr. Harry said that's because they don't have toilets, but I said monkeys don't use toilets!"

"Well." Greta didn't even try to hide her smile this time. "This is going to be an interesting trip."

Two and a half hours later, that proved to be the understatement of the day. Harry couldn't decide what bothered him more: the overabundance of people talking, pointing, screaming, eating, or the caged animals in their supposed "natural" habitat. Say what you wanted, the poor bastards were trapped. A cage was a cage, even if it had a nice view and a manmade watering hole. These animals couldn't take a crap or fornicate without people gawking. It was unnatural and left a pit in Harry's gut that made him worry he might heave. He glanced at Greta who walked ahead with Arnold while Elizabeth lagged behind, clutching his hand. Relationships might proclaim to foster a natural habitat but only through the confines of a cage. And marriage? Hell, why was he even thinking about that? Marriage was a death sentence. End of story.

"Mr. Harry, I'm thirsty." Elizabeth smiled up at him. "Can I have a lemon ice?"

"Sure. I could use a drink, too." A double. "You hungry?"

She glanced at her mother's back, turned to him, and whispered, "Starving."

"Why are you whispering?" he whispered back.

"Mama said not to ask you for anything." When he pointed at her mother, she nodded.

He winked at her. "Well, I'm hungry and Harry

Blacksworth doesn't stuff his face in front of a hungry kid. Greta," he called. "I'm hungry. Let's eat." He'd seen a kid walk by with a double-decker ice cream cone. And another chomping on a hot dog. Damn, did it have sweet onion and ballpark mustard? What about a burger and fries? Funnel cakes? Soft pretzels? Hell, onion rings? He wanted all of them, could almost taste the grease and salt on his tongue. Just thinking about all that food bumped his cholesterol and blood pressure up a few notches. He'd do an extra cardio workout tomorrow, maybe even hop on the bike. But today he was having those damn fries and a hot dog. Maybe two.

She stopped and turned. "We can eat in the picnic area. Let's make our way to the car so I can grab the picnic basket." She smiled at him. "I made you turkey on rye with a slice of avocado. Yogurt, grapes, peanut butter and jelly for the kids."

Harry didn't miss the way Arnold's gaze kept sliding to the hot dog booth. What kid would pick his mother's peanut butter and jelly when he could stuff himself with a hot dog and fries? "Save that for later." He grinned. "If you make me walk this whole zoo, I'll need a snack just to have the energy to drive home."

"It's not necessary to buy them food."

He shrugged. "If it were, I wouldn't do it."

She hesitated. "Thank you."

You'd have thought he bought her a necklace from Tiffany's. Her eyes got all bright, like she might spill a tear or two, her voice wobbled, her face flushed pink. All this for a hot dog and a lemon ice? A tiny part of him wanted to see that joy on her face every day and know that he was responsible for it. He pushed that nonsensical idea from his brain and said, "We'll hit the hot dog stand first, then we'll work our way to the cotton candy and funnel cakes."

"And the lemon ice?" Elizabeth asked, clapping her hands.

He almost said, "Hell, yes!" but caught himself. "Sure, lemon ice it is."

"And a soft pretzel with mustard?"

The boy spoke. He usually didn't talk much when Harry was around. Whether due to shyness, maternal protection, or just plain awkwardness, it was hard to tell. Harry guessed it could be a combination of all three. He didn't think he'd much like it if some man came sniffing around his mother. "You got it, Arnold."

"This sounds like an upset stomach waiting to happen," Greta said in her "mother knows best" voice. "You are not going to eat all of that food and get sick."

"We won't," Elizabeth said. "Will we, Arnold?" The boy shook his head.

"Oh, Greta, let them have what they want."

She narrowed her eyes on him as though he were kid number three in the group. "You won't think that when they throw up in your car."

Harry laughed. "I'll take my chances."

He hadn't needed to worry about Greta's children overdoing it. Apparently, their mother had trained them well, or maybe they'd barfed up too many times from overeating. No, the real person he should have worried about overindulging was himself and his inability to control his behavior, which resulted in bad consequences. Harry had his hot dog and fries, followed by a funnel cake, a generous swirl of Elizabeth's cotton candy, peanuts, and a lemon ice. He should have said no when he spotted Arnold eyeing the double-decker ice cream cones, but he knew the kid wouldn't eat one unless somebody else did. And since Elizabeth and Greta were munching on a funnel cake, that left Harry to face a double-decker ice cream cone that he knew could put him over the edge. Still, he didn't want to disappoint the kid, so he bought two cones and forced one down, bite by bite. When he finished, his stomach gurgled like a stopped-up toilet and his head spun with sugar overload. All he wanted to do was get home and lie down.

"Harry? Would you like me to drive?"

He shook his head. Greta drove ten miles an hour below the speed limit, and he couldn't afford to lose valuable minutes away from his bathroom. If he hopped on the highway, he could drop Greta and the kids off and be in his house in forty minutes. They'd just gotten on the highway when Elizabeth called from the backseat, "Thank you, Mr. Harry. I had the bestest time."

"I did, too." This from Arnold. "Thank you."

Greta slid a glance his way, her face bright with admiration. "Thank you, Harry, for a lovely day."

Something about the way she said it, her voice all soft and warm, and those eyes looking at him like he was a hero, shot to his heart, reverberated in his chest until it hurt, then landed in his gut with a bang and a thud. Harry sucked in air, tried to clear his head and his gut, but it was too late. Bits and shreds of hot dog and lemon ice slushed up his throat. Shit, he was going to puke! He pulled the car off the road, checked for cars, and jumped out before Greta could inquire if he was all right. Forget making it down the small embankment where he could puke his guts out without three spectators. Harry knelt down, opened his mouth, and hurled.

"Harry?"

Greta? "Go away." Sweat filmed his forehead, his neck, his face. He sipped in air, fought the urge to puke again.

"Here." She stood behind him, waved a tissue over his left shoulder. He grabbed it, swiped at his forehead and mouth.

"Leave me alone." He did not want her standing here, witnessing this.

She ignored him, held out a bottle of water. "I've seen people throw up before." She paused and he swore there was a hint of humor in her voice when she said, "And I usually get stuck cleaning it up. Here." She shook the bottle by his ear. "Rinse your mouth. You'll feel better."

"I doubt it." He took the bottle, sipped and swished water in his mouth before spitting it out. Three more times and he didn't feel like a walking puke zone. Harry sat back on his heels, closed his eyes and concentrated on keeping his stomach quiet.

"Mr. Harry?"

He opened one eye, squinted at her. "What?"

"You can take Mr. Squiggly home with you tonight. He'll make you feel better."

"Thanks, kiddo."

"I'll loan you my special pillow," Arnold said. "It always helps me."

"Okay. Thanks." Was he the only one who thought this whole situation was bizarre? Greta and her kids were standing within smelling distance of his barf pile and acting like it was no big deal. Who were these people? Was this what families did? Rushed in to help when one of their clan humiliated himself and acted like it was normal? Harry drank more water, spit it out in a high arc.

"I can do that, too," Arnold said, guzzling water from his plastic bottle, then arcing it past Harry's landing.

"Me, too." Elizabeth attempted to send an arc of water and ended up spraying Harry's shirt. "Ooops." She covered her mouth, looked at her mother, and tried not to giggle.

Harry shook his head and let Greta help him to his feet. "I'm driving," she said as she guided him to the car with Elizabeth and Arnold close behind.

Hmmph. He looked like shit, felt like shit, and smelled like puke, and nobody cared. He reached in his pocket, dug out his keys, and handed them to Greta. "Thanks. Thanks a lot."

Harry kept the window down and his eyes closed while Greta maneuvered the Jag toward her house. The car hadn't been handled so delicately since he drove it off the lot. One day he'd explain what a performance vehicle meant and how it should be handled like a woman: with intensity and attention. She'd think it was a line of bullshit, and she'd be right. He just wanted to get home and crawl into bed for the next fourteen hours, but first they had to stop at Greta's, so Arnold and Elizabeth could hand over their "get better" gizmos. Whatever. He couldn't think past the next curve. He dozed a bit and when he woke, Elizabeth stood on the other side of the car with a brown teddy bear peeking at him from the window.

"This is Mr. Squiggly," she said, "he'll make you feel all better. Here." She pushed the stuffed animal through the window. "Now, Mr. Squiggly, take care of Mr. Harry. He has a sick tummy." She leaned on tiptoe and kissed Harry's cheek. "Bye."

"Bye, kiddo." Harry plopped the teddy bear in his lap and worked up a smile for Elizabeth.

Arnold stepped in front of his sister and stuffed the pillow through the window. "This will help." The kid almost smiled, but he couldn't quite get those lips to work in the right direction.

"Thanks, Arnold."

Greta kissed them both on the forehead and darted to the driver's side. "I must take Mr. Harry home now and get him settled. Listen to Grandma and brush your teeth." She got into the car, buckled up, and blew them a kiss. "Prayers, too."

Harry closed his eyes again with Arnold's pillow and Mr. Squiggly on his lap. Who would have thought he could feel like crud and be okay with it? Or almost okay? He gave Greta directions to his condo and listened to her soft voice as she chatted on about the day and how much the kids enjoyed themselves. She said she did, too. Was this what couples called "bonding"? Hell if he knew, but it had a peacefulness about it that he kind of liked. It sure beat listening to Bridgett going on and on about her cardio workout and laser surgeries.

"This is where you live?"

He inched an eye open. Luxury condos, gated and secure. Lots of flowers and landscape. "Yup. This is it." Harry pointed to a parking spot in the first row. "Park there." He hoped she thought it was a random spot and not his, but one look at her pinched brows told him she knew. If she thought the parking space was overdone, wait until she met the doorman decked out in full uniform. Harry grabbed the pillow and the teddy bear and hefted his weary body from the car. Greta hurried to his side and guided him along the sidewalk to the ornate entrance and yes, the uniformed doorman. "Stevens, how are you?"

The older man nodded and opened the door with a flourish and a bow. "Very fine, sir. Ma'am?"

"Thank you," Greta murmured, smiling at him as she passed.

"Lecher," Harry said under his breath. "He's after all the young skirts. Ignore him."

She shot him a look. "Hmm. He probably says the same thing about you."

Harry's lips twitched. "Probably."

"And I'm not that young anyway." She tilted her head and studied him. "He's probably wondering what happened to your twenty-something sex partner."

And there it was, slapped right back in his face, like a boy caught with his hand in the candy jar. Greta probably thought about him and Bridgett that way, with Bridgett being the candy jar and Harry's, ahem, "hand", being somewhere it didn't belong. The woman might come across all soft and demure, but she wasn't to be messed with, that was becoming quite clear. He bet if needed, she could wield a meat cleaver and not on a cut of meat. Harry jabbed at the elevator button and waited for the ding. He'd done a few things in this elevator that might cause Greta to sharpen her meat cleaver.

When he fit the key in the door and eased it open, he waited for Greta's response. His place had been decorated with two things in mind: relaxation and sex. Leather couch, chairs, geometrical area rugs, stainless steel accents, and white. Lots of white.

"My." Greta stood in the middle of the living room. "This could be in a magazine."

"Yeah, well, it's okay." He wouldn't tell her it had been, that once upon a time he'd bedded an interior designer who decorated his house and won a spot in a magazine with it. What did it matter? It was beautiful and impersonal; no photos or expression of personal tastes, nothing but a designer's opinion of what his house should look like. How sad was that? Sadder still he'd only just acknowledged it? Maybe the barfing had drained rational thought from his brain and left him half delirious and too damn vulnerable. He'd go with that because, dammit, he was not turning into a weak-kneed baby looking for the meaning of life.

"Would you like some tea?" She'd worked her way to the kitchen, her gaze darting from cabinet to stove, to refrigerator, as if assessing where he might keep tea if he were to have it in the house.

"Top cupboard, to the right of the stove." He leaned on the marble island as she reached for the box, her top lifting to expose a scrap of skin. Had any of his other women ever cooked him a meal in this kitchen? Oh, they'd talked about it, but had they done it? Even a piece of toast? Of course, he didn't even own a damn toaster, but if he did, would they have offered? No, they were not like Greta, but then that wasn't what he'd wanted them for, was it? And exactly what did he plan to do with Greta? Oh, yes, he remembered. Attempt to have a "relationship" with her. Sweat broke out on the back of his neck and forehead, drizzled along his temples.

"Harry?" She fussed over him, blotting his forehead with a wet paper towel. "Are you going to be sick again?"

"I'm fine." He moved out of reach. "I need a shower; I stink."

She smiled. "I'll fix your tea. Should I bring it to the bedroom?"

Sure, Greta, bring it to the bedroom and set it on the nightstand...then, slide out of those shorts and that top... "No, I'll sit at the table."

"I'll have it ready for you."

The warm shower and mint soap relaxed him, but it was the toothpaste and toothbrush that made him feel like a human being again. He pulled on a pair of silk pajama bottoms and a T-shirt and glanced in the mirror. The pathetic-looking bastard staring back at him didn't look like the suave and charismatic man who could talk a woman out of her panties in ten sentences or less. This guy looked worn and used up, a sad commentary to a life of excess and abuse. Harry grabbed a comb, ran it through his hair, and turned off the light. He made it as far as the bed before his body gave out and he fell onto the bed.

He had no idea how long he slept, but when he woke, Greta was curled beside him, her breath soft and even against his chest, her arm thrust around his waist. His little warrior woman, come to protect him against himself. A surge of something he could only guess might be contentment spread through him, landed on his weary soul. So this was what couples did, shared time and a bed that had nothing to do with sex? And he, Harry Blacksworth, avoider of relationships with women who wanted more than sex and money, was actually lying next to a woman in his bed, with his clothes on. Hers, too. He closed his eyes, breathed in her scent, and smiled.

Chapter 7

Miriam sliced a cucumber and tossed it into the wooden salad bowl. "Why would your mother venture all this way and not try to see you?"

That was the question that had no answer. Not quite true. Christine knew there was an answer buried deep in her mother's actions, but what? Why would Gloria duck in and out as though her sole purpose was to see Nate? The cruel words, the harsh accusations, and demeaning comments were all signature Gloria Blacksworth. She liked having the upper hand, but to travel this distance and ignore Christine when she'd been calling, writing, and practically begging to see her? "She's up to something. I can feel it."

"Christine, I know you're still upset with your mother, but at some point, you're going to have to let it go."

Would Miriam feel the same way if Christine told her the truth she'd been carrying around for months? *Oh, by the way, I might not be my father's daughter. No, what I mean is I might have a different father; the one I thought was my uncle. How did that happen? The usual way. You see, my mother, the illustrious Gloria Blacksworth, slept with my uncle and he might be my father*. It was too messed up to think about, so Christine blocked it out and pretended her mother was dead.

"Christine? Are you ever going to forgive her?"

"Probably not."

Her mother had made her choices and chosen her path, a path that did not include her daughter. Christine had Nate, Lily, Miriam, and Uncle Harry. They were her family, and soon they'd add another Desantro. She had the new addition to the family on her mind the next morning as she and Nate lay in bed. "I've got a surprise for you tonight."

"Oh?" Nate ran a hand down her naked back, his fingers settling on her hip. "You got Pop to convince his cronies to support you?"

"No, that's not it, but Pop does think we're close." Christine sighed and snuggled next to her husband. She cherished this post-lovemaking closeness almost as much as making love: simple touches that were more caring than sexual, words that soothed rather than ignited, love that spread through her in a quiet, steady flame. Who would have thought she and Nate would be so perfect together, despite their differences, background, and rocky beginning? They belonged together, and tonight she'd show him just how much.

"Are you going to give me a clue?"

"Uh-uh." She made tiny circles on his chest. "If you guess, it won't be a surprise."

"Hmm. Good point." He pulled her close and whispered. "I've got a surprise for you, too."

Christine lifted her head and looked him in the eye. "For me? What?"

His dark eyes sparkled with humor and a bit of mischief. "If I tell you, it's not a surprise. You'll just have to wait and be patient." His lips twitched, and his voice dipped. "And we both know patience is not your specialty."

She inched up and kissed him on the mouth, slipping her tongue inside. When he groaned and tried to lift her on top of him, she pulled away and said, "What was that about patience?"

He laughed and flipped her onto her back, entering her in one swift thrust. His strokes eased, tormenting her with their calculated slowness. Nate knew how to please her, how to drive her wild, and make her moan with pleasure. She knew how to do that to him, too. Christine grabbed his shoulders and thrust her hips to meet his, harder, faster, coaxing him deeper inside. He could never resist that temptation.

"Screw patience," Nate muttered as he pumped into her, full and deep, again and again, until Christine moaned her release. Seconds later, he followed with a groan and spilled himself inside her. After, she held him close, arms clasped around his back, pressing him against her. Nate was her solid ground, her soul, her husband. And tonight, she would tell him he was going to be a father.

***

Just because Greta had witnessed him puking his guts out and just because she had spent a few hours in his bed—clothes on and not having sex—did not mean she had a direct path into his screwed-up head or his equally screwed-up life. But she sure thought she did, oh hell yes. Here they were, two days later and she'd called him up and informed him she planned to fix him dinner—at his place. He'd asked if Arnold and Elizabeth would be coming, too, but she hadn't even pretended hesitation when she said "no". Didn't she understand he couldn't be trusted alone with her in his home, that he was being chivalrous because he knew what could happen if she came alone? Hell, he knew what would happen. Even if he locked the bedroom door, that wouldn't stop him from switching into hunting mode and talking her into sex on any one of the several other, if not slightly less comfortable, choices: there was the couch, the two chairs, the table, even the damn rug. Any one of them would suffice in a pinch.

Greta hadn't been interested in the first seven excuses why she shouldn't come to his place without her pint-sized bodyguards. She'd merely laughed and said she was a big girl who did not need protecting. She had no idea. He only agreed because he couldn't resist her lasagna and she'd promised to make a double portion. Hell, who was he kidding? He wanted to see her and if this hare-brained idea of hers was the only way to spend a few extra hours with her, then he'd strap a damn chastity belt on her if he had to, but sex was out of the question. Maybe soon, just not yet, and he was not going to psychoanalyze his hesitancy. End of story.

"Harry, would you mind setting the table?"

Setting the table, as in fork to the left, knife and spoon to the right? Hell yes, he minded. That was domestic crap that a guy did to help out. If he started doing stuff like this now, what would she ask next? *Can you carve the turkey?*

"Harry? Thank you." She smiled at him and he forgot all the reasons he should deny her. He smiled back like a lovesick idiot and headed toward the silverware drawer. They were going to have a talk about the rules and boundaries in this "relationship", as in he was in charge and she was second-string. But not until after dinner.

Harry's vow to set Greta straight didn't last past the first bite of lasagna. Throwing a few pieces of silverware and a plate or two on the table wasn't such a big deal, was it? Not when one of the place settings belonged to Greta. Hell, he'd even helped with dishes, something he hadn't done since freshman year in college, and then only for two weeks until he hired a sophomore named Lisa to take care of his dishes and take care of him, too.

"This is great cobbler," he said around a mouthful of peach. "Make sure you take some home for the kids."

She dabbed her lips and said in a soft voice, "Thank you, I will."

"And I picked up some of that yogurt Elizabeth likes. Take that, too." She nodded. "I don't want Arnold to feel slighted, but I had no idea what to get the kid. He could be a poker player for as much expression as he shows about anything."

"I know." Her shoulders drooped a bit; her expression turned sad. "It's all inside and he can't get it out. He feels it, though, Harry, maybe more than the rest of us."

He knew all about feelings that were locked up with no way out. In the Blacksworth family, if you couldn't express yourself with style, eloquence, and substance, you were ignored. That had been Harry's life, while Charles had possessed the ability to say and do the right things, even if they weren't "right" for him, even if he sacrificed his own happiness.

"I worry about him," she went on, "worry he will never learn to have a relationship with someone, and he will end up alone."

"Ah, hell," Harry said, trying to lighten her spirits and also to blot out words that sounded too much like him. "Arnold's a great kid; he just needs to find something he's good at so he doesn't think about doing everything right or wrong." He paused, rubbed his chin. "And he needs a different name. Arnold is a tough name for a kid to carry around. What's his middle name?"

"James. Why do you ask?"

"A.J.," he murmured. "I like that. Ask him what he thinks about that." Yeah, he liked the sound of that name. Cool. Hip. Not Arnold.

Greta reached across the table and clasped his hand. "Thank you, Harry. Thank you for being so kind."

Right. Kind. "I think you've got me mixed up with somebody else. Take a closer look; nothing kind about me." He frowned, tried for a fierce expression, but she didn't buy it. She smiled, pushed back her chair, and ran a hand along his cheek. He caught her hand, eased it away. "What are you doing?" That look on her face told him exactly what she was thinking and what she thought she was going to do: seduction. Good grief, Greta in seduction mode? How the hell was he supposed to fight that? "Stop looking at me like that."

She moved closer, laid a hand on the back of his neck. "How am I looking at you, Harry?"

Damn that soft voice and those eyes that sparkled bluer than the Caribbean. "This is not funny. Now go sit over there and drink your coffee."

Those full lips curved into a smile. "I'm not interested in coffee." She slid her fingers through his hair. "Maybe later."

"Greta." How was he supposed to resist that voice, those eyes, that scent? "You need to stop. Now." He cleared his throat, looked away so he wasn't eye level with those breasts.

"No, Harry. I don't think so." She leaned in close, her breath fanning his neck. "We're going to go in the bedroom and I'm going to undress you." Her lips brushed a spot behind his right ear. "And then do you know what I'm going to do?"

Hadn't he imagined Greta playing seductress hundreds, no, thousands of times? But only in his mind, surely never flesh-and-blood real life. And yet, wasn't that what she was offering? Well, wasn't it? Harry opened his mouth and managed, "I have no idea."

Her gaze zeroed in on his, held it, forced him to remain in his chair, waiting for her next words. She fingered the first button of her blouse, undid it, moved to the second. Harry tried to speak but the words froze in his brain. Greta's blouse fell open, revealing a pink lace bra and lush flesh. He swallowed, caught between desperation and desire. "I'm no good for you, Greta. You know that."

She smiled, slid her blouse from her shoulders. "You're perfect for me."

He'd always wondered what her breasts would feel like in his hands, how they would taste on his tongue. "I'll screw this up. I'm a screw-up, you know that." Dammit, she wasn't listening. If she were, she'd button up that blouse and fly out of here. Now.

"It's okay, Harry." She kicked off her shoes, fingered the opening of his shirt. "I trust you."

He caught her hand, torn between begging her to continue and forcing her to leave. "You shouldn't trust me. I'll only end up hurting you."

Her smile slipped, her hand stilled. "I think you're the one who is afraid of being hurt. I won't hurt you. Trust me, Harry. Can you do that?"

Trust? In his limited and deranged experience, when people started throwing that word around, it usually meant "open up, tell me everything, and I will own you and your weaknesses." And yet, Greta wasn't like that, or she didn't seem to be. But then, how would he know unless he trusted her? He blew out a long breath and eased from the chair. "You ask a lot, Greta Servensen."

She rested her hands on his chest and looked up at him. "I ask no more than I'm willing to give, Harry Blacksworth."

His lips twitched. "Okay. Trust. We'll give it a whirl. What now?" He darted a glance at the bedroom. After a year of fantasizing about Greta, was he really this close to making it all come true? A tiny swirl of panic seized him, worked its way down his belly, and landed on the one place he could not afford for it to land. Oh, hell no, not now. He was a stallion in bed, had been since he was a teenager, and now, minutes before the most important sexual experience of his life, his equipment was going to fail?

"Harry? What's wrong?"

"Huh?" This could not be happening. "Nothing. I think I'd like another glass of iced tea."

"Sure." She clasped his hand and led him away from the kitchen toward the bedroom. "Later."

Harry slowed his steps. "What are you doing?" What was she doing? Taking him to bed? Trying to seduce him? Greta?

His Greta?

"I'm doing what you're too much a gentleman to do." She paused, wet her lips, and murmured, "Taking you to bed."

Her words meshed with her actions, pulsed through him, exploded in his brain as the reality of her intent took shape. Greta wanted him and she intended to have him.

"Come, Harry." His seductress stroked his cheek, ran a finger along his lips. "Let me make love to you. Let me do this just for you."

What man could say no to that offer? No woman had ever invited him to experience pleasure without expecting something in return, whether in the form of a touch, or a tangible good, such as jewelry, clothing, or money. Not Greta. She really wanted him just for his miserable self. He was through fighting her, through denying what they both obviously wanted, and though he should be honorable and send her away, right now honor had nothing to do with it. Desire and need were what they were both after, and dammit, they were not leaving that bed until both had been satisfied. Several times.

"You're beautiful, Harry." Greta eased the shirt from his shoulders, let it slip to the floor, her mouth on his neck, his chest, his belly. This was heaven and hell wrapped into one, a pleasure-pain that started and ended with her touch. She unfastened his belt, stroked his legs, unzipped his pants. It was too fast, too slow, too much. Harry sipped in tiny bits of air, fearful he'd explode before they got started. When he tried to touch her, she shook that luscious blonde head and murmured, "Not yet. Just enjoy." Off came the slacks and boxers, and still she stroked him with those exquisite fingers, ran her tongue along his belly. Low, lower. That damnable appendage jerked and jumped, all signs of its earlier indecision gone. When she touched him there, he groaned with such intense pleasure, he thought he would explode, but then her breathy laughter spilled over him, made him harder.

"Greta—"

"I know." She planted a soft kiss on his belly and stood. "Lie down."

She didn't need to repeat that request. Harry flipped back the covers, tossed the extra pillows on the floor, and slipped into bed. Ready and waiting. Her eyes were on him, over him, stopping here and there, settling on certain areas of interest, sliding to his hip, his chin, his belly, back to that area of interest. "Like what you see?"

"Oh, yes." The sultriness in her voice told him she did indeed. She reached behind her back, unfastened the pink lace bra, and let it slip from her shoulders. Her breasts were large and beautiful, her nipples pink and hard. She unzipped her shorts, shimmied out of them, and stood before him half-naked in pink lace panties. "Like what you see?" she asked seconds before she stepped out of the panties.

"Hell, yeah. Come here."

She slid onto the bed and leaned over him, her blonde hair brushing against his belly. "I have thought of this many times." She sighed, stroked his cheek, and murmured against his mouth, "So many times."

"Not half as many as I have." He eased her on top of him, settled her so she straddled him. "I've wanted this since the moment I saw you."

"And now you can have me. All of me." She rubbed her breasts against his chest, moaned as their tongues mated in a deep kiss of passion and need. Her words were as tantalizing and seductive as her body, shivering through him. He wanted her and he had to have her. Now.

"I need you." He groaned and jerked against her. "You're torturing me."

"Then let me end your torture." She clasped his face between her hands and slid onto his sex with a deep, lusty sigh.

It was over after that. Harry didn't remember who came first or how it even happened. There were moans and whimpers, cries of delight and pleas for release. Who rode whom, how, where—at one point, they were on the lush carpeting—it was a blur, and it was the most incredible sex he'd ever known. Once wasn't enough, twice would never be enough. After the third time, he pulled her close and for the first time in too many years knew true peace.

Chapter 8

Nate sanded the cherry wood, pleased with the initial results. He'd selected this type because of its tight grain and smooth texture. He'd have to be careful with the spindles; he didn't want any rough spots. It had to be perfect. He'd started the project three weeks ago, borrowing Gino Servetti's workshop so Christine wouldn't know what he was doing. It had been a real challenge to get here after work and on Saturday mornings, and he'd hated like hell lying to Christine, but it was her surprise. If he'd built it in his own workshop, the chances that she'd snoop around or end up finding out by pure coincidence were too risky. Gino hadn't been his first choice because of his past relationship with Natalie, but he'd been desperate to get this piece done for his wife.

Three more nights, four at best, and he'd be finished. The next challenge was how to give it to her. Should he just put it in the spare bedroom, take her by the hand, and when she spotted the cradle in the middle of the room say, "What do you think about a baby?" Did that sound ridiculous? Did he care? They hadn't talked about a baby, but then they hadn't *not* talked about one either. It didn't have to be tomorrow or even next month, but Nate would be forty in a few years; they should at least start talking about it.

And he hadn't missed the way she'd looked at Bree Kinkaid's swollen belly when they'd run into her last Saturday. Or the smile she gave Bree's two-year-old, Lindsey. Christine was thinking about it; he'd bet his wedding ring on it. Nate grabbed his beer, took a long pull, and admitted he was thinking about it, too. He spent the next hour wiping down the wood and putting the first coat of varnish on it. One day, his child would sleep in this cradle. The thought slowed his hand as he pictured Christine's belly swollen with their baby.

"Nate. What are you doing here?"

He'd recognize Natalie Servetti's voice anywhere, like sex served up hot and ready. Nate glanced up, spotted the tank top and jean shorts, and shrugged. "Working."

"I see that." She moved close to him, too close. Natalie always had a game, but he was no longer interested in playing it. "What is it?"

She wasn't stupid; she knew it was a cradle. He dipped his brush in mineral spirits. "It's a cradle."

"Hmm."

He worked the brush in the mineral spirits, letting the bristles saturate. Maybe if he ignored her, she'd get the message and leave. Probably not. That was one thing about Natalie: She really believed no man could resist her. What she didn't know was they all thought she was an easy target who could be had with a cheap dinner and a six-pack. That used to be Nate's style, quick and uncomplicated. Until he met Christine and life changed; he'd changed.

"I miss you." She eased her hand down his back, slid her fingers in the back of his jeans.

"Hey!" Nate jerked away and glared at her. "What the hell are you doing?"

She smiled, her full lips glistening pink. "Playing," she said, her voice soft and low. "You used to like it."

"I'm married."

She shrugged, fingered the neckline of her tank top. "I won't tell if you won't."

"Don't. Look, you need to find somebody else."

"I don't want anybody else, Nate." Her dark eyes grew bright as she whispered, "Just you."

Carmen and Marie Servetti did their daughter no favors by granting her every whim. They should have taught her the value of *no* just as they'd taught their sons. Nate wrapped the brush in plastic wrap and placed it on the workbench beside him. "I gotta go." He grabbed the empty beer bottle and said, "If you see Gino, will you tell him I'll be back tomorrow night?"

"Sure." She eyed the bottle in his hand. "Can you at least have a drink with me? For old times' sake?" She didn't wait for him to respond but turned and made her way to the refrigerator in the corner.

Damn, he was not going to get out of here without having a drink with her, probably some idle chit-chat, too. Oh, hell, he might as well do it and be done. Nate waited while Natalie peered inside the fridge, her shorts riding high and exposing a splash of butt cheek—for his benefit, no doubt. She straightened, pulled out two beers, and waved them at him. "Just a sec." She turned her back to him, set the bottles on the counter, and fiddled with the opener. "One more sec."

How long did it take to open a bottle of beer? Nate sighed, regretting his decision to spend one extra second with her. The old Nate would have ignored the puppy-dog sad eyes and high-tailed it out of here, but Christine had softened him up, taught him about compassion for other people, even ones he didn't particularly like.

"Come and get it." Natalie burst into his thoughts with a sultry command that did nothing but annoy him. She'd eased onto the old plaid couch that had been in the place for at least fifteen years and had no doubt seen more than its share of X-rated entertainment. Gino had thrown a sheet over it and that's where his dog, Hound, slept while he worked. Except Hound wasn't here right now and Natalie was in his spot looking all cozy. Nate moved across the room, snatched the bottle from her, and took a long pull on his beer, calculating the amount of time it would take to finish it and not appear rude. Six minutes? Seven? No more than eight. That was his limit. Natalie sipped her beer, eyes on him. "Sit down."

He shook his head. "I'm good." He was not sitting on that couch with her. Ten grand said if he did, she'd latch onto him and head for his zipper in three seconds. How had he ever thought her desirable? He pictured Christine, warm, welcoming, not filled with subterfuge or scheming. She didn't need to throw sexual innuendos at him; she was damn sexy all by herself. Just being her.

"You really don't want to be with me?"

No, I never wanted to be with you. "I'm married, Natalie. I love my wife."

Her dark eyes grew bright, and he knew the second before the tears started that he should have just shut up and finished his beer. "You used me, didn't you?" She sniffed, swiped a hand across her cheek. "You never cared about me."

"Natalie—"

"Don't pretend." She crossed one long leg over the other. "We were good together. You know we were."

Those eyes challenged him to deny it. How could he tell her the truth. *You were about filling a need, like getting a caffeine jolt. You were never long-term.* He took another drink, debated the best way to salvage her self-esteem and escape in the next five minutes. Damn, but he'd been here too long already. He settled on a meaningless response. "It doesn't matter now, does it?" She bit her lower lip, sniffed again. Was she playing him? Getting him to feel sorry for her? For what?

"It *does* matter, Nate." The tears started again, slipping down her cheeks onto her chin. "I love you."

"Hey, don't talk like that." He glanced at his watch. Damn, he'd been in this spot almost eleven minutes but he couldn't leave on a comment like that. He had to set her straight. "Natalie, listen to me." He gentled his voice. "It's never going to happen between us, okay? Whatever we shared is done. Gone."

"Is it because she's rich? Is that why you picked her?"

The tears kept coming, but her tone had switched. Anger? Jealousy? Hell, he was no good at this crap. "I picked Christine because I love her. That's it." And then, because he was tired and wanted to get the hell out of here and home to his wife, he said, "I don't love you, Natalie. I never did."

She buried her face in her hands, let out more sobs and maybe a wail or two, her shoulders shaking. "Come on, don't do that. There are a lot of nice guys out there. You'll find one." *If you stop sleeping with them the second they look at you.* More sobs, more shoulder shaking. Damn. He glanced at his watch again: another eight minutes wasted. "Hey." He moved to pat her shoulder, stumbled toward the couch.

"Nate?" Natalie's voice echoed in his head as though she were in a tunnel and not a foot away. He tried to take another step but grew dizzy. "Let me help you." She slid the beer from his hand and guided him to the couch. "There. Just relax." Her face was fuzzy, her words, too. He rubbed his eyes, refocused. More fuzziness.

"I don't know what's wrong."

"Nothing's wrong, Nate." The tears were gone, the sadness, too. "Nothing at all."

Hours or maybe minutes later, Nate woke up with a kink in his neck and a sore back. His head wasn't in great shape either. What the hell had happened? He worked his eyes open, fought a wave of dizziness when he tried to straighten, and fell back onto the grimy couch cushion. The last thing he remembered was Natalie's voice, telling him something. What was it? He ran a hand over his face, tried to piece it together. He'd been working on the cradle when she showed up and started with her song and dance about missing him and loving him more than her own breath. That part, he'd be happy not to remember. She'd insisted he have a beer and because she was not going to leave him alone until he did, Nate agreed. The crying jag started again and when he moved to pat her shoulder, he stumbled. Did he land on the couch? Had she helped him? What the hell had happened? He glanced at his watch: 1:30 a.m. He had to get home. Christine knew he was working late, but not *this* late.

He should tell her what happened. Anytime a person was involved with an ex-lover and blocks of time he couldn't remember was not a good thing. Nate dragged his gaze to the cradle resting on the workbench. He blinked until it came into focus. One day it would hold their baby. In four days when the last coat of varnish had dried, he'd take it home and confess everything: the real reason for the late nights, Natalie Servetti's visit, the blackout. He would tell Christine because he couldn't *not* tell her. All he needed was a few more days and then he'd make everything right. Nate stood and took a step toward the door. The room spun and he stumbled, his stomach bouncing and threatening to erupt. When the extra saliva pooled in his mouth, he knew he was going to puke. He made it to the 2x2 box Gino called a bathroom, knelt down, and puked into the rust-rimmed commode until there was nothing left but dry heaves. When he could move, he crawled out of the bathroom and leaned against the wall. The truth hit him as he sat there, sweating, cotton-mouthed, and groggy. *Natalie had drugged him.*

***

Christine spent the rest of the day caught between visions of Nate in bed with her this morning and picturing how he would react when she told him they were going to have a baby. She'd driven to the next town to purchase a pregnancy test lest the store clerk at Sal's spill the news. Had Christine imagined it, or had Nate pressed a possessive hand on her belly the last few times they'd made love? Had the action been intentional, maybe a subconscious desire for a child? In the last few months, he'd begun sliding a smile her way whenever Miriam began dropping not-so-subtle hints about expanding the Desantro family. Even Lily had started asking when she was going to get a niece; apparently that was her preference. Once Christine told Nate about the baby, they could tell Miriam together. Lily might have to wait until after the first doctor appointment, since telling her was like publishing it in the *Magdalena Press*, and naturally, Uncle Harry would want to know, not the details of course, just the outcome.

She would not tell her mother, and whether that was cruel or childish was not the point. Gloria Blacksworth was not a part of her life anymore. Maybe if she had stopped playing the victim in life and had taken responsibility for the disasters she'd created, she would have been more human, thus, more forgivable. This baby would be brought up in a home filled with love and commitment. And respect.

The afternoon sped by with two loan applications and a budget. The budget happened to be Mimi Pendergrass's niece, and while she was a nice girl with a "can-do" attitude and a teaching degree, she'd spent the first two years of college sucked in by credit card debt. Christine explained the need to consolidate debt and how to do it. When the young woman left, spreadsheet in hand and a follow-up appointment for next week, Christine wondered if Mimi had sent her. *Bring it on, Mimi. I can handle anything you throw my way.* Pop said he'd work the crowd at The Bleeding Heart Society the way he used to do when he was selling raffle tickets at the St. Guadalupe Festival. Well, he'd done more than that when he offered her services in the fund-raising department. Pop had told her afterward not to worry if she wasn't well schooled in fund-raising because he was, and with him backing her, they couldn't lose. The man sure had energy and a mind that never stopped.

Pop would be excited about the baby. He'd tell her a story or three about when his wife was pregnant and the stories would include food, namely pizzelles. There would be tears and such longing that Christine would hope she and Nate could grow old with feelings like that.

Tonight was a new beginning for the Desantro family, a celebration of life and love. She'd stop at the grocery store and pick up a pork tenderloin, one of Nate's favorites. By the time he got home, she'd have it ready with a salad, baked potato, and a cold glass of beer. Tonight she'd fill his belly and his heart.

When the doorbell rang at 4:18 p.m., the pork was in the oven, and Christine had sliced cucumbers and red onion for the salad. Cherry tomatoes were next. She set the knife aside, wiped her hand on a dishtowel, and made her way to the front door. Maybe it was the deliveryman with the charm bracelet she'd ordered for Lily: a gift in a string of gifts for her sister. Each one delighted Lily, no matter how small. Christine opened the door, expecting to see the deliveryman with a box, but the person on the front step was a beautiful woman in a melon-colored sundress with a tote slung over her right shoulder.

"May I help you?"

"Christine?"

The woman's voice was low and sultry. "Yes?"

"I'm Natalie Servetti." The brunette paused, flashed a wide smile. "I know Nate."

"Oh." Oh. And then, because she'd been raised to respect politeness, no matter the situation, she asked what she would later regret, "Would you like to come in?"

The woman's smile spread. "Thank you." Christine stepped aside as Natalie Servetti glided past her in a haze of perfume and self-assurance. She beelined to the fireplace mantel, her gaze latching onto the photos of Christine and Nate's wedding: sharing a kiss, holding hands, standing next to Lily, Uncle Harry, and Miriam.

"Nate always did take a good picture." The woman turned away, dismissing the rest of the photos that included more glimpses into the lives of Mr. and Mrs. Nathan Desantro, and sat on the couch.

Why was she here? And how fast could Christine get her to leave? Today was a special day, one she and Nate would remember as the beginning of their family, and no woman from his past was going to ruin that. Still, etiquette crept through her determination to be rid of the woman.   "Would you like something to drink?"

"As long as it's not a shot of Jack, then sure." Of course she'd said that so Christine knew she was familiar with Nate's habits. "Water's fine."

Christine made her way to the kitchen, poured two waters, and tried to think of a way to get rid of the woman. She glanced at her watch. Nate would be home in a little over and hour and his ex-whatever was not going to be here. In fact, if Christine had to spray the entire house with disinfectant and light candles to rid herself of the woman's scent, she'd do it.

"Here you go." Christine handed her a glass of water and tried not to notice the glossiness of the woman's hair, the long legs, the large breasts. But mostly, she tried to ignore visions of Nate knowing these body parts, enjoying them with great familiarity. Past was past; none of it mattered but now.

Natalie sipped her water, set it down on the walnut end table Nate had made, and crossed one leg over the other. "I like what you've done to the place." Her comment was just another reminder of the past relationship she shared with Nate. "Quieted the testosterone buzz a little."

"Thank you."

She sighed, placed a hand on the tote that rested beside her. "I'm sure you're wondering why I'm here."

Spoken as someone who knew that was exactly what Christine was wondering.

"I'm curious." She kept her voice even, her expression bland. The woman could lambaste her with all the innuendos she wanted and she would get no reaction. Years of living with Gloria had taught Christine how to mask her true emotions.

"I had to come." She batted her dark lashes, locked her gaze on Christine and pulled her in. "There are a few things you should know."

She paused, her voice dipping in sympathy as though to imply, *Since you haven't figured them out yet, I'll help.*

"Nate and I go back a long way. He was friends with my brother, Gino, in high school. I was younger, but I always had an eye on him." Her lips pulled into a slow smile. "He always had an eye on me, too. We got together and it was good, but explosive. You know how that can be when there's so much passion, you can't contain it." She flung both hands in the air and laughed. "Fireworks. In bed and out. It was exhausting."

Christine sat very still as Natalie Servetti's words seeped through her pores, swirled to her brain, and settled in her soul. It was one thing to imagine the man you loved with another woman but quite another to receive a testimony from the other woman.

"I appreciate your need to enlighten me on your past relationship with my husband, but you're forgetting one important fact." She squared her shoulders, leveled her voice. "Nate chose me."

"Chose. An interesting term." Nate's ex-lover eased back

against the cushion, the very spot where Christine and Nate first made love, and shrugged. "He chose his first wife, too, or maybe circumstances did. We'd had a horrible fight, and she was in the right place. Patrice. Did he tell you about her? It didn't last, though. We both knew it couldn't, no matter how much he told himself it would. The second she left him, he came right back to me. Stayed, too."

Her voice gentled. "And then you came with your fancy education and prim ways. Oh, I'll bet that turned him around. He probably didn't know quite what to make of you. I imagine it was a real thrill to bed the daughter of a man he hated so much, but it won't be any different with you, Christine. You can call yourself Mrs. Desantro all you want because Nate will come back to me. I understand him, understand what he needs, and I can give it to him. We belong together; we always will."

"Get out." Christine stood, sipped what bits of air were left in the room. "Now."

Natalie sighed and stood, grabbing her tote. "The truth is always hard to swallow when you're so hell-bent on denying it. But," she opened her tote and pulled out a manila envelope, "I'll just leave you with these in case you have any doubt or any questions." She worked her lips into a tight smile. "But I think they're pretty self-explanatory." She handed the envelope to Christine who took it and tossed it on the chair. "Thanks for the water, Mrs. Desantro." With that, she headed for the door and slipped out.

Christine waited until Natalie Servetti's car rumbled down the driveway before she snatched the envelope and sank into the chair. The contents of the envelope would be dangerous, no doubt intended to poison Christine and Nate's relationship or, at the very least, damage it. The wise action would be to throw it in the fire pit outside and watch the flames destroy Natalie Servetti's attempt to hurt them. She traced the edges of the envelope, caught between logic and emotion. Logic told her to get rid of the insidious poison fast, that one more minute in her hands could prove deadly. Emotion demanded she rip it open, right now, and deal with whatever smoldered inside.

Minutes passed as Christine battled between trust and doubt. Nate would not betray her. He loved her. He wanted a life with her. People like Natalie Servetti thought nothing of destroying lives to get what they wanted. The contents of this envelope were merely one jealous woman's attempt to take something that didn't belong to her. Nate would not betray their love. Whatever was inside might make her doubt him, and he'd done nothing to deserve that. She closed her eyes, rubbed her belly. They were going to have a baby and she'd planned to tell him tonight as soon as he walked in the door. They would talk about a nursery, names, and how to tell Miriam, Lily, and Uncle Harry. She opened her eyes, stared at the clasp on the envelope. If she peeked inside, the contents would leach into her brain. If she did not, the wondering could prove worse. Before she could torment herself with more doubt, she unfastened the clasp and slid the contents onto her lap.

Natalie had been correct. There was no need for explanation, not when the colored glossies included half-naked shots of Nate sprawled on a couch, jeans undone, ex-lover on top of him. There were six photos, 5x7s, with a date stamp of last Tuesday in the bottom right corner. Had someone taken these? Had Nate been drugged, forced, coerced? If only it could be that simple, but that happened in books and the movies. Real life was more deceitful, more tragically sad. Christine studied each photo, memorized the scrap of dark skin exposed by the half-unbuttoned shirt—the shirt she'd bought him for Christmas. His eyes were closed in all of the photos— to pretend he was somewhere else, somebody else? The last photo honed in on his left hand and the absent wedding band. Nate had told her he didn't wear his ring at work because the risk of getting a finger caught in a machine was too great. He'd said he carried it in his right jeans pocket to have it close. Apparently he took it off when he was working on other things, too, like Natalie Servetti.

Hope for a future with him burned that afternoon along with the forgotten pork roast. Christine slid the photos back into the manila envelope and refastened the clasp. The images were part of her memories now, as permanent and painful as the moment in Thurmon Jacobs's office when she'd discovered her father had a secret family. Another betrayal, as heartbreaking as the first. Was she doomed to care about people who disregarded her? Or was she simply unlovable? Maybe the people she cared about were too invested in their own wants to consider her at all. That possibility was the most painful.

She clutched the corner of the envelope when Nate's truck rumbled up their drive a half hour later. *Time for the truth.* She didn't move when the truck door slammed and he bounded up the steps, whistling. Nor did she speak when he thrust open the door and burst in, calling, "Christine! Ready for your surprise? Whew! What burned? Christine?" He glanced toward the kitchen, spotted her in the chair, and rushed over. "What's wrong?"

How did a person pretend such concern when it was all a grand show? Had he thought she'd never find out? And now he stood over her, dark eyes filled with worry, mouth pulled into a straight line, body tense. At this moment, she didn't even hate him; that would come later when the numbness wore off and she understood what he'd taken from her.

"Baby." He knelt and placed a big hand on her leg. She cringed. Baby was gone. "What happened?"

"I had a visitor today." Spoken with such control, as though her heart had not been shattered by six photos.

"Oh?" He raised a brow, waited. When she didn't continue, he stroked her left knee. "Who came? It better not have been your mother."

She glanced at his hand on her knee, the glint of a wedding band shining back at her in betrayal and deceit. Their vows had been nothing more than words strung together, one after the other, to produce a pleasant sound that held no meaning. At least not for Nate. Whatever happened once he saw the photos would be a lie. The truth spoke from the glossies, forcing her to acknowledge she didn't know the man she married, not at all.

"No, not my mother." She handed him the envelope. "Natalie Servetti came to see me."

"What?" His eyes narrowed on the envelope as though it might strangle him. "What did she want?"

He could pretend annoyance, even disgust, but he couldn't pretend what was in those photos: unzipped jeans, half-open shirt, ex-lover crawling on top of him. She nodded at the envelope. "She wanted to give us a belated wedding present."

Nate snatched the envelope and jerked open the clasp. He pulled out the photos, his face growing paler as he flipped through them. "What the hell is this?" He stuffed the photos back in the envelope and threw it across the room. "Christine, listen to me, I have no idea what those are."

"Really? I have a pretty good idea what they are and I wasn't even there."

"This is crazy. It's a set-up." His dark eyes grew wild and bright. "I didn't do anything with her." He placed his hands on either side of the chair, leaned closer. "I swear to God, on our marriage, I never touched her."

"Never?" Why did people think they could lie their way out

of the truth just because the other person loved them? "That's a strong word, and that is not what Natalie Servetti told me," she paused, "in fairly intimate detail."

"She's a liar. She wants to break us up." His voice dipped, turned desperate. "There's been no one since you; you've got to believe me."

"But you were with her before, weren't you?" She had no business asking but she wanted to hear him say it. Probably so she could torment herself with it.

A slow flush crept up his neck, landed on his cheeks. "We were together, but we weren't together, if that makes any sense."

"You mean you had sex with her but she wasn't your girlfriend."

The flush spread to his ears. "Yeah."

"The nights away these past few weeks, the Saturdays, you were with her, weren't you?"

"No!" He actually sounded mortified and disgusted. "I love you. I don't want anybody else." His voice dipped, softened. "Only you. You've got to know that."

A tiny part of her wanted to believe his sincerity, but that was the problem when lies seeped into relationships. Nothing could be trusted anymore. Everything was suspect. "The photos are time-stamped with last Tuesday's date."

"I never touched her." His gaze pulled her in. "I've been working in her brother's shop these past few weeks, making your surprise." He looked away, ran a hand through his dark hair. "I hated telling you I was at work, but I couldn't risk ruining the surprise. Natalie showed up last week, started saying ridiculous things. I told her I was married and I wasn't interested. She asked me to have a beer with her, for old times' sake, she said. I remember thinking I could drink the beer fast and get out. And then she started crying, I think, and after that

I don't remember anything until I woke up a few hours later. She had to have drugged me and taken the pictures then."

"Please. Don't insult me." Drugging and photos? "Nice company you keep."

He ignored her. "I know she did it. What I haven't figured out is who helped her, and why."

"Why don't we call her up and ask her?"

He threw her a disgusted look. "I've been trying to get in touch with her but she's avoiding me."

"Hmm. Well, she wasn't avoiding me. Obviously." The whole scene was too much. Adultery, lies, betrayal. "It doesn't matter." Her gaze slid to his belt and she imagined Natalie undoing it, reaching for his zipper...Her stomach lurched and for the first time since he'd entered the house, she thought of the baby. Pain and loss seared her heart.

"What do you mean, it doesn't matter?" he asked. "It *does* matter. We have to talk about it, get it out in the open, and deal with it." He touched her hand and she yanked it away. "Like adults." He paused, his words spilling out in what seemed like pain. "Like people in love."

Christine dragged her gaze to his. "I need time." She flipped to business mode because that was her comfort zone; that's where she couldn't get hurt. "I'll move out."

"What? What the hell are you talking about?"

"I'll move out," she repeated, not looking at him.

"You *can't* leave. We have to get this straightened out." His voice cracked. "I love you. I did not touch her."

"I hear what you're saying, but I know what I saw. I need time away from you to sort this out."

"And I don't have a goddamn say in any of this?" Anger seeped through his desperation.

She wanted him to feel her pain, know what it was like when someone ripped your heart apart. "You've done enough, don't you think?"

Nate backed away. "What are you going to do when you find out this was all a set-up and you didn't trust me enough to believe me? How are you going to fix us then?"

Chapter 9

"Nathan?"

It was his mother. Damn. Christine hadn't been gone two hours and Miriam was at his door, and he'd bet she had a thing or two to say to him. He should have gone straight to Jack Daniels instead of beer; that way he'd be so mellow by now, he wouldn't care what his mother said. Hell, he probably wouldn't even *hear* what she said. But he hadn't. He'd sat around like a fool, nursing a beer and hoping his mother had convinced Christine to come home and talk it out. That's what married people did, wasn't it? Forget married, wasn't that what people in love did, so they stayed in love?

"Nathan." His mother stood before him, hands on hips, frown on her lips. "How *could* you?"

How could I? His own mother thought he'd done the deed with Natalie. "Hi, Ma," he said, lifting his beer and taking another swig.

She advanced on him, the frown deepening. "You're my son and I love you with my whole heart, but dear Lord, what have you gone and done?"

It was a sad commentary when your own mother thinks you're guilty of a crime you didn't commit. What about faith in humanity, trust, and commitment to one another? Was that only good so long as there wasn't a speck of doubt?

"Answer me, Nathan."

"What did Christine tell you?"

"When she could talk between her hysterical crying, she told me about you and Natalie." Her voice shook with anger and disappointment. "And the pictures," she spat out. "You and Christine were perfect together. Why did you have to go and ruin it? Could you not let yourself be happy, just this once?"

"Thanks for the vote of confidence, Ma. Every son should be so lucky to have you by his side."

She shook her head and paced the room as though she were a ball of energy about to explode. When she landed near him, she touched his arm and said in a gentle voice, "A mother knows her children, their good qualities, and their weaknesses. I love you, Nathan; I've loved you when you were hard to love and when you didn't even like yourself. And I will love you until I draw my last breath because that's what a mother does, but I can't stand by and watch you destroy the best thing that's ever happened in your life." She clutched his hand, squeezed. "Christine's heart is breaking right now, she doesn't know what to think, what to feel." She sighed. "And neither do I."

Nate sucked in a deep breath and looked into her eyes. Bloodshot, puffy. She was trying to keep the tears in, but he'd bet she'd already shed a fair amount, and he was the cause. Seeing her like this reminded him of all the times Charles Blacksworth left her behind and all the tears she shed for him. "I didn't do it, Ma."

Her bottom lip trembled, and she nodded. "But how do you explain the photos, Nathan? That's what's so hard to get past." He glanced at the manila folder lying on the floor where he'd thrown it. The truth was in those photos and he'd find it.

"I knew that Servetti girl was trouble the first time I laid eyes on her at St. Gertrude's. She was still in high school, but you'd have thought she was twenty-two with the way she wore her makeup and those skirts hiked up to her behind. And the men that trailed after her like she was offering a piece of candy," she paused and scowled, "which I'm sure she was."

"Do we have to talk about this now?"

She threw him one of her "if you had used better judgment, we wouldn't have to talk about it" looks. "Yes. We do. Your refusal to have a real relationship made you think you could call her when you wanted something"—the look again—"and discard her when you didn't. I'll bet she didn't see it that way. I'll bet she thought since you went back to her after Patrice, you'd end up with her again after Christine."

"I don't care what she thinks. She can go to hell. I'm not interested." *I have a wife, a woman I love.*

"This is a big mess, Nathan, and I don't know how you are going to get out of it, but you'd better find a way." She sighed, rubbed her temples. "I have no idea what to tell Lily."

"You can't tell her."

"She's no fool. How long do you think she'll buy Christine's 'I missed you and wanted to spend time together' before she starts asking more questions?"

"Don't tell her." Lily was all that was good and pure and he would not have her heart tarnished by something as nasty as this.

"I don't plan to, but you better think of something." She shrugged. "Tell her you're sanding the floor or painting or doing something that would require Christine to stay at the house. And you'd better come for dinner and spend a little time there or Lily will get suspicious. You know how she is."

"And Christine's okay with this?" She didn't want him in the next state, let alone at the same dinner table.

"I'll talk to her. In the meantime, you'd better find this Servetti girl and get your stories straight."

What did she mean by that? "Ma? You don't think I cheated on Christine, do you?" When she didn't answer, he knew she didn't believe him. "I see."

"You and Christine are good for each other. I don't want to see bad judgment on your part ruin your lives."

Bad judgment? She really thought he'd done it. "Don't you think it's odd that Natalie waited until now to come after me?

Why not before Christine and I got married? There was plenty of time and Natalie was around. She was shacked up with Alec Mentino until a few months ago."

Miriam sighed. "Which only goes to show you should never have taken up with her in the first place."

He was not going to have a discussion with his mother about his past hook-ups. "I think somebody put her up to it."

"A set-up?" Her hazel eyes widened at the possibility. His mother was so naïve to the darkness that lived in people.

He nodded. "Yeah, a set-up. Think about it. If somebody wanted to come between me and Christine, what better way than to insert a woman from my past, have her drug me, and take pictures that reek of infidelity."

"Nathan, do you know what you're saying?"

Her tone implied he was either desperate or a hair short of crazy. It did not imply she believed him.

"Natalie was too anxious to get me to have that beer. I was on my way out the door, but she insisted, said for old times' sake and all that crap. I know she did it. You don't black out after one beer and wake up not remembering anything. She had the perfect opportunity to do anything she wanted."

His mother's expression softened as though she wanted to believe him. "That woman has never been one of my favorite people, but drugging someone and taking pictures? That's a pretty big accusation."

"She didn't act alone. I'll bet it wasn't even her idea, but I plan to find out who's behind this, and when I do, it won't be pretty." His gut filled with the gnawing possibility that Gloria Blacksworth was behind this trouble, and if intuition proved correct, heaven help her.

***

There was no escaping him. He'd be here any minute and unless Christine wanted Lily to find out what was going on with Nate, she'd have to pretend Miriam's story were true: Christine was spending a few days with them so Nate could refinish the oak floors. *He doesn't want your sister in the dust and mess,* Miriam had said. *She'll stay with us for a little while; won't that be nice?*

Lily hadn't looked farther than her own desire to have Christine to herself and dove right into pleading for a checkers and card game partner. It was easy to pretend the truth when the source of the conflict was miles away. Stories could be stretched and reworked to resemble whatever truth a person wanted, even when they bore no resemblance to the truth at all. But when the source of the conflict was in the same room, breathing the same oxygen, well then, the pretending was not so easy. In fact, Christine had no idea how she would smile and make idle chit-chat with her husband when she could barely stand to look at him and certainly didn't want to hear his voice. Or smell his woodsy scent. And what if he tried to touch her? She glanced out the kitchen window, eyeing the empty spot where his truck would be.

"Is Nate here yet?" Lily called from behind her. "I'm hungry."

Christine forced a smile. No matter what she had to do, Lily was not going to find out that two of the people she cared about most were miserable because one of them had broken his vows.

"He'll be here soon. And your mom will be back from the dentist any minute. Why don't we get the drinks ready?"

"Nate will have iced tea." Lily moved to the cupboard and pulled down four glasses. "Do you think he'll like the spices we put in the tea?"

"I think so." But what did she know? She'd thought her husband loved her enough to remain faithful and look how that had turned out. He hadn't even made it a year. The photos of

Nate and Natalie lived in the center of her brain, making her question everything she thought she knew about him.

"And I know he's going to like the chicken pot pie," Lily chatted on, "because that's one of his very favorites. Mom says he's going to turn into a chicken pot pie one of these days." Giggle. Giggle. "How would you like to be Mrs. Chicken Pot Pie?"

Oh, Lily. The child did not deserve the sadness threatening to burst into her young world if Nate and Christine couldn't work things out. And yet, how could Christine live with a man she didn't trust? It had been almost twenty-six hours since she'd seen the photos. Anger had seeped through the numbness, settled in her gut and lay in wait, ready to attack. She would have her say, and she would find out the truth, even if she had to pull it from his lying mouth to get it.

"They're here!" Lily banged open the screen door and ran outside as Miriam's station wagon pulled into driveway with Nate's truck close behind. Was it coincidence that they both arrived at the same time, or had they met up somewhere to talk?

When Nate stepped out of the truck, there was a half second when Christine's heart swelled with longing as she took in the red T-shirt, jeans, the wind-blown hair. How many times had he come home like this, framed her face with his strong hands, and kissed her "hello"?

"Nate! Nate!" Lily flung herself at him and he hefted her into his arms, laughing as he twirled her around. He set her down, kissed the top of her head, and glanced toward the back door. His smile slipped when he saw her. "Come on, Nate." Lily grabbed his hand. "Let's go inside. I'm hungry." She yanked him toward the door with Miriam following behind.

Christine sipped in air as her husband entered the kitchen and faced her. "Hi." It was a gentle tone, filtered with uncertainty, so unlike Nate.

"Hello." How could a simple word be so difficult to say?

"Come on, Nate." Lily clutched his hand and laughed. "You have to kiss Christine like you always do when you see her." He paled, cleared his throat, and leaned in. The kiss was feather-light and quick, so quick Christine didn't have time to prepare for it.

"No, that's not right." Lily grabbed her brother's hand and placed it on Christine's right shoulder. "Now put your other hand on her other shoulder and hug her like you always do." Nate complied, jaw clenched, mouth clamped shut.

"That's right, and now you have to kiss her on the mouth for a long time. And then, you kiss her behind the left ear until she giggles. And then—"

"Lily, that's enough." Thank God for Miriam's interruption. "Can't you see your brother is tired? He's had a long day and he's hungry."

"But, Mom, he always kisses Christine like that." Her dark brows pinched together. "Even when he's tired. And that time when he was sick." Her voice hitched and faded as she repeated, "He always kisses Christine like that."

Nate mumbled something under his breath, clutched Christine's shoulders, and pulled her to him. The kiss was hard, possessive, and over before she could decide if she wanted to respond or not. He trailed his lips along her neck, settled on the soft spot behind her left ear, and kissed it. Once, twice, his tongue circling the flesh until she squirmed and giggled, like she did every time he touched her there.

Lily clapped her hands. "That's it! Christine giggled."

Nate pulled away and stepped back. "I'm hungry," he said, his eyes still on her.

Miriam jumped in. "Good. Chicken pot pie is meant to be eaten when it's fresh out of the oven, not sitting around so the crust turns to mush."

"I wanted pizza, but Mom said we had to make chicken pot pie for you." She scrunched her nose at him and he mussed her hair. "Spoiled boy."

"Right." Nate sat down next to Christine. "You, Miss Lily, are the most spoiled young lady in Magdalena."

She grinned and added, "In the state of New York."

He shook his head. "In the United States."

She threw her arms wide and said, "In the world."

"Lily." Miriam gave her daughter a stern look. "Not at the dinner table. You and your brother can continue your silly shenanigans after supper." Lily flashed a grin at Nate who smiled back. They bantered like this often, and for just a second, it felt like any other day. Normal. Relaxing. Peaceful. And then Christine remembered it wasn't.

Thankfully, Lily kept the conversation going with her talk about Pop Benito's new tennis shoes from his son in California and the postcard his granddaughter sent him from Spain. Christine made a few comments, toyed with her food, and actually ate a few bites. She did not look at her husband or speak directly to him. The next time Miriam invited him to dinner, Christine would make sure she wasn't home. Pop said she could stop over whenever she wanted to strategize about ways to get The Bleeding Heart Society's support or just chit-chat.

What would he say if he knew about Nate and Natalie Servetti? Quite a bit, and it wouldn't be sugarcoated either. After peach cobbler and cleaning up the kitchen—Nate insisted on washing—he kissed his mother and Lily and made some lame comment about getting back to sanding the floor.

"Christine, can I see you for a minute?" He had his hand on the doorknob and when she nodded, he opened it and motioned her past him. She made her way to the truck, out of earshot and partially blocked from view, in case Lily was in one of her inquisitive moods. Nate leaned against the truck door and crossed his arms over his chest. "Are we going to talk about this?"

She stood a few feet from him, just out of arm's reach, in case he got the urge to touch her. "Eventually."

"That could mean anything." He shrugged, his voice guarded. "Two days, ten? A year?"

"I don't know. It's too soon." That was the truth. Her emotions wouldn't settle down so she could think logically, and aside from Miriam, who pushed for her to work it out with Nate, there was no one she could talk to. She certainly couldn't confide in Uncle Harry who might get it in his head to drive to Magdalena and confront Nate. There would be a scene because Uncle Harry didn't do anything on a small scale. It would be in the *Magdalena Press*, and the whole town would read about the photos of Nate and Natalie Servetti. And then there was the baby that no one knew about: their baby. She would have to tell Nate, but not yet, certainly not under these circumstances.

"What's going to happen when you find out I've been set up and you didn't believe me?"

The fact that he wasn't giving up that story unsettled her. Was he telling the truth? Or did he merely think he could make her believe it was the truth if he said it with enough conviction? She needed answers and time.

"Why were you at Gino Servetti's? What was the big surprise that you would risk running into your old lover for it?" He looked away, his expression unreadable.

"Well? Can you at least tell me that?" When his gaze met hers, she could have sworn she spotted a flicker of pain in those dark eyes.

"It doesn't matter now."

"Yes, it does. What was it?"

"Forget it." When he spoke in that tone, he was done with the subject. She knew him well enough to know that.

"Fine." A few days ago, she could share anything with him, had been planning to tell him he was going to be a father. Today, she could barely maintain eye contact.

"Call me when you want to talk." He opened the truck door, turned and said, "The longer you wait, the harder this is going to be to fix, until one day, it won't be able to be fixed."

***

Pop watered the first of three pots of basil, careful not to drench the delicate leaves. They'd need transplanting soon so they could spread out and grow. Too many people tossed the seeds in a pot and with the exception of an occasional bottle of water, did nothing, and wondered why their basil was so puny, or died, or withered into a spindle. Where was the wondering? Plants were like people; you had to tend to them or they'd go wild or shrink from neglect. Take Nate Desantro. Pop could sure tell Christine had been tending to that young man, showing him he counted as her number one person. You can't buy that kind of love; it grew from inside a person and when they shared it, it spread, kind of like Pop's secret fertilizer that only he and Lucy knew about.

"Ah, Lucy, you'd like Christine. She's not snooty like Nate's first wife, and she loves Lily. You can see it when she talks about her."

Pop lifted the watering can to the second pot, ran a steady stream into the soil. "I took her to The Bleeding Heart's Society meeting the other day." He chuckled and pulled a weed from the pot. "She got an earful. Didn't know what to think, I could tell. Not many garden clubs talk about ways to handle an unruly fifteen-year-old or who's gonna make a Homecoming dress for Denise Bellan. I had to let her see for herself what we're all about."

He fingered the leaf of a small basil plant. "Every time I walk into that meeting room, I remember the first time you suggested starting a wish box for people to write in what they needed. Who would have thought the whole town would get behind it? I know you remember the first wish the society granted." He fingered a basil leaf and pictured his Lucy handing an envelope to the soon-to-graduate college student with four brothers and a father on disability.

"Meg Delstant never forgot that suit the society bought her so she could go on that interview. She said that's what got her the job." He chuckled and watered the Swiss chard.

"We know that brain of hers had something to do with it, but that suit gave her courage to do what needed to be done." His voice dipped, filled with a mix of sadness and love. "That was you, Lucy. That was all you and your kindness.

"What do you think about Christine? Think she's a keeper? Or do you think she'll hightail it out of here at the first sign of trouble? She really seems to love the boy and you know Nate's a hard one to love. I know what you're thinking. 'Even love that blooms eternal runs into patches of crabgrass.' You got a point, but all I want to do is make sure that patch don't explode into a football field."

Pop set down his watering can, shielded a hand against his eyes, and glanced at the sky. The blue matched Lucy's eyes. He smiled and laid a hand across his heart where his dear wife rested.

"Nate and Christine remind me of us," he whispered. "She's feisty until she talks about him. He's bull-headed but can't see nobody but her. But time and crabgrass will tell their story, like it did ours, don't you think so, Lucy?"

***

"Okay, what did you do now?"

Nate kept his head bent and his eyes fixed on the

spreadsheet in front of him. Damned if he was going to open his mouth about anything personal, especially the truth behind the reason he was at work on a Saturday morning doing the one thing he hated more than anything—inventory.

"Nobody can count anymore. Do people just make up the numbers so they don't have to move parts around and get their hands dirty?" Frustration seeped through his words, spilled over Jack's inquiry. This wasn't about numbers or inventory; hell, this wasn't about business at all. The reason he was here, the reason he'd been unable to stay at his house for longer than the few miserable hours when he tried to sleep, had to do with Christine. Falling asleep in front of the television, drinking, moodiness, extra hours at the shop—all centered around his wife and her obvious attempts to distance herself from him while she figured out her life and his part in it.

"Uh-huh." Jack moved closer, tapped a bony hand on the desk. "The last time you blamed inventory on your misery was when you fell for that wife of yours but refused to admit it."

"Leave it alone." He did not want to talk about Christine to anyone right now.

"You know, this marriage business isn't always a smooth road. Nope, sure isn't. Sometimes you get stuck in quicksand and feel like you're gonna suffocate. Other times, you gotta push uphill so damn hard, you think your heart's gonna burst." He blew out a long breath. "And then there's the times you think about getting in your truck and driving off. You don't, though, because that's not what you signed up for now, is it?" His voice turned gruffer than usual. "And you wouldn't make it past the county line because you belong together. So, what did you and Christine fight about?"

Damn, but the man would not leave it alone. Nate shoved the spreadsheet aside and looked at Jack. "I don't want to talk about it."

"Hmm."

"What?" Nate snapped.

"Nothing. If you say everything's fine, then, of course, I believe you." He scratched his jaw. "I'm just wondering if life is so good right now, why you've been such a crabass lately, and why hasn't Christine stopped by with lunch?"

"She's been busy." *Busy avoiding me.*

"Right. Busy."

"I've got work to do, so if you don't mind, I'd like to get back to it." The only way to survive right now was to keep his brain and his body in steady motion so he couldn't think about the emptiness eating his soul.

"Sure." Jack nodded, his bushy brows pulled together. The man saw more than he let on, and most times he kept his observations to himself, unless they involved Nate. Then, he made it his job to investigate the situation, put it under a damn microscope, and eventually offer a solution, solicited or not. So why wasn't he doing that now? Why was he so amenable to staying out of Nate's business? Something was up.

"I just have one question." *Damn, here it comes.* "I was back in the warehouse a few days ago and I noticed this tarp over some big contraption. Couldn't figure out what it was, unless one of the workers got lazy and covered up some material they didn't want to put away. So I investigated." He shoved his hands in his jeans pockets. "And you'll never guess what I found."

Nate looked away. "I have no idea."

"Really? Sure as hell looked like your work."

"Huh." He picked up a pencil, fiddled with it. Jack's inquisitiveness was closing in on him. It was only a matter of two or three more sentences before he called Nate out.

"Yup. Nice piece of work." He tipped his baseball cap back and scratched his forehead. "What I can't figure out is what's a

125

cradle doing back in the warehouse."

Damn Jack Finnegan and his intuitive nosiness. "Okay, you got me. It's my work."

"Christine's pregnant?"

Nate shook his head. "No. It was just something I wanted to make, for when the time came." He should have started the cradle months ago and given it to her. Maybe by now she'd be pregnant. That would have given her the extra reason to work things out instead of what she was doing now, which was stalling and avoiding him. Why was it luck was always a stroke behind him? Just this once, couldn't things roll in his favor?

"Why did you say 'for when the time came', not 'for when the time comes'?" Jack had worked his way back to Nate's desk. "What's going on, boy? I'm a good listener and sure as hell not a gossip trap like Betty. Whatever you tell me won't leave this room."

It wasn't that he thought Jack would broadcast Nate's marital problems throughout Magdalena because the man was as solid and trustworthy as they came. No, this was more about voicing the accusations and the current state of his screwed-up marriage. He didn't want Jack giving him that pitiful look that said, *The worst is yet to come*, or even *It's not irreversible, but damn close*. Once you started talking about it, it became a reality; sometimes other people's reality, and everybody had an opinion. *Let her go. Fight for her. Stand your ground. Get a lawyer. Never trust a woman, especially an estranged wife.*

He'd said these words a time or two himself, but dammit, this was different. This was his marriage; this was Christine they were talking about. Nate opened his mouth, willing the truth to spill out, but he couldn't do it.

"I'm sorry, Jack. I can't talk about it right now."

The old man nodded, his expression somber. "I understand.

How 'bout I move that piece of furniture to the computer room, so nobody sees it and starts asking questions? Tom ain't gonna say nothing seeing as it doesn't have a keyboard or a monitor attached to it."

Tom Finnegan, ND's computer man and Jack's nephew. "Sure."

"Okay then." He made it to the door but couldn't quite get to the other side without one more word.

"You know, years ago, Dolly and I had a bout of difficulties. Mostly from my stupidity. We'd just had Jenny and I was feeling trapped, unappreciated, and steamrolled by a pack of kids who needed this and that, and a wife who didn't want nothin' to do with me. I came within a hair of making the biggest mistake of my life." He sighed and shook his head. "Thank God I woke up before it was too late. Don't wait until the hurt's gone on too long that you can't go back. You'll regret it for the rest of your life." He turned the knob and disappeared down the hall.

It didn't take a psychiatrist to figure out the biggest mistake Jack almost made had to do with a woman. Didn't it always? Maybe he'd had a Natalie Servetti type in his past, too. Maybe Nate should have confided in him. After all, Jack had been around a long time and, other than Miriam, knew the pieces of Nate's life better than anyone. There'd been the death of his father, the presence of Charles Blacksworth, the divorce from Patrice. All twisted and torn with anger, grief, sometimes despair, and Jack had been there to guide him and make sense of it all with his backwoods philosophizing. But this thing with Christine was different. Nate needed to make this work because if he lost her…he would not even consider it. He wasn't going to lose her. Christine was his wife, his partner, until they drew their last breaths.

He was well into the spreadsheet again, caught between

steel bars and steel plates, when there was loud chatter in the hallway and seconds later, Lily burst into his office, a grin on her face, a lunchbox in her hand. "Hi, Nate. Hungry?"

Truth? He hadn't been hungry since the afternoon Christine packed up her suitcase and moved to his mother's. But he couldn't tell Lily that, so he forced a smile and said, "Sure, what's in there? Liver and onions? Cow tongue and cabbage?"

His sister giggled and hefted the nylon lunch box onto his desk. "No, silly. Me and Mom made them." She unzipped the top and lifted out two sandwiches covered in an excess of plastic wrap, an apple, a plastic baggie filled with chips, and two chocolate chip cookies. "A peanut butter and banana for you." She placed a sandwich in front of him. "And a peanut butter and jelly for you." She leaned over and whispered, "It's Mom's peach jelly, the one I'm not allowed to eat."

Peach bourbon jelly. He knew it well and, yes, it was his favorite. "Mom makes you strawberry and cherry, so don't be complaining. And it's not like you share those with me." He unwrapped the peanut butter and peach bourbon jelly sandwich and bit into it.

"I'm not complaining and I do share." Her lips twitched. "Just not with you."

"Thanks. Thanks a lot. I'll remember that the next time you want me to take you fishing or beg me to play the piano so you can dance."

"Just teasing. I shared the cherry jelly with Christine this morning." She reached in the bag and pulled out a chocolate chip cookie. "I wanted to give her something to make her smile."

Oh? "She's not smiling?" *Is she as miserable as I am?*

Lily shook her head and bit into the cookie. "Uh-uh." She chomped on the cookie and said, "Mom said she needs to eat more, but Christine says she's not hungry." Lily paused, looked at her half-eaten cookie. "Why is she not hungry, Nate? Do you think she's sick?"

"No, honey, I don't think she's sick." He reached across the desk, clasped her small hand and squeezed. "Maybe she's just got a lot on her mind and isn't thinking about food right now."

She peered at him through thick glasses and he could almost see that brain working. "But Mom says food feeds our souls. Doesn't Christine's soul need to get fed?"

Miriam and her sage words. Let her explain that one to Lily. "Yes, but some people need more time than others." Learning his wife might be as miserable as he was created mixed feelings. On one hand, he never wanted her to know a second of pain, but on the other, well, if she had trouble sleeping and wandered about with a hole in her stomach, maybe that would make her more eager to get this whole mess resolved.

"You know what?" Lily stuffed the rest of her cookie in her mouth and held up a hand while she chomped away. Nate smiled and popped a chip in his mouth. She always lifted his mood and made him realize there was still good in this often screwed-up world. "You know what?" she repeated, now that her cookie was gone.

"No, what?"

She brushed her hands together to get rid of cookie crumbs and leaned toward him. "I think I know why Christine's not eating, but don't tell Mom, okay?"

"Sure. What is it?"

Lily cast a quick glance toward the door and, satisfied no one was around, turned back to him and whispered. "I heard her crying the other night after we went to bed. I think she's sad." Her eyes grew bright, and her voice cracked. "She misses you, Nate. You're supposed to be with her. Every night. Sleep in the same bed."

"Lily."

The tears started, slipping down her cheeks to her chin. She swiped at them from behind her glasses, but still they fell. "How long do you have to work on that stupid floor?"

Nate pushed back his chair and made his way to her. He knelt down and clasped his sister's hand. "It'll be okay, Lily. Don't cry."

"You better come for dinner tonight." She sniffed. "And you better sleep in the same bed."

Chapter 10

Christine slouched against the wall in the tiny bathroom at Miriam's and wiped a hand across her sweaty forehead. She'd thought the term *morning sickness* meant sickness in the morning, but the doctor she met with three days ago had not only clarified that misunderstanding, he'd provided her with several pamphlets for the "expectant parent" that she'd hidden in her oversized handbag. When he'd asked where the father was, she'd stumbled around and grabbed the first tidbit that landed in her brain. *Traveling. Hopefully, he'll make the next meeting.* Dr. Elliot Conrad, middle-aged, quiet spoken, and clearly versed on every manner of excuse regarding absent significant others, had merely nodded. At least she'd chosen a town twenty minutes away, one that was *not* Magdalena and would not contain well-wishers ready to spread the word about the upcoming addition to the Desantro family.

Dr. Conrad said the baby was due in December and talked about the importance of taking prenatal vitamins, getting plenty of rest, and reducing stress. How much more stress could a woman be under when she wasn't living with the baby's father, and there was no resolution in sight? And healthy eating? If her stomach didn't calm down soon, Miriam would figure out that the situation with Nate wasn't the only thing making Christine heave her dinner. Thankfully, Nate's mother was too preoccupied with her son and daughter-in-law's predicament to see what was right before her: Christine was pregnant with her grandchild.

It was a good thing Uncle Harry wasn't around because he might not know a thing about babies, but he knew Christine, knew her moods, knew when she was holding back, and when something bothered her. One look and he'd issue a command in that gruff voice sprinkled with a curse word or three, and she'd tell him everything. But Uncle Harry wasn't here. As a matter-of-fact, his phone calls lately had been sporadic, and when they did speak, he sounded like he was in a rush, or preoccupied, not in a bad way, but still, not totally present. Was it Greta? Maybe something was finally happening between them and, if so, Christine was not going to ruin his happiness with her misery.

What a mess. Before Nate, she hadn't really thought about children other than as add-ons to an already full and busy life that would get busier and fuller with children but would certainly not be *consumed* by them. But from the second she'd taken the home pregnancy test, she'd imagined Nate holding their baby, Lily and Miriam's excitement over the new addition, even Uncle Harry, uncertain but proud as a grand-uncle. There would be Christmases filled with pine trees, popcorn garlands, and homemade ornaments, and birthdays with handmade cards, cake, and balloons. Their house would flow with love and tradition and when the next child came along, and even the next, that love and tradition would swell and grow, filling their hearts, their lives.

But now? Christine squeezed her eyes shut and sipped in air. Now there was too much uncertainty to see the future, and even less to understand it. She had to tell Nate about the baby, and soon. He had a right to know and she wouldn't keep this from him, but neither did she want a child to force them back together. Too many of her parents' friends had done this and she'd witnessed the fallout from patched-up marriages "for the sake of the child". Kids weren't stupid; they sensed when the love wasn't real, when respect turned to animosity no matter how nicely it was presented. She wouldn't do that to their child, or Nate, or herself. There'd been no sign of Natalie Servetti or her family, according to Miriam, who found this odd since the Servettis were a clannish sort who never ventured past a two-hundred-mile radius and were now supposedly vacationing in Disney World. Even a less suspicious mind would find this bizarre and out of character. Had Nate been set-up, drugged as he claimed? If so, by whom?

If she'd never seen the pictures, it would be easier to believe him and move on. But she had to know who was behind this, if someone was, and why. Then she could believe him, *then* she could tell him about the baby. She pressed a hand across her belly. And it had better be soon, because one way or the other, this baby would be here by Christmas.

When she was fairly certain her stomach would cooperate, Christine dragged herself off the floor, brushed her teeth, and pinched her cheeks. Miriam would wonder what had happened to her, and Christine couldn't afford her mother-in-law's assessment skills to kick in just now. She found her in the kitchen, of course, rolling biscuits for dinner. "Hello, dear. I hope you're hungry. I'm making those buttermilk biscuits you love so much."

"Oh." Christine eyed the biscuits, swallowed. "Of course." And then, because she'd sounded like a sick bird, she corrected, "Thank you. I do love those."

Miriam nodded, grabbed a small glass, floured the top, and pressed it into the dough. She continued this process and then gently lifted each biscuit with a spatula and placed it on a baking sheet. "Next time, I'll let you make these." Her voice dipped. "Nate loves them."

What to say to that?

"Lily called a few minutes ago." Miriam glanced up, held her gaze. "She invited Nate to dinner. He called when she was in the bathroom and said he couldn't get out of it. She was pretty forceful. And Christine? Lily told him he needs to stay with you tonight—in your bed."

***

Who would have thought Nate would dread sleeping with a beautiful woman, a woman who happened to be his wife? From the second Lily demanded he share a bed with Christine, his gut had twisted and churned so hard he could barely get a buttermilk biscuit down his throat, let alone the chicken and gravy. And the apple crisp? Wasn't happening. He'd excused himself and headed for the garage with a lame excuse about checking the lawn mower.

Lily had a bead on them, like she was an investigator and he and Christine were under suspicion for lack of affection to one another and not sharing a bed. How the hell did his sister even know about this stuff? Maybe it was more intuitive. Lily *sensed* there was a hole in their usual closeness. Gone were the random kisses on the neck, the slow smiles, the laughter. Oh, they faked it pretty well, but apparently Lily had begun to notice, and once she did the expectations to return to "normal" came along with it. Hence, the demand that he and Christine sleep in the same bed, which would have been more than fine if they'd actually had a conversation in the last several days. But they hadn't, and now, here they were, him in his T-shirt and athletic shorts—no nakedness tonight—and her in the oversized Beauty and the Beast T-shirt Lily had given her for her birthday. *She's Beauty*, Lily had told him when Christine pulled the T-shirt from the gift bag. *And you're The Beast.* Yeah, that's pretty much what everyone thought right about now.

"So," he eased onto his side of the bed, careful not to trespass on the imaginary line separating his half from hers, "this is awkward."

Her lips twitched and for a millisecond, he spotted the old Christine, the one he missed so much his chest hurt. But then those lips flattened and she looked away. "It is, but we can't hurt Lily."

"But we're going to, eventually." He folded his pillow in half and rested his head on it, so he could study her reaction. "Aren't we?"

"I hope not." She slid into bed beside him, and when she met his gaze, there was pain in those eyes and a mountain of sadness. "I'm so tired of this. I know if we're going to get past what happened, I have to trust you. Common sense tells me that. You can't explain those photos other than to say you were drugged. It's your word against hers. I get that, believe me, I do. But now she's disappeared with her whole family." Those blue eyes grew bright. "And I'm trying to deal with it, but I can't get those photos out of my head." Her voice cracked, but she pushed on. "I see her on top of you, picture her moving over you, your shirt open... your...your jeans..." She sucked in a breath and finished. "I see it all and I *think* it all, and I don't know how to get rid of it."

Nate wanted to pull her into his arms and take away the pain, but all he could do was stay on his damn side of the bed and talk. "Trust never comes lightly. I know that."

She swiped a hand across her face. "I don't want to end up like my mother and father, living a lie for a lifetime and ignoring the truth."

"Neither do I." He willed her to see inside his heart to the love he had only for her. "On Lily's life, I did not betray you. I swear to God I didn't and I'm going to prove it. I'm going to find Natalie and she's going to tell me why she tried to ruin my marriage."

The tears started then, falling onto her cheeks, to her chin, along her jaw line. She tried to brush them away, but they kept coming. Nate waited, hoping she would let him comfort her. It was a small step, but he'd take it. Hell, he'd take anything she had to offer right now.

"Nate." She spoke his name seconds before she threw herself at him with a muffled sob. He pulled her close, whispered her name, and held her against his heart—where she belonged.

***

"I'm so pleased you could join me for lunch." Gloria offered a hand to Connor Pendleton. The last time they'd met at The Presidio, she'd convinced him to propose to Christine. Sadly, that had not worked out. Yet.

Connor flashed a bright smile and slid into the seat next to her "You know I always have time for you, Gloria." The smile slipped a bit as his expression turned serious. "But I was a little confused about your message. You said it had to do with Christine. Is she all right?"

All right? That was a relative term, dictated by time and emotion. At the moment she suffered a minor heartache that Connor would certainly cure once Christine saw the futility of staying married to that Desantro man. A quiet divorce should not be so difficult to obtain. What judge in his right mind would think Christine and that mountain man belonged together? That union had been wrong on so many levels, beginning and ending with the Desantro name. "Let's say my daughter has come to her senses." Gloria smiled and sipped her champagne. Nothing like a nice bottle of Dom Pérignon for a celebration, and the beginning of the end of Christine's short marriage was indeed call for a celebration.

Connor tilted his blond head and once again, Gloria pictured the children he and Christine would have: fair skinned, light-colored eyes. Civilized, not some backwoods offspring with dark eyes and insolent manners. "You're going to have to elaborate a bit on that. I don't even want to try and guess."

Gloria laughed and nodded. "Yes, Christine's behavior has

been a bit erratic this past year, hasn't it?"

"I'm sure it had to do with Charles's death. I can't imagine losing someone you love so suddenly." He frowned, toyed with his champagne glass. "A person can lose his mind for a bit." He glanced up and met her gaze, his handsome face a mix of curiosity and puzzlement. "You think that's what happened to her?"

"I'm certain of it." She leaned in, clasped his hand. "It was devastating to all of us. So tragic. But we all handle misfortune in different ways. Christine chose to run from it, and when the man she married turned out to be less than honorable, well," she shrugged, "you can't get away from your breeding, now can you?" She'd vowed to make Nathan Desantro pay for his disrespect, and she'd done it on a grand scale. He was on the verge of losing Christine and it had only taken a few reports from Lester so she could develop a strategy, plus twenty-five thousand dollars to that Servetti girl to drug her ex-lover. Lester had taken some charming shots. Ha! Let that Desantro man try to weasel out of that. He couldn't prove a thing, and that was the beauty of it.

"Is Christine planning to come back to Chicago?"

Oh, she had his interest now. Connor didn't like to lose and it had been a blow when Christine dumped him for that mountain man. If he saw an opportunity to steal her back, Gloria would bet her Mercedes he'd latch onto it with the same aggressiveness he went after a deal.

"I see no reason why she'd stay in that godforsaken backwoods town once her marriage is over." She sipped her champagne, paused long enough for him to assimilate the possibility of Christine returning with winning her over.

"If you're still interested in a union, I think I might be able to facilitate that." Once her daughter realized she had no place in that town, she'd head back to Chicago, and Gloria would be waiting for her, arms wide, sympathies flowing. She would not even bring up that ugly bit of past that created such a rift between them or this past year. They would put it all behind them as though it had never happened and start fresh.

"I'd like that," Connor said, his eyes bright. "Christine could be a valuable asset to me."

"I do hope you think of her as more than an asset to boost your company's net worth." She had him right where she wanted him; Connor Pendleton and his family were always about bottom line first, emotions second.

"Of course not, but she does have the uncanny ability to get my clients talking. They all love her, even the difficult ones." He paused. "Should I head to New York and visit her?"

"No! You can't rush her." Of course, that wasn't the real reason to keep him away from New York. Gloria did not want him anywhere near Magdalena and the secrets that could tarnish the Blacksworth name. How long would it take before he learned of Miriam Desantro, and worse, her daughter? Charles's memory must be preserved, but of course it was more than that, much more. Gloria was not going to let that scandal destroy the image she'd spent years creating: a loving wife with a devoted husband and daughter. A perfect family.

"How do you see this playing out?"

"Give her a little time. She's filled with so many emotions right now and she needs space to figure them out." Gloria reached across the table and patted his tanned hand. "Once she does, she'll come home and you'll be waiting for her."

"I'm not a patient man. I don't wait for things to happen," he paused, met her gaze with will and determination. "I *make* them happen. I might be able to convince Christine to end the charade of a marriage if I can see her face-to-face."

Not in Magdalena. She had to divert his plan while there was still time. "I spoke with Christine yesterday and she indicated the last thing she wants is for anyone to tell her 'I told you so'. I certainly wasn't going to say anything other than offer support. If you show up there, she'll think we plotted against her and Nathan Desantro, and that could actually bring them back together." She paused long enough to let the lie permeate his brain. "Don't you think?"

"Hmm." He rubbed his strong jaw and once again Gloria imagined the beautiful children he and Christine would have. Two was a nice number. A boy and a girl. "I'll have to think about that."

"Please do." She sighed and lifted her champagne glass. "Life has a funny way of correcting itself, evening out the rough edges and changing course when we least expect it. If we're prepared and vigilant, we won't miss the opportunity, fleeting as it may be." She sipped her drink and considered how things would change over the next few months. By Christmas, there could be a pending engagement, by next spring, a wedding. "You and Christine are meant to be together, and while I stopped believing in fairytales long ago, I do believe in creating destiny." Her lips pulled into a smile of assurance and knowing. "You'll see."

The luncheon continued with more champagne and a vigilant Armand anticipating her every need. Amazing what fear could do to make a person more agreeable. Last year's fall on the steps of The Presidio had not resulted in a lawsuit or even the threat of one, but the fact that it *could* happen elevated Gloria's status at the restaurant to one who must be treated with the utmost care and respect. It was quite enjoyable to wield such power without having to actually use it, and there was that other tidbit that elicited equal joy: her presence had driven Harry Blacksworth from his favorite restaurant. He'd loved the place, visited it often, which was why she'd made a point of showing up when she thought he might be there and force him to suffer through Armand's solicitous behavior toward her. It was a small victory for the years of antagonizing he'd caused her, but it did give her pleasure. Oh, he'd gone and bought a restaurant and handed it over to that little piece he was obsessed with, but it wasn't The Presidio. That was her turf.

Gloria arrived home in a delightful mood. This Christmas would not be like the last one, filled with elaborate festivities, scrumptious meals, and gifts, but no one to call family. This Christmas would be different because Christine would be home in Chicago, where she belonged. The knowledge spread through Gloria, making her almost giddy. Perhaps she should start making a guest list for her annual Christmas party. It might be sweltering outside, but one could never begin preparations soon enough.

Gloria tossed her keys on the kitchen counter and called out, "Elissa?" The girl had begun staying later to take over some of the other duties that had belonged to another servant who quit when Gloria refused to give her three weeks off to visit family in Italy. No one understood that employees had responsibilities to an employer. Businesses were run on sound decision-making and there were tough calls that had to be made. Why did people believe that just because they asked nicely, the request would be granted? That was not life. Hadn't she been a good wife for years, reworking her daily existence to accommodate her husband? And for what? He'd grown more distant by the month until finally, she'd lashed out and taken action by having an affair with his brother. What a horrible, painful, and unforgiveable mistake that had been! Charles had never known the man she slept with was Harry, but it hadn't mattered because he withdrew from her as surely as if he'd divorced her, and eventually, turned to *that* woman.

"Mrs. Blacksworth? You were looking for me?"

The girl smiled, her youth and beauty making her plain white uniform glow. "Yes, I was. Tomorrow morning, I want you to move all of the orchids from the bedroom they're in and place them in the one next to it. Then wipe down the walls, clean the blinds, change the sheets. Everything." The orchids had survived all of these months and so had Gloria.

"Is it your daughter, Mrs. Blacksworth? Is she coming home?"

Gloria had fired a servant for mentioning Christine's name, but that was when desperation had taken hold and she'd worried she might never see her daughter again. Desperation and worry had fled a few days ago with Natalie Servetti and been replaced with confidence and certainty. Christine would be home soon. Life would return to its new normal, without Charles, but it would be more bearable because her daughter would be here with her, forging a relationship where she belonged. Gloria smiled and did not attempt to hide the joy simmering inside. "Yes, Christine's coming home."

***

Christine pulled *The Wall Street Journal* from her purse and spread it on the tan Formica table at Lina's Café. She'd ordered a toasted cheese sandwich and if she kept that down, she was going for the coconut cream pie in the glass case by the register. It had been three days since she and Nate spent the night together and though no one had mentioned it, especially Nate, she'd been able to think of little else. When she'd fallen apart and cried, he'd held her, whispered soothing words in her ear, and stroked her back until she fell asleep. In the morning he was gone, nothing but a note on his pillow that said *I hope you feel better. I'm thinking of you.* No pressure, no demands.

There were still no answers as to what happened that night between Nate and Natalie Servetti, and maybe there never would be. Maybe it really was about blind faith and trust in the person you loved. Oh, but that left a person open to such pain and heartache. Betrayal even. People didn't always survive it. Could Nate betray her? Her heart told her *no* while logic demanded proof. This time, her heart was going to win. After lunch, she'd head back to the office and work on a strategy that would involve being at Nate's by dinner and telling him about the baby tonight.

"Christine?"

She looked up, startled to see Connor Pendleton standing beside her, his blonde good looks dwarfing the table. "Connor? What are you doing here?"

He flashed a smile and slid into the booth across from her. "I missed you." The smile spread, pulled out two dimples, and made his eyes sparkle. "And I thought why not visit the place that stole you from me?"

What was he talking about and why was he really here? "That's not exactly what happened." She'd broken up with him because they wanted different things in life and coming to Magdalena made her realize that.

He shrugged. "We all remember things differently." He glanced around the small café, his gaze landing on the gray-haired waitress Christine liked to chat with during lunch. Her name was Phyllis, a widow with five grandchildren, and a Pomeranian-mix named Belle. "I prefer to think a place rather than a person pulled you away."

Connor would think that because he hated being bested by anyone in business or in his personal life. He would never consider that *he* might be the problem. His gaze swung back to hers and he frowned. "I'm not seeing anything here that has the hum of Chicago. Is it the coffee? The air? Or do they have the freshest water this side of the Mississippi? What is it, Christine?"

How could she possibly explain it to him? "It's a different

way of life: calmer, slower paced, more centered."

"And you like that?" She might as well have told him she liked watching water fill in a bathtub. The wrinkled brow and puzzled expression told her he didn't get it. His next words proved it. "Are you saying you actually enjoy a place that doesn't even have a major hotel chain or a five-star restaurant?"

Before she could answer, Phyllis slid Christine's plate in front of her and plopped a stack of napkins in the middle of the table. "There you go, hon. Anything for you, darlin'?" she asked, eyeing Connor with a combination of interest and humor.

He flipped open the menu and scanned the right side. "I'll have a turkey burger, wheat bun, light on the mayo, extra red onion, lettuce, and a tomato. Can I have a side salad with that? No cheese, and bring the oil and vinegar. And an iced tea, as long as it isn't sweetened."

Phyllis snapped her gum and nodded. "Sure. Anything else?"

Connor had never been good at detecting sarcasm and Phyllis had just unloaded a deep-fryer basket of it on him. "No, I think that will do it."

"Great." She nodded her gray head and turned away, but not before she threw Christine a look at that said, "Darlin', you have got to be kidding."

Christine offered half of her toasted cheese sandwich to Connor and when he shook his head, she squirted ketchup on her plate and dipped the sandwich in it. She and Lily made these at night sometimes and always dipped them in ketchup. "Connor, how did you know where to find me?"

He cleared his throat. "You mean the restaurant?" Long pause. "Or the town?"

"Actually, both."

He cleared his throat again, a habit he employed when he was trying to avoid a question or prolong an answer. "It wasn't hard to find your office. The first person I asked knew who you were, where you worked, even what kind of car you drove. That's just a little too friendly for me." He shook his head and said, "You would really write, 'Gone to lunch at Lina's, back at 1:30'."

It sounded ridiculous when he said it, but when Pop suggested she make a sign informing prospective clients of her whereabouts, it had made perfect sense. The town prided itself on unity and closeness, and this had been her way of telling them she *wanted* to be one of them. Whether she'd succeeded or not remained to be seen. "It's a small town. I like to be available."

Connor glanced around the café, taking in the customers. It was mostly gray-haired senior citizens dressed in cotton and elastic, their sneakers white, shoelaces double-tied. She recognized many of them from church, the grocery store, the post office. There was Violet Peterson in the third booth with a man some said had been her high school sweetheart and now, sixty years later, had regained that title. And Patch McGregor, a scratch golfer at seventy-two, who walked five miles a day and had never had a cup of coffee.

Aside from the seniors, there were young mothers attempting to feed children whose tiny fists pounded on the tray tops of highchairs. Christine recognized Tammi Reed and Rhonda Brunelli, two of the women she'd helped work on reducing debt a few weeks ago. A smattering of "business people", dubbed such because they were not dressed in jeans and happened to have a newspaper in front of them, sat at the counter. One looked an awful lot like Dr. Pickering, the town optometrist. Miriam said he had seven children, all of them home-schooled.

"What are you doing here?"

"Huh?" Christine dragged her gaze from the man she thought was Dr. Pickering. "What?"

"What are you doing in this godforsaken town?" He leaned toward her, lowered his voice. "You don't belong here."

"It's my home now." It *was* her home; she did belong here.

"Christine." His eyes filled with what could only be pity. "This isn't for you. None of it. Where are the lights, the big city, the fancy parties? Where's the brain stimulation? I'm not seeing it here."

"Connor," she enunciated his name like she used to when she had something important to say and he wasn't listening. "This is my home now. I like it here." His expression said he didn't believe her, but before he could tell her so, the waitress delivered his lunch, which gave her a five-second head start on her next question. "You haven't told me how you knew I was here in Magdalena."

He shrugged. "The art of the good business deal is knowing the questions to ask and how to get the answers." A slow blush seeped up his neck, settled on his cheeks.

"Meaning?" *What had he done?*

"I paid a visit to your company, chummed up with Harry's secretary, and all it took was a smile and lunch for her to spill that you were here. I don't even think she realized what she said."

"You used Belinda?"

He removed the top of his bun, poked beneath the lettuce with his fork. "I think they put relish on this."

"Connor. You used her, didn't you?"

"I like to think of it as information gathering. Your mother didn't want me to come, but you know I'm not a patient person. When I decide on something, I don't want to waste time waiting." He picked up his knife and scraped bits of relish from the turkey burger. "This is definitely relish."

"What does my mother have to do with this?" He'd bitten into his sandwich and took his time chewing—to come up with a story, no doubt.

"Look, I heard about you and," he paused, "that guy you married. Your mother said things weren't working out and it looked like you'd be heading back to Chicago before Christmas."

"What? Why would she say that?" Why *would* she say that? Did Gloria have spies in Magdalena watching her every move so she could plot and plan a way to break up her marriage? A rush of anxiety pulsed through her, settled in her gut. Was Gloria behind Natalie Servetti's deeds and her disappearance? Good Lord, was she capable of that? Had Nate been telling her the truth all along?

"Christine, you've got to know how I feel about you. Gloria is only the facilitator, so don't blame her."

"Don't blame her? She's butting into my life, Connor. Did you hear me? *My* life, not hers, and she had no right to tell you anything about my marriage."

"Was she wrong?" His words dared her to refute it.

"Yes, she's wrong." Christine pushed her plate away, the half-eaten sandwich saturated in ketchup. "I'm married to Nate. I love him, Connor, do you hear me?"

He stared at her as though she hadn't just spread her heart on the table. "That's emotion speaking, not logic and common sense. You and Desantro have nothing in common. He's a loser who will drag you down with him. Cut him loose now and team up with me." His lips pulled into a bright smile. "We'll own the world."

"Do you hear yourself?" How had she ever considered marrying him?

"What? It's the truth."

"I don't know what my mother told you, but she's wrong." *Hadn't she always been wrong, manipulating people and events to achieve the reality she wanted, even if it wasn't true?* "You've wasted your time; I'm not going anywhere unless it's with my husband." She had to find Nate now and tell him Gloria was somehow mixed up in the whole Servetti mess. "Don't contact me again."

***

Small towns had their secrets and they held them close, but there was a hell of a lot of information they offered up for public consumption. Betty was big on this, jabbered on and on every day about one thing or another, until Nate had to close his door or risk a headache. Jack said Betty was like this because she lived alone with her two dogs and had to use up her daily word quota. *She talks to those dang dogs, but one-sided conversations don't yield much in the way of burning up your daily word allotment.* She certainly worked on using it up when she was at the office. Damn, but that woman could talk.

Today, however, Nate was glad Betty was a busybody, glad she'd taken it upon herself to rush back from Lina's Café and tell him what she'd seen: Christine having lunch with a very handsome, very citified, blond-haired businessman. It was a bit curious since Nate knew everyone in town and Magdalena wasn't actually a "passing through" kind of place. Betty was more intrigued than he was.

"He was a looker, Nate, all tanned and dapper in that fancy suit of his. I tried to stay incognito so I could get a better feel about him, but dang, I just don't know who he was. Maybe you can call Phyllis at the café and see if the man charged lunch on a credit card. You can get him that way, but he probably walks around with a roll of hundreds in his pocket. Looks the type." She'd been on her way out of his office when she stopped and said, "And that was some car he had. A

Mercedes. Black. Illinois plates."

That's when Nate knew the man was Christine's ex-fiancé. What the hell was Connor Pendleton doing here? He'd hopped in his truck and barreled down the road toward Lina's, pulling in just as Pendleton opened his car door. Betty was right; that was some car. Nate slammed his truck door and called out, "You Connor Pendleton?"

The man turned and faced him. "I am." Confusion gave way to understanding and his gaze narrowed, his jaw tensed. "Nathan Desantro."

"That's right." Nate shoved his hands in his jeans pockets to fight the urge to punch Pendleton's pretty-boy face. "What are you doing here?"

The jerk stared at him as if annoyed by the question. "Isn't it obvious? I came to see Christine."

Let him be annoyed, because if Nate didn't have answers that made sense soon, this guy was going to learn what annoyed really meant. "It's not obvious or I wouldn't have asked. I'm wondering why you'd come from Chicago to see my wife."

Pendleton's lips twitched. "I understand there's a bit of trouble in that area."

"Where'd you hear that?" Had Christine said something to him? She wouldn't, would she?

"I can't divulge my sources." He shrugged and jingled his keys. "I give them up and the information stops, but word has it there are problems between you two, and she'll be back in Chicago by Christmas."

"That's a lie." Pendleton shrugged again. What would the asshole look like with a black eye? Or a bruised jaw? He acted as though Nate and Christine weren't even married, or if they were, not for long. Was he really so arrogant to assume he'd swoop in and sweet-talk Christine out of her marriage? Yeah, he looked the type. That took a lot of guts, though, and this guy seemed more calculating, like he'd want some assurances before he'd commit the time and effort to win Christine back. Had someone given him a reason to think he stood a chance? He'd bet the business Gloria Blacksworth was behind this.

"Did my mother-in-law send you?" The look on Pendleton's face gave him his answer. "Damn her."

"Nate! Nate!" He turned and spotted Lily moving toward him as fast as her small legs could carry her. When she reached his side, she peered up at him and smiled. "Want a chocolate shake? Mom said I can get one while she shops." She hazarded a shy glance toward Connor Pendleton who watched her with a mix of curiosity and wariness.

"No, thanks, honey. You go on inside and I'll see you in a few minutes."

"Okay." Her gaze swept over Pendleton again. "Hi." She inched closer, studied him from behind her thick glasses. "Are you Connor?" she asked in a soft voice. "Christine's old boyfriend?"

The man cleared his throat, apparently uncomfortable with the implication of past tense. Or maybe it wasn't that at all, maybe what had him so jumpy was Lily. Nate tensed as the possibility surged through him, igniting a rush of anger. Pendleton nodded and said, "Yes, as a matter of fact, I am." His voice gentled. "And who are you?"

Lily beamed, her smile spreading with innocence and excitement as she thrust out her hand at Christine's ex-boyfriend. "Lily, Lily Desantro. Nate's my brother." She paused, the smile grew. "And Christine's my sister."

It did not take a psychologist to analyze Connor Pendleton's reaction. He dropped Lily's hand and stepped back. "What?"

"Nate's my brother and Christine's my sister," she

repeated, in a patient voice. "And they got married."

"Oh. Oh, I see." Pendleton laughed and shook his head. "You mean she's your sister because she married your brother. That makes sense."

"That's not what she means at all." Nate turned to Lily and said, "Go order your chocolate shake and I'll see you in a minute. Okay?"

"Okay. See you in a minute." She raised a hand and waved. "Bye, Connor."

"Good-bye, Lily."

When she disappeared inside the café, Nate faced him. He'd bet Gloria hadn't planned on Pendleton running into Lily. That was the thing about duplicity; you just never knew how it was going to play out. "Lily's my sister, but she's Christine's, too."

Pendleton's hands fell to his sides, the keys jingling against his thigh. "But…how can that be?"

"You're a smart man, figure it out." The tone in Nate's voice must have given Pendleton the answer, because Nate spotted the exact second when the guy put it all together. "Charles Blacksworth was her father?" The question reeked of dread and improbability.

"Like I said, you're a smart man."

Pendleton stared at the door to the café as though he could see inside, to Lily, to her life. "Do you know…who had the…" he stopped, started, "…the condition?" he finally managed. "Is that on your mother's side?"

The jerk wanted confirmation that the Blacksworths hadn't been responsible for that extra chromosome. Why? So he could continue to pursue Christine? "I have no idea." It was the truth. "Does it matter?" That was the bigger question.

Pendleton ran a hand through his perfect hair, making it stick out and look not quite so perfect. "Of course it does."

"Well, it shouldn't." Nate blew out a disgusted sigh. "I guess that means you're not so interested in my wife anymore, worrisome genes and all that. Can't have a glitch in the Pendleton dynasty now, can we?" The man turned red and looked away. "Get the hell out of here, and make sure you tell Gloria I'm waiting for her."

Chapter 11

"Blacksworth residence, may I help you?"

Christine clutched the phone and forced out the dreaded words. "I'd like to speak with Gloria, please."

"Yes, ma'am. May I ask who is calling?" The voice on the other end was young, fresh, innocent. How long until Gloria suffocated its owner with her demands and complaints? Created an environment that was both hostile and uninhabitable? She'd done it with everyone else; she would attempt to manipulate this person, too.

"Christine."

A second extra air exchange before the young woman's voice filled with excitement. "Just a moment. I'll get her for you right away."

Poor thing. She obviously knew Christine was the long-lost daughter, but who knew what Gloria had told her about the reason behind the absence? Whatever it was, it would be a grand lie, weighted in Gloria's favor to make her appear the unselfish mother, the giver of love, time, and life with no expectation in return. And what had she received for such devotion to her only daughter? Abandonment at her greatest time of need: the death of her husband. Poor, sorrowful mother. What the young woman who had answered the phone didn't know was that Gloria had most likely plotted to break up her daughter's marriage. Nice mother.

"Christine?" Gloria's cultured voice held a hint of surprise.

What an actress. Surprise indeed. "Hello, Mother."

"It's wonderful to hear from you." A pause and then a cautious, "Are you in town?"

"No, and don't pretend you didn't expect me to call the second Connor left."

"Connor?" That *did* sound like unrehearsed confusion. "Is he there?" There was a slight hesitation before the next question slipped out. "In Magdalena?"

"He was, but I expect he's on his way back now. How could you do this?"

"Connor was in Magdalena? Does he know about the girl?" Pause. "And the mother?"

"Of course not." She would not subject her sister to Connor's insensitive gawking and inquiries.

Gloria blew out a long breath. "I had no idea he would travel to that place. I told him to wait…"

"Really? Told him to wait and see if my marriage fell apart because of your little deal with Natalie Servetti?"

"Who? I'm to blame for your marriage issues? I'd say it's more to do with marrying beneath you than whatever you think I've done."

All these months, and nothing had changed. "You would try to break us up because you don't like the man I chose."

"I don't like anything you've done this past year, but what can I do about it, other than wait for you to come to your senses? It's a terrible thing to put a mother through, especially after your father's death." She sniffed. "You abandoned me, Christine, left me all alone with no one." Another sniff.

"Stop it, Mother. Those tactics don't work on me anymore."

"You have no idea how it pains me to hear you talk that way." She sniffed louder, more compelling.

It had been a mistake to call. Mother or not, Gloria wasn't going to confess to anything, especially not her role in Natalie Servetti's photo shoot. "Good-bye, Mother. I won't be calling again."

Click. Christine tossed the phone on the desk and stared at the wedding ring on her left finger. Some people were not meant to be parents and her mother was one of them. What did she know about unconditional love and sacrificing for the good of family? It had always been Gloria's needs first, second, third, and everyone else's after that. That kind of selfishness bred dysfunction and discontent. Christine didn't want that with Nate, couldn't stand to think about a life where their children were treated as possessions to be manipulated and filled with guilt. Her relationship with Nate must be based on genuine trust and respect, even if that trust might at times require blind faith.

She snatched the phone and dialed Nate's cell, but when it went into voicemail, she hung up and decided to try Betty. That woman knew everyone's whereabouts, even when she wasn't supposed to. Before Christine had a chance to finish dialing, the door to her office burst open and her husband appeared. "Nate. I was just trying to call you."

"Guess I saved you the trouble." Something in his voice bothered her. Was he angry? Since the night they'd slept together, there'd been a shift in the relationship, a calming that hinted at reconciliation. Surely he'd felt it, too. She watched as he flipped the Open sign to Closed and locked the door.

"Nate? What's wrong?"

He didn't respond until he was a foot away, close enough to touch her if he chose to, which he did not. His mouth stretched to a thin line, his eyes narrowed and turned cold. "I just met Connor Pendleton."

That was the last thing she expected to hear. "What? How?"

Nate leaned against the desk, crossed his arms over his chest. "Betty said she spotted you in Lina's having lunch with Mr. GQ. I didn't think much of it until she mentioned the Illinois plates. That's when I knew it had to be your old fiancé."

"Nate." She didn't like the way he was looking at her, as though he'd already shut her out and there was no chance he'd let her back in. "I didn't know he was coming. He just showed up."

"That's a long drive to just show up and damn convenient, isn't it? The ex-boyfriend suddenly appears at a time when things aren't exactly going well for us, and what, promises to take you away from the misery of living with me?" Anger mixed with pain seeped into his words. How could he believe she was interested in anyone but him?

"What Connor is or isn't offering doesn't matter because I'm not interested. And just so you know, my mother put him up to it."

His jaw tensed. "Of course she did."

"She led him to believe you and I weren't getting along and there was hope for him."

"Right." He rubbed his jaw and studied her. "She's one busy woman, isn't she? What about Natalie? Was Pendleton in on that, too?"

Christine shook her head. "No, but I'm almost positive my mother was. I called her a few minutes ago and confronted her. Of course, she denied everything, but I know she was lying."

"Hmmph. Nice."

She was tired of talking about an ex-boyfriend and a manipulative mother who were part of a past she would rather forget. Nate and the baby were her future. "Look, I'm sorry for doubting you. Trust has never come easy to me, especially when everything points in the opposite direction. Can we move past this and forget about it?" She stood and placed her hands on his shoulders. "Can we start again? Please?" She leaned on tiptoe and kissed his mouth. He did not reciprocate.

"Pendleton knows about your father," he paused, "and Lily."

"What?" Her hands slid from his shoulders and she stepped back. "How would he know?" She'd wanted to protect Lily from people like Connor who would never understand or appreciate her.

"I told him." His gaze challenged her. "He won't be coming after you, and do you know why?"

He wanted her to ask; she could tell from the way he'd pushed the question out of his mouth. Fine, she'd ask. "Why?"

"Because he was more interested in which side of the family carried that extra chromosome."

Of course, Connor would be concerned with genes. "I don't care about him. I care about us, what we share. Our future." *Our baby.*

"Our future? You wouldn't believe me when I told you I'd been set up, but you believed that stuffed suit with the smile?"

"No! I'd already decided I was going to come to you and I planned to do it after work today. I knew I had to trust you; it was the only way we were going to work." She ran a hand along his jaw. "And I very much want us to work."

He clasped her hand, eased it from his face. "Will more people be coming from your past to infest our town with their superiority and judgment?"

His words pinched her bruised heart. "What does that mean?"

"Your people don't fight fair, Christine." He moved away from the desk and paced the room. "They hire investigators, set people up, ruin reputations," he paused, "and marriages. And they don't give a damn as long as they get the results they want. They don't care who they hurt or how much money it costs. People and money are expendable, the people more so than the money."

He'd fallen into the old pattern of Nate Desantro against the world. There'd been a short period of time when he'd let her into his heart and the anger and resentment over bad luck and misfortune had fallen away. Then her mother visited and with her came threats and airs of superiority. Following that, there'd been the photos of Nate and Natalie Servetti that by all indications had been spearheaded and paid for by Gloria. And now Connor, venturing into town and homing in on Lily and her genetics? No wonder Nate didn't have much use for any of them. They were rude people who didn't care about feelings and doing the right thing. They only cared about results and getting answers to the questions they asked, even if they weren't the right questions. She wasn't one of them, never had been. Not really. Surely Nate saw that. If not, she had to make him see. "I'm not like my mother. You know that."

He shrugged as if to say, *No, I don't.* "My mother always says you can't get away from your genes. She's got a point."

"What's that supposed to mean?" *Say it; say what's really on your mind.*

He eyed her, his expression cold, not like the man who fell asleep in her arms at night. "Just that. Certain things are in your blood, and you can't get away from them."

"Like what? Hair color or being rich? What exactly are you talking about?"

Another shrug to imply it was of no consequence, which, of course, meant it was. "All of it."

"Right." He could be so unbendable, so damn stubborn, even to the point of damaging their relationship. Didn't he see that? Didn't he care? *We're going to have a baby, she wanted to yell at him. Our baby.* She held back because she had to know where they stood before she told him something that would tie them together forever. "Are you angry that I didn't believe you when you told me the photos I saw weren't the truth? Even though I just admitted I planned to talk to you about it tonight and put it behind us?"

"Should I be?"

"Why are you being so ridiculous? You've wanted me to get past this and forgive you since I found out, and now you're acting like you don't care if we get back together or not. What's wrong with you?"

"I don't like people coming into my town and making me feel like a piece of scum, unworthy to associate with you, let alone marry you."

"Did I ever act like that? Even once?" The left side of his jaw twitched but he didn't answer. "I've wanted to be with you since the first time we were together. You pushed me away then and you're pushing me away now. I'm your wife. Don't do this, Nate." Her voice cracked, but she continued, "Stop, before it's too late." When he didn't respond, she made one last attempt.

"You're the one who doesn't think you're good enough for me, and if you keep shutting me out, I'll start thinking you're right."

He stared at her, eyes bright, body tense. A stranger. "I need to think," he said in a gruff voice. "I just need to think." With that, he turned and walked out, leaving Christine alone, the news of their child buried deep in her heart.

***

"Mr. Harry, I'm scared. Can I sit with you?"

Harry popped an eye open. Lizzie Servensen stared back at him, close enough to spot the bristles of his five-o'clock shadow. Her usual lightheartedness had vanished, and in its place, was fear. "What wrong, Lizzie girl?"

"I don't like the witch. Her face is green and she's mean."

Harry glanced at the flat screen hanging on his living room wall. The Wicked Witch of the East cackled and threatened, darting around the screen in her black dress and pointy hat. Hmm. She kind of reminded him of Greta's mother. "Okay, but no fidgeting like last time."

The child grinned and lifted her arms. Harry hefted her onto his lap and plopped an arm around her. "It's just makeup," he murmured into her hair. "And don't worry, she'll get what's coming to her soon enough."

Lizzie snuggled against him and flung her small arm around his waist. "I'm not scared when I'm with you, Mr. Harry. You'll keep me safe."

"Yes, I will." Harry stroked the child's soft curls and glanced at Greta who sat on the leather couch with Arnold, a bowl of gourmet popcorn between them. Her smile covered him, heating his insides faster than a couple shots of scotch. Who would have thought there'd come a day when Harry Blacksworth would actually look forward to spending a Saturday night watching *The Wizard of Oz* with a woman and her two kids? Not him, that was for damn sure. But here he was, and here they were, and there really wasn't any other place he'd rather be. Since that night three weeks ago, when he and Greta took their relationship to a "clothes off" level that still amazed him when he thought about it, Harry had been more relaxed, maybe *calm* was the word.

It wasn't from the sex, though that was a mind blower on its own. He guessed it was the feeling of belonging somewhere that mattered. Arnold and Lizzie—he'd started calling her that the day after the zoo trip, to her delight and her grandmother's disgust—enjoyed spending time with him and loved playing with the gadgets in his house. The first day they'd visited his condo, Lizzie pushed the button to open and close the blinds at least fifty-two times, and Arnold fiddled with the sound system, checking to make sure music did indeed filter through *every* room, including the bathrooms. He'd taught the boy to play chess and poker, the first to impress the mothers of his future girlfriends, the second, because poker taught life lessons. Knowing when to fold meant having the brains to realize when it was time to get out. A poker face could save you from all imagined and unimagined situations.

"Mr. Harry?" Lizzie whispered into the softness of his shirt. "Can we stay here sometime? I want to sleep in the blue room. I like the pillows." She meant the room painted the color of the Caribbean with a four-poster bed mounded with blue and green pillows in various shapes and designs: squares with stripes, round with polka dots, triangles with swirls. How in hell he'd ever let the designer talk him into that was beyond him, but when you're sleeping with the person making the recommendations, the noncerebral head usually makes the choices. Still, the room was a conversation piece and every female who had seen it, from Christine to Lizzie, fell in love with its random bizarreness.

"Sure. We'll plan on a sleepover." He probably should get Greta's okay before promising anything. She'd already scolded him for the Cubs' tickets he bought without her permission. What was the big deal about a baseball game?

"Tomorrow?" She lifted her blonde head and looked him in the eye. There was trust and faith in those blue eyes, and an innocence that twisted his gut. In ten years it would all get wiped away, destroyed by a world that lied, cheated, and did not keep its word. Harry didn't want that for Lizzie; he wanted to keep her safe, protected from the harshness that seeped into everyday living like a cancer, snuffing out innocence, replacing it with doubt and suspicion. "Okay, Mr. Harry? We can have a sleepover here tomorrow?"

Harry darted a glance in Greta's direction. Good, she was absorbed in the movie. He lowered his head until he was inches from Lizzie's sweet face. How could Greta's ex-husband abandon his kids? Didn't he want to keep them safe? Hell, didn't he know what he was missing? Harry opened his mouth to tell her the sleepover depended on her mother's permission, but the words that fell out of his mouth were quite different. "Sure. Now, do you want chips and dip or a soft pretzel?"

Lizzie squealed and threw her arms around his neck. "Soft pretzel. Thank you, Mr. Harry. Thank you so much."

The movie ended forty minutes later and Harry thought about mentioning the sleepover to Greta but it was late, and he didn't really want to have this discussion in front of the kids, just in case she got pissed at him—which she probably would. Why hadn't he been able to say "no" or "we have to wait" when Lizzie asked him? Parents were supposed to be parents and make the tough calls, right? They were not supposed to be friends. Good thing he wasn't a parent because he'd make a horrible one. He'd give the kid everything he wanted and then wonder why he couldn't think for himself and forge a life on his own. Isn't that what had happened to him? Everything handed over, even his thoughts, and when it was time to use reason and common sense, there were none, because he'd never been asked to develop them? Greta had her head on straight; she was firm but fair, and consistent. That damn consistency was what really mattered. You couldn't tell a kid no ice cream before dinner and then turn around and buy him a hot fudge sundae because he gave you that sad face.

Harry planned to wait until morning to tell her he messed up and promised Lizzie a sleepover, but when the phone rang twenty minutes later with an unhappy Greta on the other line, he knew there was no postponing anything.

"Elizabeth told me you promised her a sleepover tomorrow."

She didn't even offer a "hello", which meant she was ticked. He rubbed the back of his neck and tried to figure out if he should just let her rant or start the apologies now. "I'm sorry. I screwed up. I knew I should check with you first, but damn, when she looked at me with those big blue eyes, I couldn't say no."

"We talked about this. Several times. You're not to go about promising them things, Harry. It's not fair to them. Kids believe what people say; they expect when a person says something, he'll keep his word and when he doesn't, they think it's their fault."

"Who says I wasn't going to keep my word?"

Silence. "Don't."

Okay, so he'd screwed up, but she was acting like he'd lied to them. "I get it." He paused. "Just because I never had a kid, I'm not a complete idiot."

Long sigh. "I know you mean well, but they're my children, and I have to protect them."

"Protect them?" *What the hell was she talking about?* "From me?"

"From getting hurt."

"I'm not going to hurt them." He actually liked Arnold and Lizzie, which perplexed him since he'd never cared much for kids, except for Lily. Her he liked. When Greta didn't respond, Harry pushed through the silence. "Did you hear me? I said I wasn't going to hurt them; at least give me credit for that."

"Oh, Harry." Her voice slipped through the line, soft and sad. "I don't want them to come to depend on you."

"Why the hell not?" Did she think him such a loser that she couldn't count on him to do right by her children? Well, he wasn't a loser and he could be trusted. "Answer me, dammit."

"Because one day you'll leave."

Chapter 12

"Good afternoon, Mrs. Blacksworth. How are you?"

"I don't know; why don't you open that file on your desk and tell me how I am?" She stifled a cough and cleared her throat. It would not do to have a doctor witnessing her hacking her way into a full-blown coughing fit. She cleared her throat again. "I'm fine."

Dr. Andrew Bating nodded, adjusted his glasses, and attempted what might be a half smile. Could these doctors not learn a bit about socialization and etiquette? Did they really not possess the ability to make a patient comfortable with the proper intonation and use of words and facial expressions? *Body language, dear boy, didn't you learn about that in medical school?* He looked too young, probably younger than Christine. She wondered at his education. Yes, he'd come well recommended but what did that mean? He played golf at the same country club as Roger, who quite inconveniently suffered a minor heart attack that required several weeks away from his practice. That proved sticky, especially when it came time to refill her pain pills. Of course, this new doctor required a complete history and physical—not that she'd been completely truthful with the history—before he would prescribe so much as an aspirin.

She hadn't missed the way he looked at her when she admitted to smoking a pack of cigarettes a day. Last year it had been a pack and a half, so this was an improvement. The doctor hadn't said anything, but she'd spotted the lecture in his eyes, even if it didn't work its way to his mouth. Well, she'd be damned if she'd tell him about the Crown Royal. "I'm a social drinker," she'd said, even when her liver studies came back indicating she might be a bit more than that. And the pills? "I fell off a horse years ago and suffered a horrible injury. I only take the pills on bad days." She did not tell him all days were bad days.

Gloria had wanted refills on those prescriptions and if subjecting herself to a physical was the only way to get them, she'd do it. But she hadn't expected he'd find spots on her lungs that required biopsies, necessitating yet another doctor visit.

"Mrs. Blacksworth?"

She glanced at him, offered a cool smile. "I'm fine."

"We received the results of the biopsies."

He did have a nice speaking voice though—well modulated, concerned, probably could make a nice audio…

"They're malignant."

…had he taken public speaking? His delivery was actually quite good; even tones, no hesitation, he got right to the meat of it. Most people danced around—

"It's cancer, Mrs. Blacksworth."

She jerked. "Cancer?" She, Gloria Blacksworth, had cancer?

He nodded, the dark eyes beneath the wire frames turning darker. "I'm sorry there isn't better news."

"Hmm." She sat back in her chair, hooked her gaze on a photo behind the young doctor; two children, a woman, a dog staring back at her. Was he a father, a husband? A pet owner? Did it matter? She had cancer. She would lose her hair, eyebrows, a few dress sizes. Her hair stylist could recommend someone to help with the wig that anyone would swear was Gloria's own hair, and pencils made eyebrows in any shape and color. The tailoring would require some thought; petite women who wore size two did not seek further weight loss, but the clothing could be adjusted to hide her thinning body. Cancer? She clasped her hands together to keep them still. "I want surgery as soon as possible." She did not want it in her body one second longer than necessary.

Three days later, she sat in another doctor's office, this one a middle-aged oncologist with a shock of red hair and an underbite. His name was Paul Quinn, and once again, Gloria repeated her earlier demand. "I want surgery as soon as possible."

Dr. Quinn cleared his throat, fixed his gray eyes on her, and said in a quiet voice, "That's not really an option, Mrs. Blacksworth."

"Oh." And then, "Why not?"

His expression turned more sympathetic, sadder. Maybe this doctor had taken a few classes on being human and delivering bad news to patients. "Did you come here alone?"

Alone. What a horrible, treacherous word. There were those who chose to be alone and there were others who had it chosen for them. Gloria belonged to the latter group and bitterly resented it. She unclasped her hands, gripped the edge of his desk. "Yes, I came alone. Now stop dancing around the answers and tell me exactly what's going on."

"The cancer is in the upper lobe of the lung. It's not operable, and it's spread to the lymph nodes and the mediastinum." He paused, his next words filled with concern. "Did you not have any shortness of breath or bloody sputum? Maybe loss of appetite, chest pains? Any unusual symptoms that would indicate something was going on?"

"Chest pains? Shortness of breath? Loss of appetite?" She bit out the vile words. "I lost my husband last year in a car accident. One minute he's heading home to dinner and the next, he's in a coffin, and he's never coming home again. Do you know what that does to a person? Do you have any idea?" She gripped the edge of the desk harder to keep from lunging at the man. "I couldn't eat. When I thought about the seconds after the accident, I obsessed over whether he suffered, or if it was an instant death. You tell me if that wouldn't give you shortness of breath and chest pains? And you play it over and over in your head until you think you'll go mad."

"I'm very sorry for your loss, Mrs. Blacksworth."

He did appear sorry, well, at least there was that. She relaxed her grip on the desk and sighed. "Thank you."

"And the bloody sputum? Maybe coughing?" he said in a gentle tone, almost a whisper. "None of that?"

She eyed him and spit out the bold-faced truth. "I smoke and I drink and I take pills, and I've had a nagging cough for at least five years. And the blood? Well, I figured what was a little blood considering what I was doing to my body?"

"They were signs."

"I was not looking for a sign, dammit, I was not interested in signs." She'd only been interested in getting through the day, before Charles's death, and definitely after.

Dr. Quinn glanced at the open file in front of him and rubbed his jaw. "We can provide palliative care. By that I mean radiation to minimize the size of the tumor and, hopefully, alleviate some of the symptoms you're experiencing."

"What about chemotherapy?"

He shook his head. "It's too advanced."

No chemotherapy. No nausea, vomiting, hair loss. No chance to make it. She'd walk around bald for the rest of her life with a barf bag attached to her hip if she could have a chance to beat this damn monster. "Can we try chemo?" *Can I have a chance?*

"I'm sorry, it's not going to help."

Gloria stared at the photos on his desk: a young man and woman, two babies dressed in Christmas garb, and the doctor standing beside a black Labrador retriever. Where was Mrs.

Quinn? Had she died? Of cancer? Had that prompted him to go into this field, so he might save others when he could not save his wife? And what of the ones he could not save? Like her? She stared at the picture until her eyes rimmed with tears. *Focus and regroup. You must.*

When she spoke, her voice was calm and in command. "I'm sorry, Dr. Quinn, but that is not acceptable." She gathered her handbag and stood. She needed a cigarette, badly. "I'm going to seek another opinion." She straightened her shoulders, raised her voice so he knew she would not settle for his treatment plan, and vowed, "And I'll keep getting them until I find a different answer."

Two specialists, numerous scans and appointments later landed Gloria sitting across from Dr. Marcus Patrick. Apparently, the young buck, Dr. Bating, had been accurate with his diagnosis, and Dr. Quinn had nailed the prognosis, and especially his treatment plan. Damn.

"I wish there were better news, Mrs. Blacksworth." Dr. Patrick spoke with an empathy that told her he'd done this enough times to know when to pause, when to suggest, and when to merely listen. She'd spent weeks running from doctor to doctor and it did help that she and Charles had contributed such vast amounts to West Mount Memorial Hospital. Who could possibly turn down one of the largest contributors to the hospital and personal friend of the hospital president? Money did have a way of pushing a person to the head of the line, but sadly, it did not change the outcome.

"I'm going to die." It wasn't a question any longer; there was no need for that. Dr. Quinn had implied the grave prognosis before she walked out on him. The second doctor, Virginia Bentworth, had not even offered a tissue or a kind word with her death sentence. And now, Dr. Patrick with his "I wish there were better news." She understood what he said, but more importantly, what he did not say. Death would come to her. She would not make it to the next decade of her life, maybe not even to her next birthday. Two hundred scans would not change the outcome. Neither would another hundred doctors. "How long do I have?"

Hesitation, a breath, two. "It's very hard to say—"

"Just a guess." She met his gaze, held it. "Please. What do you think?"

He pushed the box of tissues toward her and said in the quietest of voices, "It's already metastasized to the lymph nodes. We can try radiation to reduce the size of the tumors—"

She snatched a tissue, swiped at her eyes. "How long, dammit?"

"Six months, maybe a year."

Gloria blew out a long breath, coughed. "I suppose you want me to quit smoking?" Every blasted questionnaire she'd completed had asked about her smoking habits. She'd dutifully placed a check in the box and written one pack a day, though during stressful times, such as Charles's death and Christine's departure, it had increased.

"It's up to you, Mrs. Blacksworth. Whatever will cause you less stress."

Because it's too late. No matter what you do, you're going to die. "I suppose I could cut back. Would that help, even a little?"

He offered the gentlest of smiles. "It would."

She nodded. "Thank you."

Gloria made her way home through a blur of tears and disbelief. She was going to die. Oh, it might take six or twelve months, but cancer would snuff her out. There would be no looking ahead at two years, or five, or reaching sixty. She would be dead. Everybody was going to die, but to have an indicator that narrowed the timeframe? That was a bit unsettling. Charles once said he'd want to know when he was going to die, so he could be prepared. As if anyone was ever prepared to leave this earth. He certainly wasn't. If he'd been prepared, he would not have left his affairs in such a mess, and Gloria would not be driving home alone from the doctor's after receiving her death diagnosis.

Death. What was the point of knowing when it was coming? So a person could right wrongs? Go on a do-good crusade? Eat a bag of chocolates a day? Take a trip around the world? What was the goddamn point? There was none, not so far as Gloria could see.

When she arrived home, she pulled the car in the garage, entered the house, and proceeded to relieve her entire staff of their duties, even Elissa. Two weeks' severance and the promise of a letter of reference got them out the door. Maybe she'd write the letter, maybe she wouldn't. Elissa had tried to inquire about the reasons behind the dismissal, but Gloria merely attributed the decision to a change in plans and refused to say more. Once the servants were gone, she locked the doors, closed the blinds, and made her way to the master bedroom, where she spent the next seven days smoking, drinking, popping pills, and denying the diagnosis. There was something to be said for living life in a blur of intoxication and excess, because it just didn't matter when you couldn't focus long enough to think, feel, or care.

On the morning of the eighth day, she slid out of bed, tossed the empty bottle of Crown Royal in the wastebasket and headed for the bathroom where she showered, brushed her teeth, and threw on a bathrobe. She wanted a cup of strong coffee and a piece of toast with cherry jam. Maybe an egg or two. Certainly she could manage that. She stuffed her cigarettes into the pocket of her robe and padded downstairs. The smell of over-ripe bananas hit her when she entered the kitchen and a glance toward the fruit basket told her why. Fruit flies swirled around three brown bananas that oozed a clear liquid onto the apples and oranges in the bowl. Gloria lifted the bowl, opened the trash drawer, and dumped the contents into the can. Why hadn't she thought to have the cook clean out the fridge and empty the garbage before she dismissed her? And now that the staff had been let go, who was going to cook her veal, buy her peaches, clean her toilet? When she'd arrived home after the prognosis, releasing everyone from service to ensure her privacy had seemed the logical and prudent plan of action: necessary and immediate. Now, days later and in need of a cup of coffee, she had to admit that she might have been a bit hasty.

Who would help her navigate this strange and terrifying journey to her demise? Certainly not her daughter, who might treat the news with indifference bathed in concern. That was a hopeful reaction. Christine might not even respond to whatever method of communication Gloria chose to employ: phone, e-mail, letter, text. Technology ruled the world, but conversation was still king, and if Christine didn't want to talk, the method didn't matter.

Who was left? There were no aunts, uncles, cousins. No real friends she could share the prognosis with and thereby elicit help, whatever that might be. Gloria had avoided sick and dying people, said they made her uncomfortable and put her in a bad mood. Yes, she'd said on several occasions that she did not have the "caretaker" gene in her DNA. Her friends had laughed and agreed as they sipped their drinks, flashed their diamond-studded hands, and discussed upcoming five-hundred-dollar-a plate social events.

Six months to a year was a long time if one must travel that path alone. What was she to do—sit in a chair and wait for death to claim her? Or medicate with booze and pills as she'd done these past seven days, until one hour slid into the next in a fog of cigarette smoke and drugs? That seemed pathetic and tragic, and Gloria Blacksworth was neither.

But what was she to do, and who would help her? That answer was more important than the number of days she would breathe on this earth. Gloria continued to ruminate over her situation as she fixed her coffee and spread cherry jam over her toast. Whom could she trust? What would she tell them? How much would she pay? Money would factor in; it always did. Want a person to pledge loyalty? Open the checkbook. She'd spent her life in wealth and privilege, as had Charles, and what had it gotten them? In the end, money hadn't saved them or made them happy. The happiness quotient was the most out of balance because people believed fat portfolios equaled joy. Peace. Oh, they denied such a belief, proclaiming in earnest voices how, Of course money doesn't bring happiness, and then the snide smile, but damn close. *Happiness.* What an overused and misunderstood word.

Gloria sat at the kitchen table and bit into her toast. The tartness of the cherry jam made her mouth pucker. For years, this had been her favorite jam, but maybe she should try raspberry or boysenberry. Why not? Why not indeed? She was pondering other jams and where she might purchase them, when a light rap at the back door startled her. She glanced up to find the cook, Elissa Cerdi, waving at her. What on earth was the girl doing here? Gloria stood and made her way to the door, preparing a lecture about unwelcome former employees.

"Mrs. Blacksworth, I was so worried about you." Elissa stepped inside and offered a hesitant smile. "I know you said my services were no longer required, but you seemed distressed the other day and I've been trying to call for three days." Her eyes grew bright, and her voice dipped. "I started to think something horrible had happened to you."

If you thought that, you were correct. Something absolutely horrible has happened. Gloria squelched the reprimand she'd prepared for intruding upon her privacy. *The girl worried about me. She cared.*

"Yes, well, here I am." She touched her naked face and forced a laugh. "Though had I known I would be receiving a guest, I'd have dressed and made myself presentable."

The girl's smile spread. "You look wonderful. I'm so happy you're okay."

"I did not say I was okay, but I'll take the 'you look wonderful' compliment."

No one ever saw her without makeup except for the esthetician who did her monthly facials, and long ago, Charles, when her skin was wrinkle-free and toned. Her current state of undress made her vulnerable, as though the Gloria Blacksworth who demanded and demeaned had washed away with the shower and the terrycloth robe. "Thank you. I appreciate your concern." Surprisingly, it was the truth. "I made coffee and toast. Would you care for some?"

The girl glanced at the table, then back at Gloria. "No, thank you. Would you like eggs to go with your toast? Easy over, as usual?"

How nice to be cared about. "Yes, I'd like that very much." She sat at the kitchen table, drank her coffee, and watched the cook move about with casual grace and confidence, cracking eggs, humming lightly, asking now and again if she needed anything. The girl really did seem to care and in Gloria's experience, concern without expectation of monetary benefit, was a rarity. It wasn't until she'd eaten her eggs and had a second cup of coffee that she realized this girl could help her. "Elissa?"

The girl turned from the sink where she'd been washing dishes. "Yes, Mrs. Blacksworth?"

"Come sit." Gloria patted the table. "I have something I wish to discuss."

Elissa dried her hands on the dishtowel and made her way to the table. She sat next to Gloria and folded her hands in her lap. "Yes?"

When complete participation is desired, there was only one way to obtain it: Tell the truth.

"I'm dying." The words fell out in a rush of air and anxiety. It was one thing to keep the truth inside, but once spoken? Well, that was something else altogether. That made it real.

"What?" The girl's eyes grew bright, her lips quivered. "Dying?"

Gloria nodded. "Lung cancer. Late stages."

"Oh." She covered her mouth with her hand to keep the sound inside. "I'm so sorry." Tears trickled down her cheeks, to her jaw, her chin. "So very sorry," she murmured, choking back a sob.

"Thank you." It was all she could manage and yet, saying those two words gave her strength to continue. "I need your help, Elissa." She met the girl's gaze, held it. "Can you help me?"

"Of course. What can I do?"

"Move in here. Do what needs doing. I have no idea what that is, but we'll figure it out." She drew in a breath and let the rest spill out before it dried in her brain. "The doctor thinks I have anywhere from six months to a year. It's too far gone for chemotherapy; radiation would only be for comfort. I don't want that. Actually, I don't know what I want right now, except that this stays between us."

"You mean you aren't going to tell anyone else? Not even your daughter?"

Gloria's jaw twitched. "No one."

"Mrs. Blacksworth—"

"I'm dying, Elissa. I might make it a year, maybe not. Shouldn't I be the one to decide how I live those months and with whom?" It would have been much easier to deliver the news to Christine if her daughter hadn't accused her of orchestrating that whole business with Natalie Servetti. Gloria could not admit to the bold, unthinkable act, even if she were guilty, which she was.

"I'm sorry. I'll respect your wishes."

"I appreciate that. Now, I'd like you to move in as soon as possible. You will still prepare meals and do the shopping, but I don't want anyone in the house, so you'll have to take care of the cleaning and such as well. You can hire a new lawn service and when the time comes that I can no longer drive, you'll take me where I need to go."

"I do have a class on Thursdays and once fall comes, I'll have three classes." She stopped, pulled her lower lip through her teeth. "I can try to work around your schedule."

Gloria offered a faint smile. "Of course. Education is very important." *But only if you actually do something with what you learn. If you forsake it for a man, a marriage, an empty dream, then you've lost.*

"I think we'll get along quite well, Elissa." She must call the girl by her given name; it was the least she could do. "What about compensation? Have you thought about that?"

The girl blushed. "No. Whatever you think is fair."

Gloria nodded. She would teach Elissa the art of negotiation, which started and ended with silence. "You may have one of the guest rooms, but not the one that originally contained the orchids."

"I know." The girl smiled. "That's Christine's room."

***

"See these little shoots that grow between the branches of

the tomato plant?" Pop held up a branch and pointed to a small stem with leaves. "They're called suckers and if you leave them, they'll take the nutrients intended for the main plant. Pinch them off like so,—" he pinched off the sucker—"and you'll get a bigger tomato."

Christine touched the spot where Pop had just performed minisurgery. "A sucker, huh? Makes sense."

"Yup." He found another sucker, pinched it off. "Kind of like a bad relationship that sucks the life right out of the other person." He continued pinching as he worked his way over the tomato plant. "Most people don't have the gumption to get rid of it; they just keep plodding along and get used to running half a pint low until it seems normal."

Talk of blood and pinching made Christine queasy. It had been two days since Nate had confronted her about Connor. Two days of queasiness that had nothing to do with the baby. How long were they going to go on like this, not talking, avoiding one another and the real issues buried in their hearts? She loved him, wanted to be with him, and the more time that passed, the more difficult it would be to talk things out, until there would be nothing left to talk about. They both struggled with trust and yet that was the foundation of any relationship. If they didn't trust one another completely, the relationship would limp along and eventually die.

"… and a good bean is long and tender-looking." Pop snapped a green bean and tossed it in a small colander. "You gotta get down and look for the beans because they like to hide under these big leaves." He pushed aside a few leaves, located three beans, and snapped them from the plant.

"Leave them on too long and the skin gets thick and tough." He squinted against the sun and met her gaze. "Relationships can get like that, too. If they're ignored too long, no amount of talk and 'I'm sorry' is gonna get through that thick skin."

"Hmm." Why was he comparing his vegetables to relationships, or rather, problems in relationships? Was there a message hidden between *suckers* and *thick-skinned* and was it intended for her? Did he know about her and Nate? Had Lily told him she was staying at Miriam's?

Pop straightened and wiped his forehead. "So much for getting work done before it heats up. I could do with a glass of lemonade and a pizzelle. How about you?"

"That sounds good." She'd only had a piece of dry toast and a cup of ginger tea for breakfast, and it had been an effort to finish that with Miriam's eagle eyes on her. The woman wasn't stupid; sooner rather than later she'd figure out that her son wasn't the only reason for Christine's loss of appetite and queasy stomach.

"Did Nate ever tell you about his buddy Daniel Casherdon?" Pop handed her a glass of lemonade and a pizzelle and settled into his rocker on the back porch. Something told her there would be a story and a lesson behind Daniel Casherdon.

"No, I've never heard of him."

"His name's Daniel, but everybody called him Cash. Nice boy. Awful sad about him and Tess." He bit into his pizzelle, scratched his jaw. He'd changed from his garden boots to red leather tennis shoes, new ones from the looks of them. "Cash and Nate grew up together, three houses away. His aunt raised him after his parents up and took off. Said a kid didn't fit into their lifestyle. They were going fortune hunting somewhere in Africa or Australia, one of those places that starts with an A. The kid had a chip on his shoulder and got into some scrapes, but he settled down and then he met Tess. Boy, did they have plans." His thin lips worked into a smile of remembering.

"She was going to be a trauma nurse and he wanted to

become a policeman. SWAT team. They planned to head to a city, Philadelphia, I think." He blew out a sigh. "Cash became a policeman in town while Tess finished up college. She had a kid brother who was always in trouble. Cash tried to help him out, acted like a big brother, but the kid was a mess. About a week before the wedding, the convenience store got robbed. Cash was on duty, guy pulled a gun." His words drifted off. "There was no damn way Cash could have known it would be Tess's brother."

"He shot the brother?"

"Killed him. Word had it the medics had to pull Cash away from the kid. The boy was gone but he refused to stop CPR."

"How tragic."

"Lucy and I were torn up about it. Everybody loved Cash and Tess, and most of us were headed to their wedding. Well, if you haven't figured it out, there was no wedding and nothing Cash could say to make it right with Tess. Some in the town froze him out; others gave him the evil eye. A few blamed the kid and Tess's family. It was a bad time for everybody; people taking sides, slinging accusations and cruel words. There was supposed to be a wedding, but there was a funeral and enough bad blood to fill a casket. Nate tried to talk to Cash, but he wouldn't listen to anyone. All he wanted was Tess's forgiveness and that wasn't happening. He waited as long as he could and then one day, he just left."

When Pop didn't say more, she asked, "Do you know what happened to him?"

He shrugged. "Last I heard he was a policeman in Philadelphia but can't say for sure. He could be in Wichita for all I know. His Aunt Ramona won't talk about it. She's in The Bleeding Hearts Society, the one with the black hair and sad look on her face."

She did remember the woman: small and square, with

brackets around her mouth and dark eyes. "And Tess? What happened to her?"

Pop shook his head and sighed. "Selling some kind of high-end lipstick, as if that's anything remotely like caring for the sick. She used to send Lucy boxes of the stuff." His lips worked into a faint smile. "Poppy, that was Lucy's favorite. Wore it until the day she closed her eyes for the last time."

"What a sad story."

"Worse than sad. Tragic is more like it." He snatched another pizzelle, studied it. "I wonder if they might have found a way to work things out. You gotta work through the pain to the real truth, and once you do that, there's hope." He pinned her with his dark gaze. "Anybody that's ever loved has been hurt, some worse than others. Hearts ripped, trust gone, even hope tossed in the trash." Those eyes grew brighter, the voice softer. "But if you fight for it and keep talking, you can get through it to the other side. And that's where you have another chance."

Why was he looking at her as if he were talking about her and Nate? *What did he know?* Christine cleared her throat and looked away, but that didn't keep Pop quiet.

"I don't know what's going on with you and Nate, but when Lily comes here and says you're still at Miriam's, then I got to ask myself if Nate's refinishing ten ballroom floors, or there's something else going on. I'm betting on the 'something else'." She fidgeted in her chair and opened her mouth to speak, but the words wouldn't come. The tears, however, did.

Pop reached in his pants pocket and handed her a tissue. "Go ahead and cry. I have a feeling this has been a long time coming. You can tell me if you want, or don't, but all's I have to say is you better tell him about the baby fast before somebody else figures it out like I just did."

Chapter 13

The call came right after lunch. Nate had been talking to Jack about a project when his cell rang. He almost let it go into voicemail, but answered it when he spotted his mother's number.

"Hi, Ma. What's up?" He didn't hear anything past *Christine* and *emergency room*. "I'll be right there." He hung up his cell and turned to Jack. "Christine's in the hospital."

Magdalena General was ten minutes down the road and Nate made it to the entrance of the emergency room in less than seven. His mother hadn't elaborated other than to say she found Christine passed out on the bathroom floor, and by the time the ambulance arrived, she was awake but groggy. Was he responsible for this? God, he hoped not.

He made his way to the emergency room desk and asked for his wife. He had to see her, touch her, make sure she would be all right. A nurse led him to a draped-off room and ushered him through. His mother and Lily were on either side of Christine, who lay in the middle of a hospital bed, looking small and fragile, her left arm hooked up to an IV. Her eyes were closed, her breathing faint.

"How is she?" He moved to the front of the bed and kissed his mother's forehead.

Her usual composure had vanished, replaced with worry and something that looked an awful lot like guilt. "The doctor says she's dehydrated," she whispered. "They're running blood work and a few other tests." She swiped at her eyes. "I should have kept a closer eye on her, insisted she eat, drink, get her rest. I wanted to give her privacy, so I said nothing. I'm responsible for this."

"That's crazy. If anybody's responsible, it's me." He

smoothed a hand over his wife's hair, leaned close, and kissed her temple. *Did I do this to you? Make you so weak, you got sick? I'll make this right, I swear I will. Just give me a chance.*

"Nate?" Lily said in a loud whisper. "Hi."

He turned toward his sister and offered her a high five. "Hi, honey. I'm glad you're here with Mom."

"Me, too." She placed a hand on the sheet by Christine's leg. "Christine needs us. We have to help her get better."

Nate nodded. "Yes." His voice cracked. "We have to do whatever it takes."

His mother placed a hand on his back and massaged in slow circles, like she did when he was a child and didn't feel well. "It's going to be okay. It will all work out." She wasn't talking about the dehydration; she was talking about the issues between him and Christine. The separate houses, separate beds. Separate lives. He nodded but couldn't get the words out of his mouth to agree. Maybe because he wasn't so sure, even when that's what he wanted more than anything right now. "Come along, Lily. Let's give Nate a few minutes with Christine."

"But she can't hear anything. She's sleeping."

Miriam's next words held that tone that said, *I have spoken, do not make me repeat myself.* "Lily, let's go."

When they left, Nate eased in closer to his wife and whispered, "Hey. You gave us all a big scare. Don't do that again, okay?" He traced the line of her jaw, her chin, her cheek. Her eyes fluttered open.

"Nate."

"Right here." He worked up a smile, made an effort to sound relaxed. "How do you feel?"

"Tired. And ridiculous. I've never passed out in my life."

"Yeah, well, you gave Mom a scare and not much rattles her."

"I think what happened was too much time in the sun with Pop, too little food," she paused and her lips twitched, "and too little common sense."

He smiled and clasped her hand. "There's been a lot of that last one going around. Sometimes we need a wakeup call to put things in perspective. Mine came with that phone call a little while ago." His voice dipped. "I love you and I don't want to lose you. I'll do whatever it takes to make sure that doesn't happen."

Her eyes grew bright, rimmed with tears. "Nate, we have to talk. There's something—"

He placed a finger on her lips to stop the rest of her words. "We'll talk, but not now."

A tear slipped down her cheek. "I love you. I never want to hurt you and that's all I've done lately."

He moved closer, his face inches from hers. "We'll get past this. We'll talk it out and move forward, better than ever." He brushed his mouth over hers. "You'll see."

She touched his cheek. "I want to come home."

He grinned. "I'd carry you out of here right now if I thought Mom and Lily wouldn't come after me. We'll see what the doctor says and once he gives his okay, I will carry you out of this place. Now rest." She smiled and closed her eyes while Nate held her hand. These past several weeks were a mess and all he wanted to do now was get Christine back home and take up where they'd left off before the whole Natalie Servetti incident. One of these days, Natalie would have to return to Magdalena and when she did, he'd be waiting for her. It might take time and patience, but he'd get her to admit Gloria Blacksworth was behind this whole thing. And then what? He didn't know, but that damn woman had almost destroyed his marriage and she'd have to account for that. Some people really were pure miserable. He was still thinking of his mother-in-law and her misdeeds when the drape opened and Dr. Vincent entered. James Vincent was a middle-aged Southerner from North Carolina who had married Mimi Pendergrass's niece and settled in Magdalena eighteen years ago.

"Hi, Doc. Is she going to be okay?" Christine squeezed his hand, hard, as if she were scared. The furrow between her brows and the pinched lips told him she was scared. Didn't she know he wouldn't let anything happen to her?

"Nathan, good to see you." Dr. Vincent moved to the bed and smiled at Christine. "You'll be fine, Mrs. Desantro. We'll run another bag of fluids through before we release you." He glanced at his chart. "Make sure you eat at regular intervals, stay hydrated, and get rest. Are you taking your vitamins?" When she nodded, he continued, "You've got your next appointment scheduled with your doctor?"

"Yes."

Why was she so hesitant? And what did Dr. Vincent mean by next appointment? When had she had the first and with whom? What was going on? Did it have something to do with Christine's sudden odd behavior? Nate was puzzling through this, trying to make pieces fit into some sensible order, when Dr. Vincent dropped a boulder on him. "Congratulations to both of you, and give my best to Lily and your mother." Then he was gone.

"Congratulations to both of us?" Nate turned to Christine who had gone from pale to paste. "What's he talking about?" People didn't throw out congratulations unless it was a wedding, or an engagement, or a baby… his brain stuck on the last one. "Christine?"

Her attempt at a smile fizzled. "Surprise. We're going to have a baby."

**

Harry made it to Magdalena with only two stops, three if you counted the break for the cop to write the speeding ticket. He thought about hopping in the car and heading out last night after Lily's phone call, but Greta made him see that wasn't the best plan. *Wake up early, start fresh*, she'd said. *I don't like you driving when you're tired. And slow down.* She'd hugged him tight, whispered, *I don't want anything happening to you.* So he'd stayed the night, with Greta tucked beside him until 1:00 A.M. when she dressed and went home. He didn't sleep as well when she wasn't there, and damn, he hated to admit that, but it was the truth. When you had somebody who really cared about you, what you did, how you felt, hell, what you ate, it made a difference. Who would have thought that he, Harry Blacksworth, would actually *like* a woman pestering after him? Maybe *pestering* was too harsh a word; inquiring and expecting an answer might be better.

And speaking of inquiring, what the hell was going on with Chrissie and that damn husband of hers? If Harry weren't so involved with Greta and her kids, he'd have noticed something was off. She hadn't been calling much at all and when she did, she sounded kind of puny, like a watered down scotch, no punch. When Lily called him last night, she'd spoken in a rush of worry and agitation that jumbled her words and made her hard to understand. On a good day, he had to concentrate when he talked to her on the phone, but her message last night was clear, even without the words. Something was wrong between Chrissie and Nate and Harry had to fix it. The kid gave him a lot of credit because his knowledge and success with relationships between couples could fit in a shot glass. Still, this was Chrissie they were talking about, and Lily, his two favorite girls. Or maybe they were two of his favorites, with Greta and Lizzie being the other two.

Harry decided to head straight to ND Manufacturing and

face off with Nate before he talked to Chrissie. If that husband of hers wasn't treating her right, Harry had half a mind to give him a right hook. He might only get one punch in before Desantro clobbered him with one of those beefeater fists of his, but Harry's daily workouts kept him light on his feet and quick. He might get a second punch in if he were lucky. He pulled into the plant, with Lily's garbled pleas fast-forwarding through his brain. *You have to come, Uncle Harry. Fast. Christine just got out of the hospital and she won't stop crying. Nate won't talk to her; won't talk to anybody. Hurry, Uncle Harry.*

"I'm looking for Nate Desantro."

A woman with cat-eye glasses and a look that said "nosy" studied him a second too long. "And may I ask your name?"

Damn abrupt for a receptionist, unless deflecting unwelcome visitors was her job. This one could give Belinda a lesson or two in protecting your boss. Harry got too many calls that had nothing to do with business and everything to do with his old life, starting and ending with a long line of Bridgetts. "Harry Blacksworth. His wife's uncle."

You'd have thought he said George Clooney by the way her expression softened and got all cozy. *"You're Harry?"* She thrust a chicken-bird hand at him and smiled. "I'm Betty Rafferty. You were one of Charlie's favorite people; said he admired you for following your own path."

Path to what? Sin and debauchery? Poor Charlie, he really had been messed up. Harry was not one to be admired. His soul was black and tarnished, but he had a chance to do right by Christine. He shook the woman's hand and laughed. "About the only path I follow has a fairway in it." He laughed again. "So, is Nate here?"

She darted a gaze toward a closed door behind her. "He's in there," she whispered. "Been there since before I got here and

I opened up at 7:00." The woman leaned over the counter, dropped her voice even lower. "Is something going on? When he starts closing his door and won't talk to anybody, that's never a good sign. And now with you here," she paused, tilted her head as though she were connecting dots to the truth, "well, that concerns me. Is Christine okay?"

Harry zeroed in on her, threw her a warm smile, the one women couldn't resist, and said in a voice like melted butter, "That's what I've come to find out. Now, he might not talk to you, but he'll talk to me. Damn straight on that."

Betty Rafferty nodded her curly head. "Good. That's very good. His office is right behind me. Better knock first."

"Thanks." Harry made his way past a copier and two limp plants with dusty leaves the size of a person's hand. Apparently, Betty didn't have a green thumb. He debated on whether or not to knock, decided against it, and opened the door.

"Betty, I don't want to..." Nate Desantro looked up from the clutter on his desk. "Harry? What are you doing here?"

Harry stepped inside and closed the door. "Hello, Nate." He made his way to the desk, crossed his arms over his chest, and zeroed in on the probable cause of Christine's upset. "What the hell's going on between you and my niece?" Talk about turning into a ghost. The guy paled beneath a scrub of tan and stubble. He looked like crap, from his messed-up hair and unshaven face to his rumpled T-shirt. But it was his expression—beaten, tired, hopeless—oh, that last one was bad—that made Harry uneasy. This whole thing was about a relationship and even Lizzie knew that wasn't his bag. But he had to give it a whirl, for Chrissie's sake. "Well, what's going on?"

"Have you talked to her?"

What was with all the jaw-twitching and hand-flexing like

Nate was trying not to punch something? "No. I want to hear it from you firsthand."

"She called you?"

"Of course not." Harry pulled out a chair and sat down. Hell, if he wanted to, he could probably land a few good punches on the guy's jaw because the mountain man looked deflated and weak, like his strength was oozing out of him, right onto the indoor-outdoor carpeting. "Lily called me. Seems she's the only one around here with sense enough to let me know about Christine."

Nate ran a hand through his hair, which made it stick up more than it had a few seconds ago, and sighed. "She's pregnant."

"Pregnant? Damn." Harry eyed Nate, tried to gauge his feelings on the subject, and when he came up blank, decided to ask straight out. "That's a good thing, right? As long as you're the father, and I assume you are"—that drew a cold stare—"just joking. You'll make great parents." How did he know what made a great parent? This was Greta's territory, not his. "So, congratulations."

"Thanks."

Harry rubbed his jaw, considered where to go from here. Oh, what the hell, if the conversation continued like this, it would be midnight before Harry had any answers. "Just tell me what happened. No bullshit. I hate bullshit."

Maybe he shouldn't have asked for it all at once, because once Nate opened his mouth, it all poured out like the aftereffects of bad takeout: the ex-girlfriend and the half-naked pictures, Gloria's suspected involvement, the separate houses, the visit from that ass-wipe Connor Pendleton, and ending with Christine's emergency room visit and the doctor's reference to a baby Nate didn't know existed.

"I'm damn sorry to hear all of this." Harry loved his niece, but she'd done this guy wrong. What had she been thinking? Nate deserved to know she was carrying his baby and it hadn't been right that he had to find out from somebody else, even if it was a doctor. You didn't treat people like that, even if you planned to "fix it" down the road. And he'd bet his Jag that Gloria's scheming was behind this.

"Yeah, well, there you have it. Don't fall in love, Harry. It's a damn train wreck half the time."

"Don't I know it. That's why I avoid trains." He laughed and thought of Greta. They had a good thing going: no pressure, no timetable, no issues. "Okay, so let's break it down. You love her. She loves you. How am I doing so far?"

Nate's lips twitched. "Stating the obvious? That's genius material."

That was the closest the guy had come to a smile since Harry entered the room. "Do not underestimate the importance of stating the obvious. Most people don't because they think it goes without saying, but it does need saying. Like 'I love you' and 'I'm sorry' and 'I can't live without you'. You know, that kind of bullshit."

The man actually smiled at that. "Bullshit? Yeah, I know it and I've said it, too."

"I give you credit. Then you have to consider the next issue, which is trust. She didn't grow up in a household where anybody asked what was wrong or how to make it right. Freedom of speech was not encouraged or solicited. You had to suck it up and do your duty, and if you were unhappy, well, too damn bad. Go buy a shirt or get a manicure. If that didn't work, take a trip, see a therapist, buy a car. Whatever got you past the issue, even though it never really got you past it, only buried it deeper. That's what Chrissie saw and it's going to take a lot of work, talk, and trust to get past that."

Nate didn't speak right away, his gaze focused on the

picture of Christine that sat on the corner of his desk. Smiling, happy, in love. "I'm not much better about trust. It's never come easy to me."

Harry knew all about that. Trust was a tricky thing. It was one of those all-in kind of deals that made a person squeamish. He'd only trusted a handful of people in his fifty years: Charlie, Christine, Greta. "I'm the last person to give advice on relationships, but maybe my screw-ups help me see what a good relationship should look like. You and Chrissie belong together. Don't screw it up and end up like me."

"You mean you aren't living the life?" Nate rubbed his jaw, studied him until Harry looked away. "What about that German lady? Greta, right?"

Harry shrugged. "She's a nice woman and what the hell she's doing with me, I'll never know. Still, we're talking about you and my niece. Here's what you're going to do: go home, shower, and shave so you look half human, grab some flowers, and stop by your mother's at 4:00 P.M."

"What am I doing, going to the prom?"

"You're taking your wife home. To your house. And your bed. And it's happening at 4:00 o'clock sharp."

"You think she'll agree?"

There was a hell of a lot of hope pinned to that question, and Harry had the answer. "Oh, she'll agree, don't you worry about that."

Relief flooded Nate's face. Maybe he'd just needed someone to point him in the necessary direction. "Okay then." Nate stood and extended a hand. "Thanks, Harry. I really appreciate it."

"Damn straight." Harry shook his hand and said, "I need a drink; this was damn harder than I thought it would be."

Nate opened his desk drawer and pulled out a bottle. "Jack, okay?"

"Oh, yeah. Make it a double."

A half hour later, Harry pulled into Miriam Desantro's driveway. He'd called Greta on the way over to tell her about his conversation with Nate. She gushed all over him with praise and made him promise to call after he spoke with Christine. Maybe he did know a thing or two about relationships, even if he gleaned the insight from his failed attempts.

"Uncle Harry!" Lily ran barefoot from the house, her black hair flying, small body barreling toward him. She threw her arms around his waist and squeezed tight. "I knew you'd come!"

"Of course I'd come for my two best girls." He kissed the top of her head, hugged her. She was innocence and hope wrapped up in a little girl. Lizzie and Arnold would love her, so would Greta. Maybe one day he'd bring them here.

Lily eased back and looked at him through her thick glasses. She'd gotten new ones since the last time he saw her. These were square-framed and red and provided a great contrast to her black hair and blue eyes—Blacksworth hair, Blacksworth eyes. "Mom's in the house making you manicotti." She lifted a finger to her lips. "Christine's out back."

"Let's go say hello to your mom first and then I'll see Christine." She grabbed his hand and swung it up and down as he followed her toward the front porch and the chimes dangling on either side of the steps.

"Mom, look who's here," Lily called out as they headed for the kitchen. Harry pictured Charlie in the living room, among the pottery and artwork, reading quietly and sipping some natural-herb tea.

"Harry. Hello." Miriam smiled at him from her spot at the kitchen table, a manicotti in one hand, a spoonful of cheese mixture in the other. She wore a navy T-shirt and dangly stone earrings. Her face was bare of makeup, her hair pulled back in a ponytail. Fresh, clean, honest, the exact opposite of Gloria.

He hugged her and kissed her cheek. "Another of my favorites. I know I'm staying for dinner."

"Thank you for coming," she said in a quiet voice. She glanced at Lily, who still held Harry's hand and asked, "Did you see my son?"

"Matter of fact, I did." He gave her a thumbs-up. "He'll be here at four. How about you fix a dish of that to go?"

"Oh, I see." The faintest of smiles slipped over her face.

He nodded. "Exactly."

"Mom, what do you see? And what is exactly, Uncle Harry?"

"A secret." Harry bent down and got eye level with Lily. "Christine's going home today."

A few minutes later, Harry made his way down the back steps, carrying two glasses of iced tea. Christine sat in a wooden rocker, hands folded over her stomach, sunglasses blocking the sun's glare. He came up behind her and said, "Well, if this isn't loafing, I don't know what is."

She jerked around and sprang from her chair. "Uncle Harry! What are you doing here?"

"Hold on, hold on." He set the glasses on the table and opened his arms. She fell into his embrace, buried her head against his chest, and thrust her arms around his waist, much like Lily had a short while ago. Harry patted her back and kissed the top of her head. "That bad, huh?"

"Oh, Uncle Harry." She sniffed into his chest. "I've made such a mess of things."

"So I hear." He stroked her back, welcomed the tears dampening his shirt. "Lily called me last night, all in a dither about you and that husband of yours."

Christine pulled away, wiped a tear. "Lily called you?"

"How about that?" His voice dipped with affection for his niece. "The only one with common sense around here. Come on," he released her and gestured to her chair. "Sit down and tell me your version. I've already heard your husband's."

"You...talked to Nate?"

He handed her a glass of iced tea, grabbed his own, and sank into the chair next to her. "Of course I went to him, and I was all set to throw my best right hook. Don't give me that look; that boy was limper than overcooked spaghetti. I could have taken him, thought about it, too." He eyed her over his glass. "Nobody's going to bring grief to my Chrissie, and then he started talking and I realized he wasn't the one keeping you two apart." He eyeballed her long enough to make her look away. "It's you, Chrissie, you and your damnable fears. If you don't set things straight, and soon, it's going to be your mother and father all over again."

"Don't say that."

"What's with not telling him about the baby? He's the father, for Chrissake, and you kept it from him?" He shook his head and sighed. "Not good." At seventeen, Harry's girlfriend had told him about their baby, but she hadn't given him a choice in what happened. Money and a controlling father had taken that choice from him.

"What did he tell you?"

"Enough for me to figure out you two need to square things now before the hurt thickens up and you can't get past it." He clasped her hand and squeezed. "I get the whole trust thing with the ex-girlfriend and the pictures. I'd be suspicious even if there weren't pictures; hell, I'd be suspicious of anyone looking a second too long. Don't be like that; it will eat you up and make for a miserable life."

"He thinks Mother was behind this." Her words filled with

anger and resentment. "And it took me awhile but I agree. I called her and of course, she denied it, but she had that guilty sound in her voice, even from hundreds of miles away."

"I'd sure as hell trust that husband of yours over your mother." Gloria and her manipulations really had no limitations, even to the point of risking her daughter's happiness. "I hear that pain-in-the-ass ex-boyfriend of yours graced you with his presence."

She sighed and rubbed her forehead. "He met Lily."

"Ah." So now he knew about Charlie and his other life. "What did Wonder Boy have to say about that?"

"Nate didn't tell me specifics, but I guess Connor was trying to figure out which side of the gene pool Lily had come from, since breeding is more important to those kinds of people than relationships and family."

"Those kinds of people? I hope you haven't lumped me into that category." Damn straight, he did not want to be thought of as a nose-in-the air society type who made associations based on breeding and background. Not that anyone would ever make the mistake of classifying him that way, but still, it needed saying.

She actually laughed. "Of course not. You put your heart and feelings ahead of what society says are important. I wish there were more people like you."

"Yeah, well, I'm not so sure that would be a good thing, but thank you." He sipped his tea and let the warm breeze roll over him. Leaves would turn soon and a chill would capture the night air, followed by frost, then snow. Another season would pass with Charlie gone from them. "It's peaceful here; no hustle-bustle, traffic jams, people stacked on top of one another in living quarters twenty stories high, fighting for the same air. I'd like to see this place in the spring, when everything is new and fresh."

"You could buy a place up here, you know. Real estate is cheap and even though the places aren't new, there are plenty of tradesmen looking for work. This would make a wonderful vacation spot and that way I'd get to see you."

Now why hadn't he thought of that before? He bet Greta and the kids would love this place. *Why was he thinking about what Greta and the kids would like?* That was crazy and he squelched those thoughts before they took root in his brain and spread. "I'll think about it. Right now, I want to talk about you and your husband. I want you to go inside, put on a fancy outfit and that shiny stuff on your lips, and pack up your junk. He's coming for you at four o'clock."

"What?" She sat up, bit her lower lip. "He's coming?"

Harry didn't miss the breathiness in her voice. Fear? Anticipation? Hope? Probably all three. "Yup. I told him to be here at four o'clock sharp to take you home." He paused, leveled her with a no-nonsense stare, and said, "Your home, where the two of you belong, where you're going to stay from now on. Period."

"And he agreed?"

"Of course he agreed. Poor sap just needed a little push to open his eyes, and I," he grinned and jabbed his chest, "used my excellent relationship skills to show him the way and give him that push."

Christine squeezed his hand and said, "Do you really think he'll forgive me for not telling him about the baby?"

"He already has."

Chapter 14

Nate stepped out of the truck and grabbed the bouquet of sweetheart roses. That had been Harry's idea. *Women love flowers*, he'd said. *You can't go wrong with roses*. As soon as Harry left the shop, Nate went home, cleaned the bathrooms, threw in the first of six loads of laundry, and ran the dishwasher. He tossed out pizza boxes, empty beer cans, and something covered in slime that might have been lettuce. These last several weeks had been a blur of misery that blinded him to the pigsty he'd been living in. Christine was not coming home to this, that was for damn sure. He opened several windows to let out the staleness, changed the sheets, and filled a few vases with hydrangea blooms he cut from the bushes outside. At 3:15, he showered, shaved, and put on a pair of dress slacks, a long-sleeved shirt, and a tie. He made it out the door with the sweetheart roses with ten minutes to spare.

Now he stood outside his mother's house, sweating from too many clothes and a nervousness that threatened to consume him. What if Harry had been wrong and Christine wasn't interested in moving forward just yet? What if she needed more time? What if she didn't want more time, didn't want him? What if she planned to have the baby on her own? Maybe even head back to Chicago where the child could be raised in wealth and privilege? The "what ifs" pounded his brain, giving him the beginnings of a headache. There was only one way to find out his wife's intentions and it sure as hell wasn't by standing outside. He opened the back door and entered the kitchen.

Lily spotted him first. "Oooh, fancy," she said, running toward him with a big grin on her face.

"Hey, kiddo." He gave her a hug and a peck on the cheek.

She smiled and dipped her nose in the roses. "Mmm. They smell good." She lowered her voice to a half-whisper. "Christine's getting all pretty for you, and Mom made you manicotti. And a salad, I think."

"Where is Mom?" He smelled her handiwork in the kitchen: manicotti, meatballs, bread.

Lily fingered a rose. "She ran to the store with Uncle Harry. They said you needed food."

"Why would they do that?" Probably because they figured out he wouldn't have been to the store, and maybe didn't have more than beer and butter in the fridge.

She shrugged. "Uncle Harry said you looked like a sad sack." She scrunched up her nose and asked, "What's a sad sack?"

Damn that Harry. "Just a person who's sad." The first thing Harry needed to learn about saying anything within earshot of Lily was that she'd expect an explanation.

She studied him, pulled her bottom lip through her teeth, and said, "You don't look sad. Not anymore."

"Right." He winked and flipped a pigtail over her shoulder.

"And I know why!" Her lips pulled into a wide smile. "Christine's going back to your house today. The floors are all done, like brand-new. And Uncle Harry said you'll probably stay in bed for a week." She scratched her jaw, looked at him. "You'll get hungry, Nate."

Double-damn that man and his mouth. "He was just teasing. You know how Uncle Harry likes to do that."

Lily giggled and nodded. "Yup. He's silly." She grew quiet for eight seconds before she headed for the stove and said, "I'm hungry. Look what Mom has on top of the stove. Can I have a meatball?" Nate set the bouquet on the table and moved to the stove where he lifted the lid on the pot and peek inside. "You can have one." He spooned out two meatballs set them in a dish. "Don't try to steal mine." She giggled and forked a chunk of meatball.

"Hello."

Nate swung around so fast he almost spilled sauce on his shirt. Christine stood in the doorway between the kitchen and living room, looking beautiful and shy. Maybe she was as nervous as he was.

"Hi," he said, handing the dish to Lily, no longer caring if she ate one meatball or ten. He moved toward his wife, slow, cautious, desperate to touch her, afraid to move too quickly. They had another chance to make things right, and he was not going to fail this time. His gaze darted to her belly, shot back to her face. *She was carrying his baby*. Her eyes grew bright as she reached for his hand and placed it on her belly.

"You'll make a wonderful father," she whispered.

"I love you." He brushed his lips against her mouth, slow, longing, needful.

"Hey, kiss on the neck, like you're supposed to do." Lily stood a foot away, waiting for them to follow her instructions.

"Okay, okay." He kissed Christine's neck, trailed his lips along her jaw and ended with a deep kiss on the mouth. When he pulled away, he faced his little sister and said, "It's okay to mix things up once in a while. Just so you know."

She pulled on her pigtail and considered this. "Once in a while," she repeated and then, "maybe." Nate grinned and held out his hand. "Come here, we want to tell you something."

Lily bounced forward and clasped his hand. "A secret?" she whispered.

He glanced at Christine, who nodded and said, "More like a A very happy surprise." She slung an arm around and he pulled her closer.

Desantro are going to be an aunt."

grew wide, her bottom lip quivered. "An

aunt?"

Nate nodded and said in a gentle voice, "Christine and I are going to have a baby."

"A baby!" She flung her arms around them and buried her head against her brother's chest. "I'm going to be an aunt. I'm going to be an aunt." Her head bobbed up. "When?"

"By Christmas," Christine said.

"A Christmas baby," Lily murmured. "In your tummy, right?" She pulled back to examine Christine's belly. "Where's the part that looks like a big ball?"

Nate stifled a laugh and said, "That will come soon enough."

Lily leaned close to Christine's belly and whispered, "Hi, little girl. I can't wait to meet you. I'm Lily. I'm your aunt."

"Uh, Lily, how do you know Christine's going to have a girl?"

She looked at her brother and a smile spread across her face. "It's going to be a girl, you'll see."

Nate glanced at Christine who shrugged. Girl, boy, he didn't care as long as the baby was healthy. How many times had he heard that line? Enough to make him wonder at its sincerity, but now that he was the one expecting the baby, he got it. Oh yes, he definitely understood the honesty of that single sentence.

Lily spent the next several minutes considering names, all girls' of course, and taking pictures of Christine's still-flat belly. "I want to show her what she looked like when she was in your tummy." *Click, click, click*. "Smile, Nate. Do you want your baby to think you're a sourpuss?"

Thankfully, they were spared more picture-taking when Uncle Harry and Miriam walked in the back door, carrying bags of groceries. "Well, if it isn't the Prom King," Harry said, grinning at Nate. "I didn't know you owned a tie. Or is that the one you wore at the wedding?"

"Shut up." The guy could be a real smartass.

Harry laughed. "You know I'm only joking. If I didn't like you, I'd ignore you." He threw Christine a knowing look. "Ask my niece about that one." Ah, Nate bet he was referring to that jerk, Connor Pendleton. Christine fidgeted and shot Harry a look Nate was beginning to recognize as seriously ticked off.

"Guess who's going to have a baby?" Lily grabbed Harry's hand and coaxed him toward her sister. "See?" She pointed to Christine's belly. "She's right in there."

"A girl, huh?"

"Yup." Lily nodded and snapped another picture. "A little girl."

Nate glanced at his mother who stood at the kitchen table, clutching a handful of bananas. Damn, but he could tell from the way that bottom lip quivered, the tears would start soon. Maybe if he and Christine hurried, they could get out of here before the dam broke open and his mother flooded the kitchen. She sniffed and cleared her throat.

"Harry and I picked up a few things for you." She paused, wiped her eyes. "Who wants to be bothered with shopping when you have more important things to do?" What she meant was, *I know you have nothing but beer in your refrigerator and no inclination to fill it tonight.* "And I made you manicotti and meatballs."

"Thanks." He grinned and added, "The meatballs were really good, weren't they, Lily?"

"Nate!" She set her small hands on her hips. "That was our secret."

"Ooops."

Harry kissed Christine on the cheek and murmured, "I'm happy for you, kiddo."

"Thank you, Uncle Harry." She hugged him and said, "For

always being here for me."

"You know it, kiddo. Now go home with that husband of yours and don't make me come here again to play mediator, or next time, I'll charge you."

He turned to Nate and said, "It doesn't count if you buy a woman flowers and leave them on the kitchen table. Now give her the damn things and throw in a few sweet words." He winked at Christine. "Women like that, don't they, Chrissie, the mushier the better."

Harry would have continued on if Lily hadn't darted in the middle of his comments and announced she was starving. That changed the focus from Nate and Christine to food, which was where most subjects ended up in this house. Nate took the opportunity to snatch up the groceries, the manicotti, and whatever other goodies his mother had packed and wave good-bye. When they arrived home, he insisted on carrying Christine over the threshold; this was a new beginning for them, one that would be filled with memories, love, and stories to tell their children in years to come.

An hour later, they sat at the kitchen table, a tray of manicotti, salad, and a vase filled with sweetheart roses between them. Christine forked a piece of manicotti and slid a smile at Nate. "Your mother's outdone herself again."

"Doing for others is like her oxygen. Take that away and she'll wither."

She reached for his hand, squeezed. "She seems excited about the baby."

"Oh, she's excited. I'll bet she already pulled out her knitting needles. Once she finds out if it's a boy or girl," he stopped, "do you want to know the sex of the baby?"

She shook her head. "I don't think so. There are so few things in this world that are pure surprise; let's let our baby be one of them. Is that okay?"

He slid a smile her way, his voice low and intimate. "Sure. Let's be surprised."

"Nate," she traced his wedding band with her index finger, "we're going to have to talk about what happened between us, how we got so far apart."

"I know." He rested his forehead against hers. "I was miserable without you." He brushed his fingers along her neck, trailed them over her collarbone to her chest, settled on her belly.

"Uncle Harry's the one who made me see things the clearest, imagine that?"

"Yeah, he's not as crusty as he makes out."

"He seems different somehow, calmer, more level-headed." She paused, as if considering the reasons for the shift in his behavior. "I wonder if he's seeing Greta."

"Your old cook?"

"Right. I wonder…."

Nate kissed the tip of her nose and said, "Harry's a great guy, but can we not talk about him right now? I haven't been alone with you in weeks, haven't tasted you in longer than that… "

Christine pulled away so she could look him straight in the eye. "I know you're a man of action, but we're going to talk about what happened and how to avoid it in the future."

His lips twitched. "So, no action first, talk later?"

"Uh, no."

He nodded. "Okay. Here's what I've got. I'm going to trust you from now on, even when it kills me and goes against every defensive tactic I have. Trust doesn't come easily for me, and aside from my mother, Lily, and Jack Finnegan, I don't trust anybody very much. But I'm going to trust you, *no matter what,* because I love you and I want us to work more than anything." He blew out a long breath and said, "I've never promised that to anyone. And tomorrow morning, I'll come to your office and we'll fill out the loan work for the furniture business."

She leaned forward, placed a soft kiss on his mouth, and murmured, "Thank you. I don't know much about how to have a relationship either. I didn't see it growing up, and I fought it as an adult because I didn't want to get hurt. But what I learned is that opening up to hurt is part of the equation, just like trust is." Christine framed his face with her hands. "I love you, Nate Desantro, now and until I draw my last breath. I promise, from this day on, I'll trust you, no matter what."

"From this day on," he repeated.

She wrapped her hands around his neck and whispered, "*Now*, you can take me to bed."

***

"Are you warm enough, Mrs. Blacksworth?"

Elissa tucked the afghan around Gloria and stepped back to inspect her work. Oh, but she was attentive and interested and quite sympathetic to her employer's plight. A woman with cancer all alone? No husband? No child to help her? How tragic. Indeed. "Yes, I'm fine. Thank you."

The girl nodded and arranged a few magazines within Gloria's reach. "I'll be in the kitchen preparing dinner if you need me. Don't forget about the bell." Yes, the bell. Apparently, one of Elissa's aunts had used a bell to summon assistance when cancer consumed her to the point where she could no longer raise her voice. It sounded so…debilitating, but Gloria must admit, it did make it easier on her vocal chords. Not that she'd been calling the girl every few minutes, because she hadn't, but it was comforting to know someone was here—in case.

Elissa had lugged a beat-up black suitcase and red duffel bag up the stairs three weeks ago and settled into the spare bedroom. Gloria no longer required her to wear a uniform, black slacks and a white top would do, and after the first three days, invited the girl to dine with her. What was the point of eating in separate rooms when the dining room table seated ten and nine seats remained empty? At night, Elissa retired to her room to read her homework assignments and Gloria flicked through channels, attempting to find a movie that did not involve someone dying. That was a difficult, if not impossible, task, unless one wanted to resort to half -our sitcoms that tested one's patience. A few days after the girl moved in, Gloria switched off the television and opened a book. She hadn't read an actual book in years, but word by word she became engrossed in the fictional lives of the people between the pages. As long as someone didn't die, she could read and enjoy the book. If there was a hint of death or illness, she slammed it shut and at times, tossed it across the room.

Other than a few extra naps, Gloria felt the same as she had the afternoon she learned of the diagnosis. *Cancer. Terminal. Death. Six months. One year*. Of course, she refused to attend the meetings and support groups that would enlighten her on what to expect. What was the point, so she could cross off every symptom that cropped up until her page was filled and death was the only unchecked box? No, she would not succumb to that, would not even read an article in the paper pertaining to cancer of any sort. She would live her life until the end, when the blasted cancer finally caught up with her.

What a grand plan, but how would she actually accomplish this *living* life, and what exactly did that mean? She'd spent the majority of her years waiting for the next event, the next season, the next moment when she might actually be happy. It had never happened. The posturing, organizing, and anticipating had only disappointed her in the end. And why was that? Why, why, why?

The damnable truth snuck out of her subconscious, settled in her brain, and refused to leave. Her dissatisfaction with life, people, and relationships, had been a result of trusting others to deliver her happiness. What a horrible, irresponsible mistake. It had created unrest, anger, and a self-loathing that she'd masked with pills and booze. But in the end, here she was, all alone, with nothing but a stranger to care for her and bankloads of assets.

"Would you care for a cup of hibiscus tea?"

Elissa stood before her, concern pinching her lovely face. A few months ago, Gloria would not have admitted the girl's beauty, would have forced her to wear dowdy uniforms and clunky shoes. She'd done that with Greta, but the woman's beauty had shone through. Gloria squinted, took in the girl's cheap slacks, ill-fitting blouse. *The haves and the have-nots.* As she studied the girl, an idea burst through her, bold, strong, powerful. Even six months was enough time to make a difference in a person's life if she started today. Right now. Christine might not need her, but Elissa Cerdi did. Gloria threw back the afghan and stood. "I'll take a tea; you have one, too. And put a little Crown Royal in mine."

"I'm fine, Mrs. Blacksworth, I don't need anything."

"Yes, you do," Gloria said, studying her from top to bottom. "You need a lot, and I'm going to help you get it."

The girl looked confused. "I don't understand."

Gloria smiled, a real smile, filled with genuine humor and a wisp of good will. "I know you don't, but you will. We don't have much time," she paused, "who knows when I'll be too weak or too ill to think straight. But today, right now, I'm fine."

Elissa didn't look convinced by Gloria's words. Maybe she thought the cancer had spread to her employer's brain and rendered her incapable of logical thought. Anyone who knew

Gloria might agree, but for once in too many years, she was absolutely lucid, and it was exhilarating. "We're going to change your life."

"Excuse me?"

"Come." Gloria moved toward the staircase and motioned the girl to follow. "I have closets filled with more clothes than I'll ever wear in this lifetime or the next." She proceeded up the stairs, talking as she went. "I'm smaller than you are but I wear my clothing loose, so that will make up for the difference. And I know you must be thinking you don't want to wear a fifty-some-year-old woman's clothing, but I can assure you, they're the latest designs and the simple lines are stunning at any age." She threw a smile over her shoulder as she entered the master bedroom. "You'll see."

"Mrs. Blacksworth," the girl followed her into the bedroom and said in a quiet voice, "I don't know about this."

"What's not to know?" Gloria slid open the closet and revealed a color-coded wardrobe complete with scarves, belts, and shoes. "The key to feeling good about oneself is the ability to look one's best at all times." She rifled through the peach section of the closet, a renewed energy pumping through her. This girl needed her help and Gloria desperately needed to be needed.

"Let's try this blouse, and if the slacks are too short, we'll order the proper size." She pulled out a peach silk blouse and cream-colored slacks. "The changing room is through that door." She pointed to her left and handed the clothes to her. "Peach is a very good color for you with your dark hair and fair skin."

Elissa opened her mouth to speak, hesitated, and finished with a respectful "Thank you."

Gloria sat in a chair and waited. The girl needed a haircut; she had too much hair, and curls were so bothersome and unruly. And what about makeup? While she did wear a bit, it was so faint as to appear nonexistent. She shook her head and sighed. Christine had been the same way. Maybe it had more to do with the current generation and less to do with the individual. Sloppiness was rampant and the idea of relaxation extended from hair to clothes to lifestyle to attitude. If a person possessed a thimbleful of ambition, she could be president of a major corporation. And then some.

Perhaps Franco could fit Elissa in today and work his magic on the girl's hair. If Gloria called, he'd make it happen, even if he had to bump someone else from her slot. That's what money could do and Elissa Cerdi would reap the benefit of Gloria's power. Nails, makeup application, maybe even a few pointers on how to walk into a room to gain notice, or use body language to get a point across without opening one's mouth. Oh, yes, Gloria had years of expertise and before she left this earth, she would gift it to Elissa. They would need to discuss the girl's choice of profession as well. While it was endearing that she'd chosen nursing, she really ought to consider something less demanding...more...profitable. Finance would be a good choice; a person could depend on numbers. Gloria would even consider calling that good-for-nothing brother-in-law of hers and asking him to give the girl an internship while she finished college with a job offer to follow. Of course, she'd be very firm about the "off limits" policy. If that lecher looked at Elissa twice, she'd see that he had a sexual harassment suit slapped on his dirty hands. Gloria would be long gone by the time Elissa joined Blacksworth & Company, but her threat to take down Harry Blacksworth would live on and instill just enough worry to keep him away from the girl.

What was taking so long? "Elissa? Is everything all right?"

Seconds later, the dressing room door inched open and

Elissa reappeared in Gloria's peach blouse and cream slacks. The slacks were indeed too short, but the fit was decent. The blouse hugged the girl's breasts and created a small opening that revealed a scrap of tanned flesh, enough to make a man interested, but not too much to send the wrong message. Despite the less-than-perfect fit, the girl exuded an air of elegance and style that would escalate with the proper size and tailoring. "Well? What do you think?"

Elissa bit her lip, glanced about the room, arms at her side, and finally settled her gaze on Gloria. "I appreciate your generosity, but I can't do this, Mrs. Blacksworth."

"Why, of course you can. I want you to have the clothes. We can have the pants tailored."

She shook her head. "No, it's not right."

Why couldn't she simply accept the gift and say "thank you"? Why did there have to be a discussion about it? What on this earth was there to discuss? Didn't she know Gloria Blacksworth was not in the habit of helping others? She should be honored and yet she stood there as though she were miserable, as though she did not *want* what Gloria was offering. "What's the problem?" Dammit, what *was* the problem?

"I don't want your clothes, Mrs. Blacksworth. I have my own."

Indeed. Most likely department store closeouts or hand-me-downs. "You don't have clothes like these. That's silk you're wearing, and the pants are linen. Don't they feel wonderful? Don't they make *you* feel wonderful?" The girl looked away and didn't answer. "Oh, for heaven's sake, we'll head into town tomorrow and you can pick out a few outfits."

"I'm not taking your clothes or your offer." Her words fell out as though she'd been insulted, which was ridiculous.

"You don't want to look better? You like looking like a

ragamuffin with that long curly hair that goes every which way even when you try to tie it back? And slacks that are almost threadbare?" Gloria huffed her annoyance. This was why she never tried to help the less fortunate. They were always so ungrateful. "I'm offering you a chance you'll never have again. I can dress you, fix your hair and makeup, maybe even convince you to get out of health care and into finance." She paused, her gaze narrowed and steady. "If you let me, I can give you the world."

"Thank you." Gloria smiled. The girl was no fool; she knew a good thing when it stared her in the face. "But I'm not interested."

"Not interested? How could you not be interested? Why, anyone would be honored to have me shower attention on them."

Elissa Cerdi advanced on her and stopped when she was a foot away. Her eyes flashed with sadness and disappointment. "I do appreciate your generosity, Mrs. Blacksworth, but you should appreciate my right to say no. I'm happy with my life, who I am, and where I'm headed. I don't want you offering me clothes or makeovers as though I'm not good enough as I am. And don't try to talk me out of my nursing career. It's *my* life and it's what I want to do."

"But why wouldn't you want to better yourself if you had the chance?" Could she really not see Gloria only wanted to help her?

The girl's voice turned soft, gentle. "Because a bag of clothes and a haircut isn't going to gain me the world or make things any easier. Life is tough and all we have is each other. I *want* to stay and help you make the most of your time left, but if you can't respect my right to make my own choices, then maybe you should find someone else."

Chapter 15

"Have the kids ever seen Niagara Falls?" Harry had been thinking about a short trip with Greta and the kids. Three days tops, separate rooms with adjoining doors, so Greta could sneak in to see him for an hour or two once the kids were asleep.

"No, they haven't even been to the ocean."

"You're kidding. Damn, every kid's got to stick their feet in the ocean, smell the air, taste the saltwater." Harry turned on his side to face Greta. "They've really never dipped their toes in the Atlantic Ocean?"

"Never."

"Hmm. Have you?" She shrugged and didn't answer. Something was going on with her. The sex had been great, as usual, but the connection had been off, like leaving garlic out of a pasta dish. He noticed because, like garlic, the connection with Greta when they were in bed was important to him. He sure as hell hadn't ever thought about a connection with any of his other bed partners that didn't have to do with physical pleasure, and if he had, he would have shut it down fast. Greta was different; he wanted that connection with her and when he didn't feel it, he wanted to know why. "Hey, are you going to answer me?"

"What was the question?"

Harry reached out and cupped her chin. "Look at me." She lifted her head slowly, met his gaze. Those blue eyes sparkled with tears and misery. "What's going on? You're not yourself."

She shook her head and sniffed. "It's nothing."

When a woman said *nothing* with a bucket of tears in her eyes, it was always something. "Greta, talk to me. Did your mother bitch you out again for coming here? Just let me set her straight. I know she hates my guts and I could care less, but she's not going to demean you."

A tear slipped, then another and another. She swiped a hand across her eyes and said in a voice above a whisper, "It's not my mother."

"Okay, it's not your mother. Are you going to make me guess who's causing the grief, because unless you give me a hint, I'm riding blind here."

She opened her mouth to speak but nothing came out. Three attempts later, she managed a small, "It's about us."

Crap. A comment like that was never good, with or without tears. Harry slid his hand from her chin and cleared his throat. "What about us?" He zeroed in on her, waited. Again, she opened her mouth to air and no sound. "Just say it, dammit."

"I'm pregnant."

"What?" He couldn't have heard that right. "Did you say pregnant?" She gave him a half nod. More tears spilled, accompanied by sound, great waves of sobbing, pulling him in, sucking him under with that single, dreaded word. He'd fought against it his whole life, and except for that one time at seventeen, he'd never gotten caught. And now here he was, trapped by sweet, innocent Greta. Except maybe she wasn't so sweet and innocent; maybe it had all been part of a scheme to snatch him and tie him down. More cunning women had tried, but he'd been duped by Greta's wholesomeness, her insistence that she didn't care about his money or his name. She only cared about him. Right, him and his sperm. Harry threw back the covers and grabbed a T-shirt and pajama bottoms. He tossed Greta her robe and said, "Put something on; I can't think when you're naked." And that said it all. Common sense left him when she was close and naked, her heat inviting him to take, touch, kiss. "How the hell did this happen if I used a condom every damn time?"

"It wasn't every time, Harry," she said to his back. "Remember the shower? And the kitchen?"

Hell, yeah, he remembered. "Shit." He bounded off the bed, as if he could revert the pregnancy by creating distance between them. Harry paced the room, raking his fingers through his hair, and cursing his own lack of control. Condoms were of no value if you didn't use them. "Are you sure?"

She swiped at her eyes and said in a pinched voice, "Of course, I'm sure."

"Okay, just asking." Now what? "Did you see a doctor?"

"Not yet." She'd tied the robe so tight she'd need a pair of scissors to cut it off. "It's too early."

"Oh. When is the...uh....when's the date?" He could not bring himself to say *baby*.

"I won't know for certain until I see the doctor, but I think early spring." With that, she grabbed her clothes and disappeared into the bathroom. Fifteen minutes passed and just when Harry began to wonder if she was going to hole up in there all night, the door opened and Greta appeared, dressed in jeans and a T-shirt. His gaze darted to her belly and then back to her face. The scowl she gave him said she'd caught him looking and didn't appreciate it. Well, too bad. It was his kid in there and he'd look as much and as often as he damn well pleased.

"I have to go," she announced as though she hadn't just dropped a bomb on him that would change their lives forever. Greta slipped into her sandals and gathered her purse.

"You can't leave now. We have to talk about this." Was he the only one here using common sense? That was scary.

"What's to talk about? I told you I was pregnant because you have a right to know, but that's it. I'm not asking for your opinion or your help."

"What does that mean?" He tore across the room in four steps, halted when he was an arm's length away. "If you think you're going to tell me you're carrying my baby and then just waltz out of here, you can think again. That's my kid, too, Greta."

"Harry, think about what you're saying. You don't want to be a father."

"That's not really the issue now, is it?" How many men actually wanted to be a father until they were one? He'd lost that opportunity once and he would not lose it again. "You aren't," he paused, ran a hand through his hair and said, "You aren't thinking about getting rid of it, are you?"

"Of course not."

He let out a long sigh. "I know this was never in our playbook, but I do want to be part of this baby's life." Harry settled his hands on her shoulders, met her gaze. "And yours." The truth swirled around him; he wanted Greta in his life, needed her there, and maybe this was the way to do it. "We'll go to the justice of the peace and have a small ceremony, just a witness and the kids." He brushed his lips against hers. "What do you say?"

"I can't."

"Of course you can." Harry traced her lips. "We'll get Lizzie a new dress and Arnold can take pictures with my phone, and—"

"I'm still married."

Those words were as shocking as her pregnancy admission earlier. Greta was still married?

"What do you mean you're still married?" Harry tried to process what she'd just said. She looked away, which meant either she didn't want to tell him or she was about to manufacture a lie.

"We never divorced." Her voice dipped, evened, and he

211

could tell she was miles away in her other life with her husband. "We did file but then he moved away and we never carried it through." She cleared her throat, pushed on. "My mother is very much against divorce and I figured as long as he kept our agreement, what was the point of making it legal."

"And what was the agreement?"

"He would stay away from the kids and I wouldn't ask for child support or alimony…or anything."

Anger seeped through him, slow, steady, hot. "That's not what you told me. You said their father paid child support when he could be found." Who would have thought that the only woman he'd ever trusted would be the one to betray him with lies?

She looked away. "That wasn't true. I didn't want you getting involved."

"Do you realize how screwed up this is?" And people called him messed up? This was nuts. "What did you tell the kids? Dad's on the moon for the next twenty years so he can't see you, but we're still married?" She didn't like that; he could tell by the way she pinched her lips and sipped in air like there wasn't enough in the room for both of them.

"He calls every six weeks, tells them he misses them and wishes he could be home, but duty to country keeps him away."

"Oh, for the love of God." This was like a script for a bad movie. "Let me guess. CIA? Special Ops? What is it? Some superhero-type bullshit he saw in the theater?"

She dipped her head. "Something like that."

"This is ridiculous." Harry swore under his breath and paced the room. Was Greta a whack job disguised as a normal person? Who would believe this kind of crap? Of course. Kids. They were the victims and it pissed him off. "Please tell me you did not conjure this up, because if you did that is the sickest—"

"I didn't," she spat out. "But he wouldn't leave unless he could take a superhero image with him." She dragged her gaze to his and swiped at her eyes. Tears. Were they supposed to replace his anger with compassion? Understanding? What about the damn kids? Who had thought of them?

"So you let him create a story that will live in Arnold and Lizzie's brain for the rest of their lives? And you think just because he told them he's doing something noble, that will make up for his absence? You think it will fix things?" He was nine again, waiting for his father to show up for his swim meet. *I can't, Harry. I'm expecting a call about a merger. Big stuff.* And again at thirteen, the soccer tournament where Harry scored the only goal. *Wish I could have been there, boy, but I was being honored at the country club. Can't very well skip my own party now, can I? They expect me to give a speech.* And finally, senior year. *Charlie said he'd take you to see a college or two. I'm sure you don't want your dad hanging around when you can have your brother with you.* But Harry had wanted his dad to hang around. He'd wanted that precious time so badly he stayed awake at night thinking about it until it was all he thought about. He wanted to belong to someone, somewhere, and maybe that's how he'd gotten his girlfriend pregnant at seventeen.

"I'm trying to give them a normal life."

Harry rounded on her. "Normal? You think it's normal to let a kid think his dad is Superman? That's messed up, Greta."

She wrapped her arms around her middle as though she could shut out his words. Nice try. She'd need a suit of armor to shut out what he had to say. "What's his name?"

She hesitated, then asked, "Why?"

Harry shrugged. He was not going to divulge his game plan, though he didn't really have a game plan yet. But he would. Count on that. "I want to meet him, have a little conversation."

"No."

"What? Did you say no?"

She stared at him, an open challenge. "I'm not giving you his name."

"You can either give me his name, or I'll hire a private investigator to find him." Why was she protecting the idiot? "You know I'll do it, Greta."

Apparently she did, because she deflated right in front of him; lips and eyes sank, shoulders slouched. "Lars," she said. "Lars Servensen."

"Good." Now he had a name to go with the man. He could funnel his anger into finding this guy so he didn't have to think about the bigger problem: Greta had lied to him. The one person he trusted could not be trusted. "Do you have an address?"

She nodded. "Why do you want to see him? What difference does any of this make?"

"I can't marry you until you divorce him, and I am going to marry you." There, let her try to get out of that one. This time, with this baby, he would do the right thing.

"Are you crazy?" She faced him, hands on hips, displeasure coating her face. "I can't marry you."

"Why not?" Why the hell not?"

The laugh that escaped her was not filled with humor. "You're not the marrying kind, Harry. If you were, you would have been married by now."

Good point. "And the baby? Is this going to be one of those one potato, two potato, hopping between houses?"

She ignored the question and threw him one of her own. "Can you picture taking a baby and a diaper bag on a date? Or a crib in the next room while you're pleasuring your ladies?"

Greta sighed her disgust. "I don't think so."

"What if I want to be a bigger part of its life?"

"Listen to yourself." Her voice softened. "You're in shock. The Harry Blacksworth I know would be planning an escape route, not talking about being a bigger part of a baby's life."

She was giving him a way out, nice and neat, no strings. Oh, there would be child support, but so what? He could pay for ten children, plus college, and everything in between. All he had to do was stroke a check and walk away. But he couldn't. Dammit, he couldn't do it. At seventeen, his old man had stripped him of the opportunity to be a father, and then the mess with Gloria and the possibility that his blood might be running through Christine's veins. But now, here he was again, holding the "father" card, but this time he could do something about it. He knew nothing about being a father, but who the hell really did? If "qualified" individuals were the only ones to have a kid, the population would decrease by seventy percent. This was about a chance to do the right thing, to redeem his sorry soul, if that were possible. And while he was a New Age kind of guy, he still possessed a few old school values—knock up a woman, you marry her.

"We're going to get married," Harry said. "Don't even try to argue." He ignored her blue stare and pinched lips. "But first I have to find your husband and convince him to get a divorce."

*****

Harry found Lars Servensen two hours outside of Chicago in a town the size of Magdalena. It wasn't hard to locate the jerk; the townies called him Lars the Giant, which didn't bode well for Harry if the guy had a temper or liked to use his fists. Still, what Harry planned to offer the man was more powerful than twenty-inch biceps and a strong right hook. Once Greta realized the futility of fighting him, she relayed all sorts of interesting and bizarre information about her husband. He worked out four times a day, was covered in tattoos, including a sleeve on his right arm, had once thought of becoming a minister, and had fathered two other children, all born within seven months of Arnold. When Harry asked Greta what the man did to make money—inquiring about a profession would have been a stretch—she'd blushed and said he was a male model and actor. Right. Harry might have seen him in a few "movies" but it might be hard to tell, given the man would be wearing clothes when he met him today. What a scumbag. Impregnating multiple women, running off and pretending to be a superhero?

What the hell had Greta been thinking to take up with somebody like Lars Servensen? The guy sounded like a narcissistic, manipulative bastard, only interested in his own pleasure. Damn, he kind of sounded like Harry. Maybe the real question was what the hell was wrong with Greta to take up with men like them? She appeared so squeaky-clean honest, but maybe emotionally damaged men turned her on. Was she a psycho? She was pregnant with his kid; did he need to have her evaluated? What if she tried to harm the child because she was a nut case? His brain burst with possibilities, all beginning and ending with blood and baby killing.

He sucked in air, forced his brain to calm down. Is this what being a parent did to a person? Made them so friggin' irrational they couldn't think straight? If he was this way already and the kid hadn't even popped out yet, what would he be like when the kid had to enter the world with all of its sickness and depravity? A surge of protectiveness pulsed through him and he thought he was going to puke. How was he going to keep the kid safe? How could he save him from pedophiles, disease, gunshot wounds, random acts of violence, and dammit, just being in the wrong place at the wrong time?

And if the kid survived all of that, what if he hooked up with the wrong kind of people, got into drugs, shot up, overdosed?

Harry was only one person, and so was Greta. Two people could not protect a kid from the world; sometimes they couldn't even protect him from himself. So, what the hell was a person to do? How do you deal with the knowledge that no matter if you took your kid for every medical checkup, bought him the "safest" car on the road, installed a state-of-the-art security system, and gave him an Ivy league education, you could not protect him? That realization blew Harry's mind, because now it was real, now it had to do with the child Greta carried in her belly. Their child.

By the time he parked his car in front of the three-story apartment building where Lars Servensen supposedly lived, Harry was pissed and agitated. The pissed part had to do with the futility of man and Harry's sudden sense of mortality and insignificance. He did not need or want to have those feelings jacking him up right now when he had to face Greta's loser estranged husband. But it didn't seem to matter what he wanted, the feelings were there and whenever Harry thought of his kid, he grew more agitated. He did not wish this sense of helplessness on anyone, and yet, he bet every parent and parent-to-be felt it.

Harry climbed the outside stairs of the apartment building to the second floor and knocked on 2B. "Hold on." The voice was rough, gravelly, maybe from lack of sleep, too much booze, or a combination. The guy couldn't be rolling in cash or he wouldn't be living in an apartment with pizza boxes and beer cans stacked by the stairwell and doors that looked like they'd been kicked in a time or two. The place smelled of piss and stale beer. Had Greta lived in an apartment like this? Had her kids? The door squeaked open and a monster of a man towered over him. "Who are you? I paid my rent yesterday."

Meaning, the man owed rent money. The beast behind the voice had a solid six inches and fifty pounds on Harry. Muscle on top of muscle, shaved head, nonexistent neck. And the tattoos. Lots of tattoos.

"I'm Harry Blacksworth." He kept his voice even, his expression bland. *Think of it as a business transaction, don't let emotion get involved or you'll lose your edge.* "I'm here on behalf of Greta Servensen. May I come in?"

The man's blue eyes turned to slits of ice. "What's Greta want? You a lawyer?"

Harry shook his head. "No. But I do represent her." That could mean anything and in a way, it was true. Lars Servensen considered this, muscles flexing in his neck, his shoulders, along his forearms. Harry glanced at the tattoos on the man's left arm; too hard to identify what they were unless he studied them, which he chose not to, seeing as the man attached to the tattoos was eyeballing him, and none too kindly either.

"I don't know." He crossed one trunk-sized arm over the other. "Whatever you got to say, you can say out here."

So, the man didn't want to extend an invitation into his pigpen. Well, that was too bad because Harry wasn't dealing anything from a piss-laden doorstep. "No, I really can't." He glanced to the right, then left, dropping his voice. "I really can't do that."

The man sent him an extra five-second stare, an intimidation tactic, no doubt, and stood back to let Harry enter. "Five minutes, that's all you get."

Harry entered the apartment, scanned the living room, and decided pigpen was an understatement. The place smelled like sweat and yeast and was strewn with clothes, bodybuilding magazines, and dog toys. The last one threw Harry. "You've got a dog?"

"Pixie, come here, girl." Servensen whistled. "Come see

Daddy." A brown and white shaggy dog the size of a football ran down the narrow hallway, tongue hanging out, tail wagging. Pixie wore a pink collar with sparkly blue studs. Tattoo Man scooped her up and kissed her head. "This is my baby," he said, his voice softening as he nuzzled the dog's ear.

"She's cute." Harry knew nothing about dogs, less about owners who treated their dogs like children. Still, the dog might be the angle he needed. "How old is she?"

The man smiled at Pixie and lifted a monster shoulder. "Don't know. I found her by the Dumpster last Christmas." His thick brows pinched together and his thin lips pulled into a long frown. "Can you imagine somebody just dumping her? I mean, to not own up to your responsibility, like she was nothing? What kind of person does that?"

Scumbags like you, he wanted to say. *Didn't you dump your kids and leave them for Greta?* "I don't know."

"A worthless piece of shit, that's who would do it," he growled.

"Pretty much." *And that includes you.* "Look, I know you must be really busy, so I'll be brief." Harry reached in his suit jacket and pulled out the envelope with the letter and the check that would set Greta free. "Greta wants a divorce and here are the terms."

"Who the hell are you?" Lars Servensen stared at him, the veins in his temples bulging.

Harry cleared his throat. "I'm a friend. I'm helping her out."

"Ahh." The man gave Harry a once-over, his steel-blue eyes knowing. "You're banging her, aren't you?"

If Harry didn't need this asshole to show up in court, he'd punch him in the gut. He wouldn't get a second punch because Muscle Man would floor him, but the jerk deserved one good shot for speaking about Greta that way. "What I am or am not doing with Greta is none of your business."

Servensen laughed. "Yup, you're banging her. She's a piece, isn't she? All passion and fire, makes you feel like you're the only man in the world."

"That's enough." If the bastard said one more word about Greta, Harry was going to punch him. In the nuts. "Listen here, you piece of shit. I'm going to offer you a very large sum of money, probably more than you'll make in the next ten years doing whatever it is you do. When the judge sets the date, you better damn well show up in court at the time on the docket. Not three hours late or the next day. You're going to give Greta the divorce and agree to everything in this letter." He tapped the envelope against his thigh. "Once you do, you'll get a check for ten times what I'm giving you today. Got it?"

The man stroked Pixie behind the ears, his gaze honed in on the envelope. "How much we talking about?"

Now he had him. Harry opened the envelope, pulled out the check, and held it up. "That's a helluva lot of food for Pixie, isn't it?"

***

Ninety-seven days was a long time for a man to wait when he wasn't accustomed to waiting ninety-seven seconds. But Harry did it; hell, he probably would have waited seven years to be with Greta. Who would have thought that Harry Blacksworth would actually be excited for his wedding day? Certainly not Harry, but here he was, dressed in a black suit and burgundy striped tie, his old man's pocket watch in his hand as he counted the minutes before Greta became his wife.

Greta's divorce to Lars Servensen was official eight days ago, but he and Greta began making plans for their future the night he returned from seeing Tattoo Man. Actually, Harry was the one making the grand plans while Greta hung back, asking him every sixteen minutes if he was certain he wanted to take on the responsibility of a family. After the third day of questioning, he'd pulled her to him, kissed her long and hard, and said, "I love you, Greta and I want this, more than anything." She'd pretty much melted after that, crying and telling him her heart was filled with love for him. He'd liked the breathy little hiccups that spilled out between her tears and profession of love. And then had come the sex, ahem, lovemaking, and it had been damn explosive, better than before.

They'd settled on a house in the suburbs, three-car garage, colonial, six bedrooms, four and half bathrooms, with a pool table in the basement. A.J., formerly Arnold, liked that room the best and had already asked if Harry would teach him to shoot pool. Of course Harry had agreed and damn but the boy seemed more confident. Greta thought it was because he had a man in his life, but Harry attributed it to the new nickname. Lizzie loved the swing set in the backyard, complete with a fort and sliding board. She'd conned Harry into playing hide-and-seek with her and he'd pushed aside his embarrassment and done it, but he told her he wasn't doing it again until he bought "play clothes" because he'd snagged his dress pants climbing up the fort ladder and ripped a hole in his shirt.

Greta had insisted on lugging some memorabilia from the old house: a bowl from Germany, a crocheted afghan from her grandmother, a stack of photo albums with two inches of dust. What the hell. There were enough bedrooms and closets to stash things in and he'd agree to anything, as long as Greta and the kids were attached to it. What he would not and did not agree to was Greta's mother taking up squatter's rights in the new place. Oh, he might have halfway considered it had his future wife asked him to, but she hadn't. Not once, not even when A.J. and Lizzie asked if Grandma Helene was coming to the new house. She'd told them it hadn't been discussed, but one afternoon, a week before the move, it was discussed…in great detail and in loud voices.

Harry had swung by to pick up the kids and a carload of their junk. While they were gathering their things upstairs, he made his way to the kitchen where Helene stood at the stove, frying peppers and onions. He tried to make small talk but she ignored him, pointy nose in the air, thin lips pinched into a straight line. To hell with her, she was nothing but a miserable woman, moody, obsessively critical, and cruel. He'd taken three steps toward the living room when she'd lashed out, calling him a monster, a derelict, an immoral bastard—yes, she'd sworn at him—and wishing him and her sinful daughter to hell and back. Wishing Greta to hell? That was it.

Harry turned mid-stride and told her exactly what he thought of her in loud and colorful language. When he informed Greta of the blowout that night, she'd been silent, but she hadn't scolded or frowned at him and the kids had actually seemed happier. Score one for Team Harry. Sometimes you had to fight the bullies, even if they masqueraded in the form of family.

"Mr. Harry. Mom's ready." Harry smiled at Lizzie who looked like a miniature version of her mother, hair piled on top of her head and stuffed with baby's breath, white lace dress falling just below the knees, and tights with patent leather shoes.

"Okay, kiddo. Let's get this show on the road." Harry remembered nothing after that as his brain clogged with visions of Greta gliding down the aisle, A.J. at her side. If angels walked this earth, his Greta was one of them in a shimmery ice-blue dress, tummy round and full with his child, her blonde hair piled on top of her head. She wore his wedding gift to her, diamond drop earrings and a diamond drop necklace. Of course she'd had a fit when he handed her the

Tiffany boxes, but he wasn't backing down. This was his wedding, dammit, and she was going to wear them—and like it, too. He hoped. They'd already had the discussion about Harry buying her extravagant and unnecessary gifts, but the fact that she really didn't care about them made him want to give them to her. Wait until she saw the new car he was having delivered next week: a four-door Lexus sedan. He would stop after that. Maybe. All Greta wanted from him was his love, commitment, and fidelity. For somebody who had spent his whole life estranged from those things, it was easy to promise them to the woman who owned his heart. His Greta.

"...do you take this man..."

Harry stared at those blue eyes, fell into them.... She smiled and said, "I do."

"....until death do you part..."

"I do," he murmured.

Husband and wife. The kiss came next, long, slow, spreading from Harry to Greta, joining them in a lifetime of love, commitment, and fidelity. "I love you, Greta Blacksworth, and I plan to spend the rest of my life showing you."

Chapter 16

Five inches of snow fell the day of The Bleeding Hearts Society monthly meeting, but Pop wouldn't hear of staying home. A little snow wasn't going to keep him from attending. Today they were turning in the gifts they'd made or purchased for this year's family in need, and he was just nosy enough to want to see what everyone brought. Christine picked him up at his doorstep and refused to drive him to the meeting until he went back inside and changed out of his tennis shoes and into winter boots.

The group spent most of the meeting removing price tags and wrapping gifts. Pop inspected each item, inquired as to the donor, and made an occasional noise of approval or, in a few cases, disapproval, if he thought the gift-giving was skimpy. When the meeting adjourned, Pop snatched a sugar cookie and bee-lined for Ramona Casherdon. Christine guessed it had something to do with Ramona's nephew, Cash, who had become the buzz about town. Everyone wanted details of the accident that would soon send him back to Magdalena so they could formulate an opinion and an appropriate sentiment, should the occasion arise. Pop said some still judged him for what happened all those years ago, said Cash was a lost soul smothered in bad luck. Others sympathized, said if Cash had stood up and challenged his fiancé's biased and exaggerated version of the story, maybe he wouldn't have felt the need to run from the town and himself, and maybe this latest tragedy wouldn't have happened. The residents of Magdalena might not ask Ramona a straight-out, no-sugar-coated question about her nephew, but Pop Benito would, and no doubt, that's what he was doing in the far corner of the room as he munched on a cookie and nodded his white head.

"Christine? Mind if I sit?" Mimi Pendergrass flipped her reading glasses onto her salt-and-pepper curls and smiled.

"Of course." An audience with Mimi was a good thing. Pop had stated with certainty that today was the day Mimi Pendergrass would grant the big thumbs-up that would filter through the community and send residents to Christine, portfolios in hand.

Mimi perched sideways on the edge of the folding chair, one small hand resting on the table next to Christine's water, the other clutching the back of the chair. "We'd like you to join The Bleeding Hearts Society. We think you could do some real good here and we'd be pleased to have you."

Join the club? Was that code for, You're in, we'll back your business? "Thank you. I'm honored."

"We'll send a formal invite next week. Ramona's in charge of that," her gaze skittered to the far corner of the room where Pop continued in earnest conversation, "but she's got her hands full right now."

"I know. I'm so sorry to hear about her nephew." All she knew was that Cash Casherdon had been in an accident while on police duty. The details were sketchy and well guarded. She'd asked Nate about his old friend, but her husband hadn't talked to him since the day he left town eight years ago.

Mimi pinched the bridge of her nose and shook her head as if to clear it. Her dangly leaf earrings brushed her neck, tinkled in a gentle rhythm. According to Pop, this woman had known her share of pain, but her faith and her flowers had kept her from falling into a compost heap of self-pity. "Cash was a good boy and what happened was beyond tragic." She cleared her throat and sat up straight. "Never mind about that, this is a happy time for you." Her gaze settled on Christine's stomach and her voice grew soft and gentle. "There's nothing like a new baby in the family. I'm so very happy for you and

Nathan."

"Thank you." These past few months had taught Christine what real love meant as they prepared for the baby's arrival. Nate painted the baby's room a pale yellow, Miriam made draperies and a comforter and added a new crocheted item to the stack on the baby's shelf each week. She promised to "customize" items once Baby Desantro entered the world. There were a few moments when Christine wished she knew the baby's sex, but they were outweighed by her desire for a true surprise. Of course, Lily continued to insist the baby was a girl and said it with such certainty, Christine started to believe it, too, referencing "she" on several occasions, prompting Nate to slide her a "what in the hell are you talking about" look.

Mimi leaned forward and whispered in Christine's ear. "Pop gave his okay this morning, so it's a go."

Okay for what? "A go?"

"Yes." More whispering. "We'll put the word out; expect the phone calls to start this week. It might be a bit slower than usual with the holidays, but things will get cranking. And don't worry about taking time off with the baby because everybody expects you to do that. They're not going anywhere and neither is their money."

"Mimi?" Christine shifted in her chair so she could look the woman in the eye. "What exactly are you talking about and why does Pop have anything to do with it?"

The older woman's thin lips pulled into a grin. "Pop gave us the okay to do business with you."

"*Pop did?* Why would he be doing that? He said you and this group were the ones who had to give me the thumbs-up, with you as the lead."

Mimi laughed. "He did, huh? Well, he's a sneaky one. Pop was the one doing the vetting and you must have passed his eight-point approval system or we wouldn't be having this discussion."

"Eight-point approval?" She slid a glance at Pop, who had his head bent toward Ramona but his eyes on Christine. He lifted a bony hand, gave her a thumbs-up, then turned back to Cash's aunt.

"To pass Pop's test, you have to exhibit the following qualities: loyalty, integrity, honesty, compassion, forgiveness, dedication, humility, and, of course, a sense of humor. Not many people do it so quickly, so you must have really impressed him."

"I have no idea what to say." Darn that man. He'd spent hours telling her what she needed to do to win Mimi Pendergrass's acceptance, how the society loved volunteers and organizers, how his opinion was only part of the approval process. Wait until she got him alone. Pop had some serious explaining to do and he was not going to appease her with a box of pizzelles.

Mimi patted her hand and said, "He told me you're the daughter he never had. Praise doesn't get much better than that."

Christine told Nate about Pop's shenanigans later that night and the way the old man apologized for the sneakiness, but insisted there were times when those tactics were necessary. *A person's real self comes out when he thinks others aren't watching, or the person he's with doesn't matter. That's when you get your best information, little details that, pieced together, make the big picture. I had my doubts until you and Nate worked out the kinks and got back together. That's what true love is—fighting through those rough spots like a rototiller plowing through clay.*

"Pop's got a soft spot for you," Nate told her that night as they sat on the couch, drinking hot cocoa with miniature marshmallows and admiring the blue spruce in the corner.

He'd just finished playing his nightly serenade for the baby. Tonight was a combination of Bach, Mozart, and a little Billy Joel. Lily would be over tomorrow to help string popcorn and cranberries for the tree, and Nate had promised she could pick out the Christmas carols for him to play. Of course, that would involve dancing, but Lily would have to do a solo on the floor because Christine could barely walk, let alone think about dancing. Nate smoothed his hand over her belly and kissed her temple. "Feeling okay?"

"Other than looking like the bed of a wide-load truck?" She smiled and covered the hand that rested on her belly. "I'm fine, but I'm ready for this little Desantro to make an appearance." She wasn't technically due for another ten days, but the doctor thought she might delivery early.

"You think it will be a girl?"

"Maybe. Lily has never wavered."

Nate leaned forward and kissed her belly. "Hello, baby," he murmured against the soft flannel of Christine's shirt. "Can't wait to meet you." He laid his head on her belly and sighed. "I have never been happier or more content than I am right now."

"I know. Your mother says we should enjoy it now because the next eighteen years will be chaos."

"Yeah, I was not the most pleasant kid to be around."

"So I've heard." She laughed and ran her fingers through his hair, enjoyed the softness of his curls. Would their child have its father's hair? His eyes? His feet? The miracle that lived inside of her might share some of their characteristics, but the child would be her very own person and Christine would work hard not to interfere with that uniqueness. Her mother had attempted to stamp that out of Christine's personality, but thankfully, she'd not succeeded.

"If you think we're going to go crazy, what about Harry? Can you picture him with a kid?" Nate chuckled. "Harry

Blacksworth with spit-up on his custom-made shirts, carrying a designer diaper bag."

"That's mean. He's excited. I wish we could have made the wedding." She'd asked Dr. Conrad but he'd said absolutely not.

"Greta promised to send the video and while it's not the same as witnessing his agony in person, we will have the benefit of replay." He chuckled again. "Think the new husband is ready to ditch everybody and head to Bermuda?"

"I think Uncle Harry is going to surprise us all," she said. "Greta's perfect for him and he really seems attached to her kids. He said they were talking about buying a place here for the summers."

"Oh, boy. One big happy family." He sighed. "Can't wait."

Christine leaned forward and tried to see his expression. "Are you serious?"

Nate sat up and studied her. "What if I am? Would it matter?"

"Of course it would." She waited, and when five seconds passed without a response she said, "Well?"

His lips twitched. "I like Harry. He's a straight shooter, even if he's a little too hung up on his wardrobe." Nate's expression turned serious. "I'd like it if they spent the summers here, around family. It would be good for all of us."

Christine nodded. "That's kind of what he said." Well, not exactly. *That mountain man better treat you right because I'll kick his butt if he doesn't.* He'd said it with a wink, which in Harry Blacksworth lingo meant the guy passed his test.

Nate smiled and pulled her against him. "Warm enough? I can put another log on the fire."

"I'm fine. Just getting sleepy."

He checked his watch and said, "Actually, Jack's stopping by tonight with one of your Christmas presents. He should be here soon."

"Presents? We said we weren't doing that this year because of the baby." There'd been so many things she wanted to get him but he'd insisted on no gifts and now he'd gotten her one? That didn't sit well at all.

"I made it a long time ago before I even knew about the baby."

"Nate—"

Tires screeched up the driveway, followed by three quick honks. "Sounds like Jack's here." Nate stood and gave Christine a quick kiss. "Stay right here and no peeking. I'm going outside to help Jack bring it in."

"It takes two men to carry my present inside?"

He grabbed his jacket and said, "You have no idea the trouble this thing has caused me. Be right back."

And with that, he was out the door and stomping down the steps toward Jack and her present. Her husband was full of surprises lately, from the hardbound edition of *Aesop's Fables, Mom said every kid should have one,* to the pink cactus in full bloom he brought home, *because it made me think of you.* She rubbed her stomach and wished her father were alive to know his grandchild, and yet, if he were, she might never have met Nate. Life was a strange mix of twists and turns, where incomprehensible loss often led to paths of unimaginable joy.

The door opened bringing with it a rush of cold air and Jack Finnegan's gravelly voice. "Hello, Christine. How's the little mama?"

"Hi, Jack," she called from the couch. "I'd turn and greet you, but apparently I'm not allowed to see my present yet."

"Hell, no, can't ruin this surprise. Been a long time coming and a lot of heartache. If this boy would have just fessed up from the start, he could have avoided a lot of trials, but can't knock no sense into that thick head sometimes. Hey!" He grunted and muttered, "Hold on, Nate, I ain't as spry as you. This hip don't move so well."

"Less gum flapping and you'd have the energy to do the job."

"Don't let him get hurt, Nate. Jack's got to cover for you when the baby comes."

"Yeah, don't forget that, boy," Jack said. "Be nice or I'll tell that little wife of yours you ain't as great as she thinks. Hey now! That hurt." The back and forth insults continued until their voices faded. Were they in the baby's room? Christine waited and listened but she couldn't tell what they were doing or where. And what had Jack meant about Nate fessing up and saving heartache?

"Okay, all set. See you, Christine. Don't take any crap from this boy."

"Aren't you going to stay while I open my present?"

"Nah, snow's gonna start any minute. I want to get home and tucked in. These bones don't take the cold the way they used to. Besides, Nate don't want me around when he starts blubbering all that love and commitment fiddle-faddle."

Jack laughed and when Nate spoke, there was humor in his voice. "Thanks, Jack. Appreciate it."

The old man's voice cracked with his next words. "Anytime, boy. Anytime at all." Then he was gone, his truck barreling down the road toward home.

Nate came up behind her, pushed aside a hunk of hair, and kissed the back of her neck. "Ready for your surprise, Mrs. Desantro?"

"Absolutely." She stood and made her way to the other side of the couch.

"This has been a long time coming," he said as he held out his hand and led her to the closed door of the baby's room. His dark eyes grew bright, his voice hoarse. "I hope you like it."

He opened the door and she entered. A cradle rested in the center of the room, its rich wood gleaming under the soft light. The spindles were carved with delicate precision, the headboard outlined in a simple scrollwork design, the base, sturdy and dependable.

"It's beautiful," she breathed. She ran her fingers along the fine wood. "Just perfect."

Nate covered her hand with his, met her gaze. "This is what I was doing at Gino Servetti's."

"But…why? You didn't even know I was pregnant."

A dull flush crept up his neck, settled on his cheeks. "It was going to be the lead-in to 'What do you think about a baby?'"

"That day everything fell apart and you told me you had a surprise; this was it?" Tears flooded her voice, made it hard to speak. "This was the surprise?" He nodded, squeezed her hand. "But why did you wait until now? Things have been good between us for a while."

"I don't like to think about that time without you. It was one of the worst periods of my life, worse than when my father died and that was pretty bad. I'd actually planned to gift it to one of the guys at work who has a pregnant girlfriend, but Jack talked me out of it. Said you deserved to see what I'd been doing at Gino's." His lips inched up. "Plus, he said it was a 'damn fine piece of craftsmanship' and I should be proud of it."

"I'm so glad he convinced you to bring it home." She paused, stroked her husband's cheek. "Where it belongs. I love you, Nate Desantro. Thank you for this beautiful gift. I wish I had one to give you."

He placed a hand on her belly, bent his head, and kissed her softly on the mouth. "You've given me the best gift of all."

***

"I knew it was going to be a girl. Anna Nicolina Desantro."

Lily grinned at Pop. "I got to hold her. She's tiny. Seven pounds and something, and her hair is black like mine and Christine's."

Pop knew all about the new addition to the Desantro family. Miriam had called him two days before Christmas to tell him Christine had delivered a baby girl that morning. They'd named her Anna Nicolina. He knew why there'd been a hitch in her voice when she spoke. Nobody had to remind Pop who the child was named after because he remembered the baby Miriam delivered that only lived a few hours. Anna Nicolina had been her name. Some said it was the beginning of the end for Miriam and Nick Desantro because when a man chooses a bottle at O'Reilly's over his dying child, well, that's pure disaster in a shot glass.

Six days had passed since Anna Nicolina entered the world and according to Miriam, Nate had learned to change a diaper, burp the baby, and even taken to singing her to sleep in the rocker Harry Blacksworth sent from some fancy-dancy furniture place in Chicago. Times were sure a-changin'. What would Lucy say about a man changing a diaper and doing night duty?

"Is it time to make the pizzelles?"

"Hold your horses, Lily girl. What did Pop tell you was the trick to making good pizzelles? Hmm?" He tapped his chin and made a chicken sound.

"The eggs!" She clapped her hands. "They can't be cold."

"You get an A plus." Pop set two bowls in front of her. One contained six eggs, the other was empty. "Now crack the egg and put it in this bowl. Be careful you don't get shells. Nobody likes shells in their pizzelles."

Lily lifted the first egg, cracked it against the bowl, and dumped the egg in. "Like that?"

"Good. Now the next one." Pop only had to dig out three

bits of eggshell, which was a lot better than the first time he showed Anthony the art of pizzelle making. His son had called on Christmas day and sent a package of frozen steaks, chicken, and gourmet hot dogs. There was no mention of Anthony visiting Magdalena, but there were several mentions of Pop returning to California on a permanent basis. Pop pretended he couldn't hear his son and after a few *Must be a bad connection*, Pop hung up.

"I like cooking with you, Pop." Lily reached for the measuring cups and laid them next to one another, biggest to smallest. "You're like a grandpa." She scrunched her nose and studied him. "Does your granddaughter in California miss you?"

"I expect she does, but she's older, in college." His granddaughter had been named after her grandmother—Lucy. She looked like her, too, with her fiery hair, pale skin, and blue eyes. A vision with a temper. Maybe one day she'd visit and spend a little time with him before the Good Lord called him home.

"I don't want you to go back there. Last time, you stayed too long and then Mom said you got hurt and couldn't come home."

"Don't worry, I'm not going back." Pop snatched a measuring cup and scooped flour in the cup. "Once was enough for me, that's for sure. Do you know I didn't see one basil plant the whole time I was there? Can't count what you find in them fancy grocery stores either."

"Mom said you might have to go live there sometime. 'When the time comes' is what she said. How do you know when the time comes?"

Pop dumped a cup of flour in the mixing bowl and measured another cup. "That means when they think I can't take care of myself anymore, they want to ship me off to my son's." To heck with that. Why did these adult kids get it in their head that they could call the shots when their parent hit a certain age? So what if Pop moved a little slower or ate toasted cheese sandwiches with salsa for lunch almost every day? That was his choice. And what did it matter if he read his newspaper at exactly 4:45 every afternoon? Or talked to his Lucy about everything as if she were sitting right beside him? He liked toasted cheese and salsa, and reading the paper at 4:45 just so happened to be when he was relaxing before dinner. And he was not even getting started about Lucy, because that dear woman, love of his life, *did* sit beside him— in his heart. Repetition calmed him as much as the garden in his backyard.

And if Anthony thought Pop was giving up his green space for a bunch of plants in clay pots—and not one of those plants had been basil—well, he could think until his brain fried, because Pop was staying put. He and Lily knew what it meant to find the joy in simple things. A piece of chocolate lava cake, gooey and warm in the middle. A pair of thermal socks, thick and comfortable. The perfect rocker, worn at the arms with a relaxing creak that calms and soothes. The ultimate pizzelle, crisy, sweet, memorable. He and Lily didn't need more, more, more. They knew how to be content with the ordinary and the simple. There was something to be said for that, and if Anthony could only learn that sort of contentment, maybe he wouldn't need those deep-breathing exercises, the massages, the therapy, the pills. Maybe if he came home to Magdalena and got a good dose of fresh air and the simple life, he'd be happy.

***

Gloria learned of Anna Nicolina's birth the day after it happened. Lester Conroy had been as diligent in his reporting of Christine's life in Magdalena as he had been with Charles's.

There was something to be said for a man who reports what he sees and does not judge. He'd informed her of Christine's pregnancy, the estrangement with her husband, the subsequent reunion, and the birth of their daughter. Knowing she would die soon had done something to Gloria; perhaps it made her more accepting, more forgiving. More human. She knew she'd been responsible for Christine's estrangement, knew too that Nathan Desantro loved her daughter, and what Gloria had done to them was incomprehensible and unforgiveable.

The days dragged into winter with blustery winds and dark nights. Gloria remained indoors much of the time, tucked beneath an afghan, with Elissa at her side. The girl had become more than a caretaker and companion to Gloria; she'd become a friend. With Elissa, she no longer felt the need to wield power or position. Now she merely wanted the girl to spend time with her, talk, share moments that were not fraught with judgment or recrimination as Christine's had been. Life could not be lived backward. There was no undoing the regret, but she could make one last attempt to seek forgiveness. She and Elissa must make the trip soon while Gloria still had the strength because despite the pain pills, there were too many other signs that told her the months were dwindling.

They arrived in Magdalena on a crisp, bright day in early February with snow packed on the ground and a cloudless sky. Gloria dropped Elissa off at the local diner and made her way to Miriam Desantro's home. She'd imagined this encounter for years, the exact moment of recognition, the hatred that would pulse through her, the disgust and fury over having been tossed aside and played for a fool. But when the door opened and the woman stood before her, the half-smile frozen in place, Gloria felt only relief. This was indeed the last step in her journcy. "Hello."

Miriam Desantro stood before her, grace and elegance in a

willowy form. There was never any doubt they would not recognize one another and this proved true when she said, "Hello, Gloria."

"May I come in?" Gloria coughed, pulled her scarf closer around her neck, and waited for the woman's response. After a slight hesitation, Miriam held the door open and ushered her into the place Charles had called home for fourteen years. It was quaint, homey, artistic, and original—everything Charles's home in Chicago was not. Miriam led her to the living room and offered her a seat. "Thank you." Gloria removed her coat and took a seat on an old but comfortable-looking chair.

"Why are you here?"

The words were cold, protective. Gloria understood this, expected it even, but the knowledge that this woman knew more about Christine's life now than Gloria ever would still hurt. "I've come with one purpose in mind. Whatever happens after that will be up to you. I did a horrible thing against your son and my daughter when I paid the Servetti girl to take pictures and act as though," she coughed, cleared her throat, and pushed out the rest of the words, "as though there had been inappropriate behavior. I know Christine will never forgive me, but I have to tell her I was behind the plan to set your son up."

Miriam Desantro's pale eyes narrowed. "Why confess now? Why not when it happened, when it really would have made a difference?"

Gloria shrugged. "Human nature, I guess. I'm not in the habit of admitting I'm wrong." The woman said nothing, merely stared. "Do you know how I might get in touch with Christine?"

"No."

She answered a little too quickly, which meant she knew

exactly where Christine was and when she'd be returning. "Please. I must tell her how sorry I am for what I've done."

"You have no idea the pain you caused. You almost destroyed your daughter. You've wasted your time coming here and I'd like you to leave." Miriam stood and moved toward the front door.

"I'm dying." Miriam stopped and turned.

"I have lung cancer," Gloria said. "No treatment, and no hope past a few more months. I don't want Christine to know. Please don't tell her. I've spent my whole life making people feel guilty, especially my daughter. I won't lay that on her now. Not anymore."

The woman hesitated, as if caught between two choices. When she spoke, her words held the tiniest bit of empathy. "Would you like a cup of coffee?"

That's how Christine found them forty minutes later, drinking coffee in the living room, not speaking, not acknowledging one another, but oh so aware of the other's presence. Just like it had always been.

"Mother?" Christine stood in the doorway, looking flushed and beautiful. Gloria had been so obsessed with molding her daughter into what she thought she should be, she'd never really looked at her. But what she saw now was grace and confidence, a woman at peace with herself. A woman in love.

Gloria set her coffee cup on the table and stood. "Hello, Christine."

"What...what are you doing here?"

Before she could answer, the back door banged open and laughter filtered to the living room.

"Hey, where is everybody?" Nathan Desantro's deep voice reached her, squeezed the breath from her. "What's going..." He stood next to his wife, their baby cradled in his large arms, but his gaze was honed in on Gloria. A predator's gaze, and she was the weakened prey. "Did you come to cause more destruction?"

"Nathan, enough." His mother cast him a reproving look.

"I've come to apologize," Gloria said. "For all the hurt and incredible pain I've caused you. I'll never be able to make it up to you, but I deeply regret my actions." She met her daughter's gaze. "Your husband was never unfaithful to you. I was behind all of it."

"What's going on? Who's that?" A young girl inched around Nathan Desantro and entered the room. She studied Gloria with keen interest. "Hello."

"Hello." *This was the girl.* Lily. Charles's daughter. Gloria's sipped in air, fought the pain stabbing her chest. It was one thing to suspect, another to know, but to actually see the betrayal in real life, flesh and blood?

"I'm Lily." She smiled and pointed to the baby in Nathan's arms. "And I'm an aunt. Her name is Anna Nicolina."

"What a beautiful name." *She has the Blacksworth eyes.*

"What's your name?"

"I'm…" Gloria darted a look at Christine, then Nathan, but they remained silent.

It was Miriam who came to her rescue and offered an answer. "Lily, this is Christine's mother."

"Oh!" The child's eyes grew wide, her face flushed with excitement. "Christine's mom." She held out her hand and waited for Gloria to take it. "Come with me." Lily led her to Nathan and the baby. "Anna Nicolina, this is your other grandma. She's sparkly, isn't she?" The girl took in Gloria's necklace and rings,and bracelets. "Yup, very sparkly." She looked up at her brother and said, "Nate, aren't you going to let Grandma hold Anna Nicolina?" Nathan's eyes narrowed on Gloria and his jaw tensed. He'd just as soon kick her out of the house than let her hold his child. Could she blame him?

"That's okay, Lily. Really." Gloria had said what she'd come to say and now it was time to leave.

"It's rude, Nate." Lily frowned and crossed her small arms over her middle. "Not good manners."

He turned to his little sister and said in a firm voice, "Lily, that's enough." Miriam stood and made her way across the room. She touched her son's arm, looked him in the eyes, and nodded. "Sit in a chair," he said, "and I'll hand her to you."

Gloria did as he asked, and he placed the baby in her arms. Lily rushed over to them and knelt beside the baby. "You make a nice Grandma," Lily said. "See, we're one big happy family. That's us."

***

"Harry? Harry, wake up. I think it's time."

"Huh? What?"

Greta shook his shoulder. "My water broke. It's time to go to the hospital."

"Shit!" Harry tossed back the covers and jumped out of bed. "Okay, okay. I'll get your bag. Do you need help getting in the car?" What the hell had the instructor said in the childbirth classes? *Calm, remain calm.* Right.

"No, but we have to call Belinda."

"Why?" What did his secretary have to do with getting to the hospital?

Greta waddled toward him, her nightgown stretching over her belly. "She's going to watch A.J. and Lizzie while we go to the hospital. Remember?"

Her speech was slow and deliberate, as though she were waiting for his brain to process the words. Yes, now he remembered that Belinda was on call to watch the kids when Greta went into labor. She'd turned out to be a real gem, as important to him in his personal life as she was in his professional one. And with the wicked witch Helene out of the babysitting picture, life was a lot more relaxed in the Blacksworth household.

"Harry?" Greta touched his arm. "We have to move. I'll call Belinda, you get the bag, and then get changed. Okay?"

Damn, he would have run out of here in his pajamas. Harry Blacksworth, making a fashion screw-up? Now he knew he was in trouble. He looked at his wife, so beautiful and giving, and knew a moment of sheer panic. What if something happened to her? Or the baby? What if she started bleeding? And there were complications? What if—

"It will be fine." Her smile calmed him, settled his heart to a normal rhythm, and made him believe everything would indeed be fine.

Harry clasped his wife's hands between his own, kissed her lips, and said, "Let's go have a baby."

Four hours later, Harry sent the following text message to Christine. *Jackson Henry Blacksworth arrived at 6:22 A.M. 6.2 pounds, 19 ¼ inches. Mother and baby fine. Father resuscitated with a double scotch.*

Epilogue

Pop rifled through the mail and pulled out two brochures. They were similar to the ones he'd been receiving for the past two months; glossy, lots of green lawn, bougainvillea running up the walls. And lots and lots of smiling senior citizens. One caption read *Retire in Ease*, the other, *Living on your own does not mean alone*. Dang-blasted retirement homes. What were the odds that every last brochure was from San Diego, the very same city Anthony lived in? Did his son think he'd been born in a bed of escarole?

"Lucy, that boy of yours is behind this and don't think I don't know it." Pop tossed the flyers in the trashcan and shook his head. "He ain't getting me out of this town, not while I'm still breathing." He poured a glass of milk and grabbed two pizzelles. Lily had done a good job making them, and other than a few crispy ones, which he happened to prefer, she'd got the twenty-second timing down just right. Next Saturday, he promised they would make chocolate ones.

"Besides we got bigger problems right now and this town's gonna need all the help it can get to keep things calm." He sank into his chair and homed in on her portrait. "Daniel Casherdon is coming back to town. He ain't walking on his own two legs either. I was talking to Ramona the other day after the meeting and she said he'll be here next month. I didn't ask what all happened but I think he might have been shot. Wonder where?" He scratched his jaw, considered the possibilities, and none of them were good. "Ramona teared up and couldn't talk about it, so I told her if she needed help, I'd sit with the boy. I know you always liked him, and we thought the town gave him a raw deal. Shoo, wonder what Olivia Carrick's going to say when she finds out. Guess you don't send a box of cookies when the person's killed your son unless you intend on sprinkling it with something deadly to return the favor." He nibbled his second pizzelle, considered all the commotion that would start soon enough.

"You always said Tess and Cash belonged together, but don't look like they'll get a second chance like Nate and Christine did. Oh, you'd like this Desantro baby, Anna Nicolina. Lots of black hair and the bluest eyes you ever seen, Blacksworth eyes, Lucy, that's what everybody calls them. Like her mama and Lily." He sighed. "Don't you worry now, I'll let you know every little detail about Cash. As a matter of fact, I might pay Olivia Carrick a visit, see if she's heard from Tess, and maybe I'll politely inquire if her daughter has plans to visit Magdalena anytime soon." His lips turned up in a faint smile. "And maybe if she does, I'll see about arranging a 'chance' meeting between Tess and Cash." His voice faded as the blueness of his wife's eyes looked back at him from the portrait, pulled him in, held him. In that instant, a wonderful, magical idea burst in his heart. "I won't disappoint you, Lucy. You'll see." The smile spread. "You certainly will see."

The End

Go to MaryCampisi.com and sign up for Mary's Mailing List to receive an email for new releases. If you want to read more about the residents of Magdalena, be sure to check out *A Family Affair: Summer*, Book Three in the *Truth in Lies* Series, coming 2014.

A Glimpse of A Family Affair: Summer

If she knew her life were about to shatter into a million bits of unrecognizable tragedy, Tess Carrick would have kissed Daniel "Cash" Cashderon with greater urgency that afternoon, savored the taste of his naked flesh, dug her nails into his back. She would have ignored Magdalena's raised brows and clung to him with the desperateness of one taking a last breath.

Because in the end, that's exactly what it was—one last pure breath of the most consuming love she'd ever known. After, despite the town's honest attempt at comfort, there was only pain. Lies. Betrayal. Too much guilt. Fate killed the memories of loving him with one shocking act, so swift, so final there would be no retracing steps to an earlier time, no recapturing innocence or second chances. There would be nothing left but survival.

Watch for *A Family Affair: Summer*—Coming 2014

About the Author

Mary Campisi writes books about second chances. Whether contemporary romances, women's fiction, or Regency historicals, her books all center on belief in the beauty of that second chance.

Mary should have known she'd become a writer when at age thirteen she began changing the ending to all the books she read. It took several years and a number of jobs, including registered nurse, receptionist in a swanky hair salon, accounts payable clerk, and practice manager in an OB/GYN office, for her to rediscover writing. Enter a mouse-less computer, a floppy disk, and a dream large enough to fill a zip drive. The rest of the story lives on in every book she writes.

When she's not working on her craft or following the lives of five young adult children, Mary's digging in the dirt with her flowers and herbs, cooking, reading, walking her rescue lab mix, Cooper, or, on the perfect day, riding off into the sunset with her very own hero/husband on his Ultra Limited aka Harley.

Mary has published with Kensington, Carina Press, The Wild Rose Press, and Jocelyn Hollow Romance.

website: www.marycampisi.com
e-mail: mary@marycampisi.com
blog: http://www.marycampisi.com/blog/
twitter: https://twitter.com/#!/MaryCampisi
facebook   http://www.facebook.com/marycampisibooks

Other Books by Mary Campisi:

Contemporary Romance

A Family Affair (Truth in Lies Series-Book One)

A Family Affair: Spring (Truth in Lies Series-Book Two)

A Family Affair: Summer (Truth in Lies Series-Book Three)
Coming 2014

Pulling Home (That Second Chance Series-Book One)

The Way They Were (That Second Chance Series-Book Two)

Simple Riches (That Second Chance Series-Book Three)

Paradise Found (That Second Chance Series-Book Four)

Not Your Everyday Housewife (That Second Chance Series-Book Five)

The Butterfly Garden (That Second Chance Series-Book Six) - Coming 2014

Pieces of You (The Betrayed Trilogy-Book One)

Secrets of You (The Betrayed Trilogy-Book Two)

What's Left of Her: a novella (The Betrayed Trilogy-Book Three)

Begin Again: Short stories from the heart

The Sweetest Deal

Regency Historical

The Redemption of Madeline Munrove (The Model Wife Series-Book One)

The Seduction of Sophie Seacrest (An Unlikely Husband Series-Book One)

A Touch of Seduction (An Unlikely Husband Series-Book Two) Coming 2014

A Taste of Seduction (An Unlikely Husband Series-Book Three) Coming 2014

Innocent Betrayal

Young Adult
Pretending Normal

26419732R00138

Made in the USA
Lexington, KY
30 September 2013